ASSAULT OF THE
MOUNTAIN MAN

ASSAULT OF THE MOUNTAIN MAN

WILLIAM W. JOHNSTONE
with J. A. Johnstone

PINNACLE BOOKS
Kensington Publishing Corp.
www.kensingtonbooks.com

PINNACLE BOOKS are published by

Kensington Publishing Corp.
119 West 40th Street
New York, NY 10018

PUBLISHER'S NOTE
Following the death of William W. Johnstone, the Johnstone family is working with a carefully selected writer to organize and complete Mr. Johnstone's outlines and many unfinished manuscripts to create additional novels in all of his series like The Last Gunfighter, Mountain Man, and Eagles, among others. This novel was inspired by Mr. Johnstone's superb storytelling.

All Kensington titles, imprints, and distributed lines are available at special quantity discounts for bulk purchases for sales promotions, premiums, fund-raising, educational, or institutional use. Special book excerpts or customized printings can also be created to fit specific needs. For details, write or phone the office of the Kensington special sales manager: Kensington Publishing Corp., 119 West 40th Street, New York, NY 10018, attn: Special Sales Department; phone 1-800-221-2647.

PINNACLE BOOKS and the Pinnacle logo are Reg. U.S. Pat. & TM Off.
The WWJ steer head logo is a trademark of Kensington Publishing Corp.

ISBN-13: 978-0-7860-2352-3
ISBN-10: 0-7860-2352-X

First printing: December 2011

10 9 8 7 6 5 4 3 2 1

Printed in the United States of America

PROLOGUE

Bill Dinkins was thirty-eight years old. Standing five feet ten inches tall with sandy hair and blue eyes, he was a man that women found handsome at first look. But there was something about him, an evil glint in his eye, the curl of a lip that, upon further examination, frightened women away. One fine fall day Dinkins, Loomis Caldwell, Gary Beeman, and Henry Kilpatrick rode into the town of Buffalo, Colorado, and went straight to the bank. While two of the four stayed mounted, Dinkins and Caldwell went inside and asked for five twenty-dollar gold pieces in exchange for a one hundred dollar note.

While in the bank the two men checked it out, noticing a back door they assumed opened onto the alley. Once they left the bank, the four men rode up and down Decker's Road a couple times, checking out the lay of the town, then they rode up the alley to see where the bank door opened.

When the four men first rode into town Glen

Davis, the town marshal, thought nothing of it. But when he saw them ride up and down the street twice, then go into one end of the alley and come out the other, he began to get suspicious. "Bobby, let's you and me go outside," he said to his deputy.

The four riders, still unaware that they had attracted attention, rode back into the alley and tied their horses to an empty freight wagon. They split up, with two going into the bank through the front door and two going in through the back door. Three customers and the bank teller were inside.

"Up against the wall!" Dinkins yelled to the customers. He handed the teller a cloth bag. "Fill the bag with money," he ordered.

With shaking hands, the teller began to comply.

Outside, Marshal Davis and Deputy Mason were approaching the bank with their guns drawn.

"What's going on, Marshal?" someone called.

"Get a gun," the marshal replied. "I think the bank is being robbed."

With that, at least four other townspeople armed themselves and came over to join Davis and Mason.

"Bill, hurry it up!" Caldwell shouted. "There is a lot of people comin' toward us, and ever'one of 'em is got a gun!"

"Give me the bag," Dinkins ordered.

"I haven't finished filling it," the teller replied.

"Give me the bag!" Dinkins ordered again. Reaching through the window, he made a grab for the bag, but the teller jerked it back. Angrily, Dinkins shot him. The slug hit the teller between the eyes, and he collapsed on the floor behind the teller's cage, with the money bag still clutched in his hand, out of Dinkins' reach.

"We got to get out of here now!" Beeman yelled.

Bells were ringing all over town. Dogs were barking and citizens were running, some for cover, and some to find a place from which to shoot.

"Everyone, out the back door!" Dinkins shouted, and the four men ran out the back door, then down the alley to their horses. Mounting their horses, they saw that wagons had been pushed across the alley at both ends, blocking them off. Their only exit was to ride up the narrow opening between the bank and the shoe store.

When they reached Decker's Road, which was the main street, the angry citizens of the town were ready for them. The first person to take a shot at the would-be bank robbers was a clerk who had come outside to stand on the front porch of the general store. Armed with a double-barreled 12-gauge Greener, he let loose. Beeman, his chest opened up by the load of double aught buckshot, was knocked from his horse. Kilpatrick's horse was killed by someone firing a Winchester rifle, and when Caldwell turned back for him everyone with a gun started shooting at the two men. Kilpatrick and Caldwell's return fire was effective enough to drive several citizens off the street and provide cover for Dinkins.

"Bill, come here! Help me get Henry up on Beeman's horse!"

Dinkins looked back at the two men, then at the armed citizens, and turned and galloped away.

"Dinkins! You cowardly son of a bitch!" Caldwell shouted angrily.

Dinkins didn't look back, but continued to ride as the shooting was going on behind him. He rode hard, until he realized nobody was giving chase. He could hear the last gunshots being exchanged between the citizens of the town and Caldwell and Kilpatrick. Then the shooting fell silent, and he knew they were either captured or killed. Dinkins had gotten away with his life, but none of the bank's money except for the five twenty-dollar gold pieces he had gotten in exchange for the one hundred dollar bill.

When Dinkins reached the town of Snyder, he dismounted, slapped his horse on the rump, and sent it on. He hoped if anyone was following him, they would follow the tracks of his horse.

He walked the rest of the way into town, then went to the depot to buy a ticket on the next train out. He was pretty sure nobody would be looking for a bank robber on a train. Bank robber. He scoffed at the term. Some bank robber he was. He had not gotten away with one red cent.

CHAPTER ONE

Washington, D.C.

Sally Jensen had been back East for almost six weeks, during which time she had visited her family in Vermont, friends and relatives in Boston and New York, and as the last part of her trip, she was in Washington, D.C. At the moment, she was sitting in the reception room just outside the Presidential Office in the White House. As she waited to meet with the president, she was reading the novel, *A Study in Scarlet*, written by the English author, Arthur Conan Doyle, in which he introduced a new character, Sherlock Holmes. Sally enjoyed the intellect and deductive reasoning of the Sherlock Holmes character. So engrossed was she in the book that she did not notice Colonel Lamont, the appointments secretary, approaching her.

"Mrs. Jensen?" Colonel Lamont said.

Sally looked up from her book. It took her a

second to come out of the story and realize exactly where she was.

"Yes?"

"The president will see you now."

"Oh, thank you," Sally answered with a broad smile. Slipping a book mark in between the pages, she stood, then followed the secretary into President Cleveland's office.

The president was rather rotund, with a high forehead and a bushy moustache. He was wearing a suit, vest, and bowtie, and he was smiling as he walked around the desk with his hand extended. "Mrs. Jensen. How wonderful to see you."

"The pleasure is all mine, Mr. President," Sally replied.

President Cleveland pointed to a sitting area over to the side. "Please, won't you have a seat? And tell me all about your wonderful West."

"As you say, Mr. President, it is wonderful. You really should take a trip out there sometime."

"I agree, I must do that. And your husband, Smoke? He is doing well?"

"He is doing very well, thank you. Right now he and the others are involved in the spring roundup."

"The spring roundup," President Cleveland said. "What exciting images those words evoke." The president glanced toward the door to make certain no one could overhear him. "Please don't tease me about it, but from time to time I read novels of the West. I find them a wonderful escape from the tedium of reports, analysis, bills, etcetera, etcetera, etcetera, ad naseum."

Sally laughed.

"And how is your family?"

"They are doing well, thank you. It was my family who insisted that I call upon you before I return home," Sally said.

"And rightly so," President Cleveland replied. "When I was governor of the state of New York, I vetoed the bill that would have reduced the fare to five cents on the elevated trains in New York. That was an extremely unpopular veto, and your father's support, even though he was not a resident of New York, helped convince several legislators to change their vote and support me when the legislature attempted to override the veto. Had I lost that veto, I believe my political career would have been finished. I do not think it would stretch credulity too far, to suggest that I am occupying the White House partly because of your father's early, and important, support."

Sally laughed. "It wasn't all altruistic on my father's part you understand, Mr. President. He had loaned Jay Gould the money to buy the railroad. He was merely looking out for his investment."

"Oh!" President Cleveland said, clutching his heart with both hands, and laughing. "And here, I was certain your father's support was because he thought me to be a brilliant politician and servant of the people."

Sally and the president visited for a while longer, then she was invited to have lunch with Frances Cleveland, the president's young wife. "Unfortunately I will not be able to attend, as I have a prior luncheon engagement with the caucus of Western Senators."

"Well, if they are from the West, then by all means you should not break the appointment," Sally suggested.

"But if it was a caucus of Eastern Senators?"

"Then I would fully expect you to join us," Sally said, and the president laughed with her as he escorted her from the office.

"Colonel Lamont, would you please telephone my wife and tell her that she will have a guest for lunch," President Cleveland asked of his private secretary.

"Mr. President, I have already done so," Lamont replied. "Mrs. Cleveland is on her way here now."

Grover Cleveland was twenty-seven years old when he met his future wife. She had just been born, the daughter of Oscar Folsom, a long time close friend of Cleveland's. When her father died in a buggy accident in 1875 without having written a will, the court appointed Cleveland administrator of the estate. This brought Cleveland closer to Frances, who was eleven at the time.

She attended Central High School in Buffalo and went on to Wells College in Aurora, New York. Sometime while she was in college, Cleveland's feelings for her took a romantic turn. He proposed in August 1885, soon after her graduation, and she accepted. Frances became the youngest first lady ever. Despite her age, her charm and natural intelligence made her a very successful hostess, a quality Sally was enjoying.

"Oh, Sally, have you seen Washington's monument?" Frances asked during lunch.

"I saw it some time ago," Sally said, "but it wasn't completed then. It was sort of an ugly stob."

"Oh you must see it now," Frances said enthusiastically. "It is all finished, and it is beautiful. If you would like, we'll drive out there after lunch."

"I would love to," Sally replied, her enthusiasm matching that of the first lady.

Sugarloaf Ranch

Even as Sally was touring Washington, D.C., with the first lady, Pearlie, the foreman of the ranch she and Smoke owned, was out on the range with three other cowboys, riding bog.

It was one of the less glamorous and more difficult jobs pertaining to getting ready for the roundup. While crowding around a small water hole, weaker animals were often knocked down by stronger ones, and they would get bogged down, unable to get up. Getting them out was called bogging.

It was easy to find them; the hapless creature would start bawling, not a normal call, but a high pitched, frightened, intense bawl.

"Pearlie!" one of the hands called. "Over here!"

Pearlie rode in the direction of the call, and saw a steer, belly deep in a pond that was mostly mud.

One of the cowboys, a new hand, looped his rope around the steer's neck.

"No!" Pearlie called. "Not the neck. Around his horns."

It took the cowboy a moment of manipulating his rope until he managed to work it up onto the animal's horns.

Pearlie dismounted, then got behind the steer and started pulling on the rope. The idea was to get the animal over on its back, then pull it backward—which was easier than trying to pull it out straight ahead, or sideways.

A couple of the other cowboys grabbed the rope with Pearlie and they pulled until the steer was free.

"You boys grab his tail and hold on until I get the rope off," Pearlie said. "Then one of you run one way and the other run the other way, 'cause this critter is goin' to turn around and charge. If you go in opposite directions, he might get confused and not chase either one of you."

"You said he might get confused. What if he don't get confused and he chases after me?" one of the cowboys said.

"In that case run like hell," Pearlie said, and the others laughed.

Pearlie remounted, then rode around and took the rope off the steer's horns.

"All right, let 'im go!" Pearlie shouted, and the two cowboys started running in opposite directions from each other. The steer took off after one of them, and Pearlie slapped his legs against the side of his horse, urging it into an immediate gallop. He closed on the running steer within a few seconds and forced the steer to turn aside, breaking up his charge.

The other cowboys were laughing hard as Toby, the cowboy who was being chased, stopped running and bent over, his hands on his knees, breathing hard from his exertion.

"Damn, Toby," one said. "I sure didn't know you could run that fast. Why, you should enter the race at the county fair this summer."

Toby was still breathing hard. "Won't do any good unless I've got a steer runnin' after me," he said, to the laughter of all.

"All right, you boys know what to do now, so keep it up, pull out all the cows you find bogged down. I'm going back to get cleaned up, then I'm going into town. Smoke wants me to pick up a few things."

"If you want, Pearlie, I'll go into town for you," one of the cowboys said.

"Yeah, I'm sure you would," Pearlie replied with a broad smile. "But like as not you would get drunk and forget what you went to town for."

"Ha, Wade, you think Pearlie ain't got you pegged?" Toby said with a laugh.

Big Rock, Colorado

Pearlie took the buckboard into town. He stopped first at Cousins' General Store to fill the list of food items needed for the chuck wagon while the roundup was ongoing.

"Hello, Pearlie," Cousins said, greeting the young cowboy as he came into the store. "Come for your possibles, have you?"

"Yes, sir, Mr. Cousins," Pearlie replied. "We'll need beans, flour, bacon, coffee, sugar, and some dried fruits. It's all written out."

"You got a buckboard outside?"

"I do."

"I'll fill your order and take it out to the buckboard for you. If you have anything else to do in town you can go ahead and take care of it."

"Thank you. I'll do that."

Food wasn't the only thing on Pearlie's shopping list. From Cousins' General Store he walked over to the gun shop where he bought several boxes of ammunition in various calibers. From there he went to the post office to pick up the mail. By the time he got back to the store, the food had been loaded onto the buckboard. He touched the brim of his hat, in a salute to Cousins, climbed into the seat, picked up the reins, and clucked to the team.

Sugarloaf Ranch

Back at the ranch, Smoke Jensen was standing in an open field by the barn. Twenty-five yards in front of him were three bottles inverted on sticks of varying heights, one as high as a man's head, one about the height of an average man's chest, while the third would align with a man's belly. The sticks were ten feet apart.

Off to Smoke's right, but clearly in his vision,

Cal was holding his right hand out in front of him, palm down. There was an iron nut on the back of his hand, and beneath his hand, on the ground, was a tin pie plate.

The full-time hands, the ones who had stayed through the winter, as well as some of the new men, the temporary cowboys who were showing up for the spring roundup, were gathered around in a semicircle to watch the demonstration.

Cal turned his hand over, and the nut fell. The moment Smoke saw Cal turn his hand, he began his draw. He fired three quick shots, breaking all three bottles before the iron nut clanked against the tin pan.

The men cheered and clapped.

"Damndest thing I ever seen!" one of the cowboys said.

"How can anyone be that fast?"

"I've read books about him, but I always thought they was just made up," another of the hands said. "I never know'd there could be anyone that could really shoot like that."

"Yeah, but this is just trick shooting," a new cowboy, one who had never worked at Sugarloaf before, said. "Seems to me folks who can do trick shootin' ain't always that good when it comes to the real thing."

Cal, who was picking up the iron nut and the pie pan, overheard the last remark. "Trust me. When it comes to the real thing, he's even better."

"How would you know?"

"'Cause I've been right there beside him when the real thing happened," Cal said.

He walked over to join Smoke, who had gone back up to the big house. Smoke was leaning against the porch, punching out the spent cartridges and replacing them with live bullets. "Better not let Sally know we used one of her pie pans for this."

"Oh, yeah, I nearly forgot!" Cal said. He examined the pie pan carefully, then breathed a sigh of relief. "Ah, it doesn't look like it was hurt any."

At that moment Pearlie came driving back in the buckboard. He came all the way up to the porch, smiling as he was holding up a letter.

"Looks like you got a letter from Miss Sally," Cal said.

"Looks like it, doesn't it?" Smoke said.

"Reckon how long she's going to be gone before she comes back?"

"Next week, I believe," Smoke said as he reached for the letter. "Unless this letter says something different."

My Darling Smoke

   I have enjoyed my visit back East, (please notice that I did not say back home, as the only home for me is our beautiful Sugarloaf) but am growing anxious to return. The weather here has been abysmal; it snowed every other day for the two weeks I spent in New York. I did get to see a play in which Andrew and Rosanna MacCallister appeared. It made me feel special to be sitting in the theater, watching as they enthralled the audience, knowing that their brother and my husband are good friends.

I visited Washington, D.C., and President Cleveland asked about you. Smoke, I am used to everyone in the West knowing who you are, but when a hotel concierge, a restaurant maitre d', a hack driver, and the president of the United States ask about you, I must say that it does give me pause.

Mrs. Cleveland, whose name is Frances, is a most delightful person. She is younger than I am, but is mature beyond her years. She took me on a personal tour of the capital, and how fun it was to see the city through her eyes.

How glad I am that I stuck to my childhood dream of seeing the wonderful West, and how fortunate I have been in finding in you, the love of my life. I shall be returning home next week, and expect to arrive in Big Rock at eleven o'clock Tuesday morning. I can hardly wait until I breathe the high, sweet air of Colorado once again, and, if I may be so bold as to put it in words, to taste the lips of the man of my dreams.

> *Your loving wife,*
> *Sally*

"Yahoo, boys!" Smoke said. "She'll be back home next Tuesday!"

"Reckon we'll be through ridin' bog by then?" Cal asked.

Pearlie chuckled. "You ain't never really through ridin' bog, Cal. You know that."

"Yeah, I know, but it's generally worse right after winter is over," Cal said. "Then it starts easin' up some."

Another necessary, but unpleasant job, would be cleaning out the water holes. It would require a team of horses and a scraper. Depending on the size of the hole, and how much weed, mud, and cow-dung there were in the water, it would sometimes take up to a week just to clean one hole.

Of course, even before the general roundup was done, there would be a roundup of all the newly born calves, so they could be branded. This was the kind of work that was keeping Smoke, Pearlie, Cal, and the other cowboys, those who had been present all winter, and those who were newly signed on for the spring roundup, busy.

CHAPTER TWO

Big Rock

When Sally Jensen stepped down from the train it was nearly midnight. Dark and cold, the little town of Big Rock was a windy emptiness under great blinking white stars. "What ever do you see in that wild and wooly West?" Molly Tremaine had asked, during Sally's recent visit with her. Molly was an old schoolmate, now married to a Boston lawyer.

"It isn't something that can be explained," Sally replied. "It is something you have to experience. There is nothing more beautiful, nothing more vibrant, than to live in that wonderful country."

Sally wished Molly could be here, right now, to get a sense of the magnificent wonder of the place—high and dry, with the stars so huge it was almost as if she could reach up and pluck one from the sky.

Sally had written to Smoke telling him she

would arrive mid-morning Tuesday, but when she was in St. Louis she took advantage of a faster connection, which caused her to arrive in Big Rock almost twelve hours ahead of her schedule. At first she thought only of the time she would be saving, not realizing it meant she would arrive in the middle of the night. She was alone on the depot platform and there was no one to meet her.

Behind her the engineer blew his whistle twice, then opened his throttle to a thunderous expulsion of steam. The huge driver wheels spun on the track, sending out a shower of sparks until they gained traction. With a series of jerks as the slack was taken up between the cars, the engine got underway puffing loudly as it did so.

As the train pulled out of the station, Sally watched the cars pass her by. Most of the windows were dark because the passengers were trying to sleep. But the windows of the day cars were well lit, and she could see the tired faces of passengers who were either unable or unwilling to pay for more comfortable accommodations.

As the train left the station, she turned to walk toward the depot. Because there would be no more arrivals or departures until the next morning, the waiting room, which was dimly lit by the yellow light of an oil lantern, was empty. The ticket window was open, but there was no one behind the counter. She could hear a telegraph instrument clacking from the telegrapher's office, so she assumed someone was there.

"Miss," someone said from behind her.

Thinking she was totally alone, Sally was startled by the voice and she jumped at the sound.

"Sorry, ma'am, didn't mean to . . . ," the man started, then stopped in mid-sentence. "Why, Mrs. Jensen, what are you doin' here at this hour of the night?"

"Hello, Mr. Anderson," Sally said to the baggage and freight agent. "I wasn't supposed to get here until tomorrow morning, but I took an earlier train out of St. Louis. I don't know what I was thinking. Of course there was no way of letting Smoke know in time to meet me, so I haven't gained a thing. It would appear that I have been hoist by my own petard."

"You been done what, ma'am?" Anderson asked.

Sally laughed. "I'm just commenting on how foolish I was to change trains, is all. Did my baggage get off?"

"Yes, ma'am. I've got it out on the platform right now."

"Could you keep it until tomorrow morning for me? I'm going to have to get a hotel room, I'm afraid."

"Yes ma'am. Well, if you'll wait until I get your baggage put away, I'll walk with you to the hotel. It's not all that good for a lady to be out on the street in the middle of the night, alone."

Sally started to tell him he needn't bother. She could shoot a gun as well as any man, and better than most, having been taught by her husband, who was one of the most proficient men with a rifle or pistol in the whole country. But even as she harbored that thought, she was aware she was not armed. In fact, she was wearing a traveling dress. It was stylish enough to have drawn many an admiring eye—though her delicate features and svelte womanly figure would have drawn as many admiring glances no matter what she was wearing. She was not wearing the more practical clothes she wore at the ranch.

"I would be happy to have you accompany me, Mr. Anderson," she said.

She waited a moment longer, then after closing and locking the door to the baggage and freight room, Anderson came back to join her.

As Sally walked down the street, escorted by Mr. Anderson, she pulled her shawl more tightly around her. The moisture clouds of her exhaled breath were almost luminescent in the dark night. From down the street a short way, she could hear the tinkling sound of an out of tune piano, loud male voices, and a woman's high pitched laugh. The noises came from the Brown Dirt Cowboy Saloon, a business that had been established within the year, and already was the scene of at least three shootings. She knew Sheriff Carson was contemplating closing it, if there were too many more shooting incidents there.

They reached the McKinley Hotel, a three-story brick structure, one of the finest buildings in Big Rock, which had a very nice restaurant on its ground floor. Inside, a dozing clerk sat behind the desk in an empty lobby. In the middle of the lobby a wood burning stove roared, and glowed red as the fuel burned.

"I'll leave you here, ma'am," Anderson said when they stepped inside.

"Thank you." Sally walked over to the desk and smiled as she saw the clerk, his head drooped forward, snoring rather loudly. She tapped the little bell, and the *ding* awakened him with a start. At first the clerk looked somewhat irritated that his nap had been interrupted, but he brightened considerably when he recognized her as the wife of one of the leading citizens in the county, if not in the state.

"Mrs. Jensen," he said. "What a pleasant surprise. You will be taking a room with us?"

"Yes, I just arrived on the train, and Smoke isn't expecting me until tomorrow. I do hope you have an available room."

"Indeed we do." The clerk turned the register around so she could sign it.

Picking up the pen, Sally saw a name on the line just above hers. "Tamara Gooding McKenzie! That has to be Tamara Gooding. Is she here?"

"Mrs. McKenzie? Yes, she checked in at about six this evening," the clerk said. "She came in on the afternoon coach from Gothic."

"Tamara is an old and dear friend of mine. Please do not let her leave tomorrow without seeing me."

"I will tell her you are here." The clerk handed a key to Sally.

As she climbed the stairs, she got a reminder

that the elevation in Big Rock was over seven thousand feet. Having lived there as long as she had, she was used to the elevation. But she had been gone for six weeks, all the while at sea level, so she would need to get reacquainted with the altitude.

The hotel room contained a double bed, a dresser, a stand with a water pitcher and basin, and one chair. There was also a small stove which had already been prepared with wood and kindling. Sally took one of the matches from a box on the dresser, struck it, then got the fire going.

Within minutes the room was warm and cozy so that when she slipped under the covers of the bed, she didn't even mind that the sheets were cold and damp. She fell asleep quickly.

Sugarloaf Ranch

As was his routine, especially during roundup time, Smoke Jensen was up before dawn. He stood in the doorway of the cookhouse. Even though he was in silhouette, it was easy to identify him. He had shoulders as wide as an ax handle, strong arms, flat stomach, and stood just over six feet tall.

For the six weeks Sally had been absent Smoke had been taking all his meals in the cookhouse, eating at a private table where he was occasionally joined by Pearlie or Cal. They believed, as did Smoke, that as they would be working closely with the cowboys, they should eat with them.

It was early enough that none of the other cowboys were awake yet. Pearlie and Cal had been with Smoke long enough to know his schedule, so they were having their breakfast with him at his table, as they discussed the roundup.

"We've got cattle scattered from hither to yon," Pearlie said. "It's goin' to take two, maybe three weeks to get 'em all rounded up, branded, and ready to drive into Big Rock to the railhead."

"Miss Sally gets back today, don't she?" Cal asked.

"Don't say that in front of her," Smoke said.

"Don't say what?"

"Don't say, 'don't she.' It is, doesn't she."

"Oh, yeah, her bein' a schoolteacher an' all, I sometimes forget what store she sets by talkin' good English."

Smoke laughed.

"What?"

"Never mind. You are incorrigible, and I would merely be casting pearls before swine."

"Smoke, I tell you the truth, sometimes you don't make no sense a-tall," Cal said.

"Miss Sally does get in today though, doesn't she?" Pearlie asked.

"Yes. I'll be going into town to pick her up this morning," Smoke said.

Big Rock

At breakfast in the dining room of the hotel, Sally and Tamara sat across the table from each other. They had been classmates at Vassar and later taught together. This was the first time they had seen each other in a long time.

"Yes, I knew you were living here," Tamara said, "but I didn't want to bother you with my troubles."

Sally reached her hand across the table to lay it on Tamara's hand. "Tamara, we are friends. Friends are never a bother. Now, please, tell me what is going on with you."

"Shortly after you and Smoke Jensen were married, I married a man named Ian McKenzie."

"Did he live in Bury?"

"No. I left Bury and went to Denver to take a position there. That's where I met Ian. He was a lawyer, and a wonderful man."

"Was?"

"He took cholera and died two years ago," Tamara said.

"Oh, I'm so sorry."

"Yes, it was awful. I miss him so. But, to make matters worse, I found out his law partner had been cheating him all along. I'm sure that Ian died thinking I would be well taken care of, but there was nothing left of his estate. I left Denver with nothing but the clothes on my back."

"Tamara! If you knew I was living here, you should have come to see me," Sally said.

"I couldn't do that. I won't be a burden to my friends or to my relatives."

"Where are you living now? And what are you doing in Big Rock?"

"I am living in Gothic," Tamara said.

"Gothic? Why, that is very close to here. Tamara, if you are that close, you should have come to see me."

"I planned to do so once I got back on my feet," Tamara replied.

"Are you teaching in Gothic?"

"No. I applied, but there is no position for me. I have been earning a living baking pies and cakes and selling them from my house." Tamara smiled. "I've actually done better than I thought I would, so that gave me the idea of starting a restaurant."

"Why, Tamara, that is a wonderful idea," Sally said. "So, why are you in Big Rock? Do you plan to start it here?"

"No. The restaurant will be in Gothic. To tell the truth, I have come to get some ideas from the people who are running this restaurant. There is already another café in Gothic, and I'm not sure they would be all that happy to have competition, so I thought I would do my research over here."

"I remember what a good cook you were, even when we were in college. You would sometimes prepare a veritable feast for us. I think your restaurant will do wonderfully."

"Thank you. I hope I can convince, Mr. Flowers."

"Mr. Flowers?"

"He owns the Miners' Bank in Gothic," Tamara said. "I will be applying to him for a loan to get my restaurant started."

"How much money will you be asking for?"

"Quite a lot, I'm afraid. From all I have been able to figure, I'm going to need at least two thousand dollars."

"You've got it," Sally said.

"No, I don't have it. That's why I'm going to have to borrow from the bank."

"No, I mean you've got the loan. There is no need for you to go to the bank. I will lend you the two thousand dollars you need."

"Oh, Sally, no," Tamara said. "I told you, I don't want to be a burden to my friends. And I especially don't want to borrow money from them. Why, what if the restaurant doesn't make it?"

"What would you do with the bank if the restaurant doesn't make it?"

"I don't know, to be honest. I haven't thought it through that far."

"That's because your restaurant is going to make it. I'll come over next week with the two thousand dollars you need. If you truly are my friend, you won't upset me by turning this offer down."

Tamara's eyes welled with tears. "Oh, Sally. What a wonderful friend you are."

CHAPTER THREE

Colorado State Penitentiary,
Cañon City, Colorado

The prison guard walked down the center aisle between flanking rows of cells, carrying a large ring of keys.

"Hey, Jack, you comin' to let me out of here? I'm innocent, you know," one of the prisoners called to him.

"Yeah," the guard answered. "There's not a guilty person in this whole prison."

"That's right," another prisoner said. "We're all innocent, so when are you goin' to let us out?"

"Two men are getting out today," Jack replied. "They aren't innocent. They've just served their time."

"Hey, tell the warden to check his books. I know damn well I've served my time," another prisoner said.

"Hell, Smitty, you've only been in here two months," someone else said.

"Is that right? Damn, I thought I had been here for ten years already."

The other prisoners, and even Jack, laughed.

He stopped in front of one of the cells, and the prisoner, as was the routine, stepped all the way back to stand against the wall.

"What's your name?" Jack asked the prisoner.

"Hell, Jack, you know who I am. I done been here for five years," the prisoner answered.

"You do want to get out today, don't you?"

"Yes."

"Then you'll do this my way. What is your name?"

"Parnell. Cole Parnell, number 1210."

Jack unlocked the door.

"Step out into the aisle, Parnell, and come with me."

Parnell did as instructed until they reached the far end of the aisle, where Jack went through the same procedure with a man named Johnny Putnam, number 1138. Parnell and Putnam marched in step with Jack toward the lock gate at the other end of the aisle. Prisoners shouted their good-byes as the men walked by.

"Good-bye, boys."

"Putnam, don't forget, you owe me two dollars."

"I'll send it to you," Putnam called.

"No need to. You'll be back inside in less than a month. You can just bring it to me."

Parnell and Putnam were taken to the warden's

office. Each was given a new pair of jeans, a denim shirt, and a wool coat. They took off their striped trousers and striped shirt to put on the new clothes.

"Here's five dollars apiece," the warden said, sliding the money across the desk. "Both of you are young enough that you have your entire life ahead of you. I don't want to see you back here again."

Neither Parnell nor Putnam answered. Dressed in their new clothes, they took the five dollars and put the money in their pocket.

"I had a gun and holster when I checked in here," Putnam said.

"Yeah, I did too," Parnell added.

The warden nodded, then opened the bottom right drawer of his desk. "Here are your guns. No bullets. I would suggest you don't use them for anything other than shooting varmints and the like."

"Don't worry none about that, warden," Putnam said as he strapped on his pistol belt. "I ain't plannin' on doin' nothin' that will get me back in here. No offense meant, but this here prison ain't exactly a high class hotel."

The warden chuckled. "Why thank you, Mr. Putnam. I'll take that as a compliment. It is our intention to make your stay here unpleasant enough that you will think twice before doing anything that might cause you to return."

Fifteen minutes later the two former prisoners walked through the door at the front gate.

They heard the door slam shut behind them, a clanking of steel on steel.

They stood for a moment, as if adjusting to the fact that, for the first time in five years, they could see from horizon to horizon without walls around them.

"Damn," Parnell said. "Damn, this feels good."

"Don't it though?" Putnam replied.

"What are you going to do now?" Parnell asked.

"I'm going to find the nearest saloon and have a beer," Putnam said. "No, not a beer, a whiskey. A real whiskey."

Bill Dinkins was sitting in the Red Dog saloon when he saw Johnny Putnam and another man come in. Dinkins knew that Putnam was getting out of prison today, and it was for that reason he had come to Cañon City. He watched as the two men stepped up to the bar to order drinks. Their new jeans and shirt, plus the five dollar bill each of them slapped down on the bar, telegraphed to everyone in the saloon that they were just-released prisoners. The other saloon patrons moved away pointedly.

Dinkins chuckled at the reaction of the saloon patrons. They lived here, and saw prisoners released every week, and they reacted the same way to all of them.

"Putnam!" Dinkins called.

Hearing his name, Putnam turned toward the caller.

Dinkins held up a half full bottle. "Save your money. You two boys are welcome to a drink at my table."

Putnam smiled, and tugged on Parnell's arm. "Come on. This is an old pard of mine."

The two men picked up their five dollar bills and walked over to the table before the bartender returned with two shot glasses of whiskey. Seeing what happened, he shrugged his shoulders, then poured the whiskey back into the bottle.

"Who's your friend?" Dinkins asked as he handed the bottle to Putnam.

"His name is Parnell," Putnam lifted the bottle straight to his mouth, took several swallows, then passed it over to Parnell. "We both got out this morning."

"Where are you goin' next?"

Putnam shrugged. "I don't know. I don't have a horse, I got only five dollars. Don't seem to me like there's many places I can go."

"You interested in a job?"

"By job, do you mean the kind of job that got me in prison in the first place?" Putnam asked.

"I can furnish each of you with a horse and saddle, and twenty dollars advance," Dinkins said.

"It is the same kind of job that got me in prison in the first place, isn't it?" Putnam said.

"You got 'ny better prospects?"

"No, I don't reckon I do."

"I don't know about Johnny, but if the offer is for me as well, I'm in," Parnell said.

"Yeah," Putnam said. "Like you said, we don't have no other prospects."

"Come on down to the stable," Dinkins said. "We'll get the two of you mounted."

The three men stood up and started away from the table.

"Don't leave the whiskey behind," Dinkins said. "It's already paid for."

Parnell walked back to the table and grabbed the bottle.

"Now, when we get to the stable, let me do the talking," Dinkins said on the way out.

"Hello, Mr. Kirkeby," the teenaged hostler at the stable said. "Back to rent a horse again?"

"Yes, and I'd like the same one if you don't mind," Dinkins said. "Oh, and I'll need two more today. These men, Mr. Jones and Mr. Brown are thinking about investing in my mine. I want to take them out to show them what it's like."

"When are you going to tell me where that mine is?" the young man asked.

"Ha, you would like to know, wouldn't you?" Dinkins wagged his finger back and forth.

"I know it's not too far, 'cause you've had the horse back within a couple hours every day."

"You're too smart for me," Dinkins said. "That'll be two dollars apiece for the horses, right?"

"Yes, sir, two dollars for a full day. And remember, no matter what time you bring 'em back, you'll still be charged the two dollars."

"Yeah, I've already found that out by comin' back early," Dinkins said. "Think I can get a break on account I'm rentin' three horses?"

"No sir. Mr. Zigenhorn, he owns the livery, and he says I got to charge two dollars per day per horse, for ever' horse that gets rented."

"Highway robbery," Dinkins said as he counted out the money.

Fifteen minutes later the three men left Cañon City, heading west.

"When you said you would supply us with horses, I didn't know you was talkin' about rentin' horses," Putnam said. "Hell, how far can we go on rented horses?"

"As far as we want, seein' as I don't plan on turnin' 'em back in," Dinkins said.

Parnell laughed out loud. "Ha! That's why you been rentin' horses there, ain't it? You planned all along to do this. You was just makin' him trust you."

"Your friend is smart," Dinkins said to Putnam. "Now, if you boys just pay attention to me and do what I tell you, you'll have more money than you know what to do with."

"Ain't possible," Parnell said. "No matter how much money I have, I'll always know what to do with it."

Big Rock

Smoke drove a buckboard into town to pick up Sally. It would not only be good for carrying her luggage—Sally never traveled light no matter where she went—it would also be good for him to pick up a few supplies he needed.

He was at least half an hour early for the train, but figured it would be better to be early than late. As he was checking the blackboard in front of the depot to get the latest telegraphic report on the train, he heard a familiar voice calling to him.

"Smoke, I'm over here," Sally said.

Smoke looked at her with a shocked expression on his face.

"Sally! What are you doing here?" He pointed to the blackboard. "According the schedule, the train isn't due for another half hour."

"That train isn't due for another half hour. But the train I was on arrived at midnight last night."

"What? Why didn't you tell me?"

"I changed trains in St. Louis. I should have known it would arrive here in the middle of the night. I just didn't think it out."

"You didn't spend the night here, in the depot, did you?" Smoke asked anxiously.

Sally laughed. "Of course not, silly. I stayed in the hotel. Tell me, Smoke, am I just going to stand here like a toad on a log? Or am I going to get a welcome home kiss?"

Smoke laughed, then went to her where they embraced and kissed deeply and unashamedly, on the brick platform in front of the depot.

"I had Mr. Anderson hold my luggage overnight for me."

"Good. But if you don't mind, we'll come back for it a little later. I have some things I need to pick up—some wire and fence posts."

Sally chuckled. "It's roundup time and you've put the fencing off until the last minute, haven't you?"

"I have an excuse for it. I hate fences." Smoke helped Sally into the buckboard.

As they left the depot, they saw a stagecoach drawn up in front of the stage depot.

"Smoke, drive over there," Sally said. "I want to tell a friend good-bye."

Smoke drove over to where the coach was being loaded. Sally looked toward the passengers, smiled when she saw Tamara, and called her name.

With a glance toward the coach to make certain she wasn't going to be left behind, Tamara hurried over to the buckboard.

"Smoke, you remember Tamara Gooding, don't you? Only, it is Tamara McKenzie now."

"Yes, I do remember you," Smoke said to the attractive young woman. "It's nice to see you again."

"Thank you," Tamara said.

"I'll be coming over in a couple more weeks," Sally said.

"Sally, are you sure you want to do this?" Tamara asked, her voice displaying her anxiety.

"I am positive I want to do it."

"Ma'am, if you're goin' on this coach, you need to get aboard now," the driver called.

"I'll write to you," Tamara shouted over her shoulder as she hurried to board the coach, the last passenger to do so.

"Heah, team!" the coach driver shouted, snapping his whip with a pop that could be heard all up and down Main Street.

Smoke held his own team back until the coach pulled out. "Want to do what?" he asked as he got his own team underway.

"Invest in a restaurant," Sally said, without further clarification.

CHAPTER FOUR

After the coach left, Smoke drove down Main Street, exchanging greetings with the citizens of the town he helped form. The Jensens were well-known and respected, and if everyone in town didn't know them personally, everyone in town certainly knew who they were.

Sheriff Monte Carson was sitting on the boardwalk in front of his office, with a cup of coffee in hand. When Smoke and Sally rode past, he called out, "Howdy."

Smoke grinned and tipped his hat and Sally smiled and waved.

"You going to stop in to Longmont's?" Sheriff Carson called. Longmont's Saloon, unlike many Western saloons, was a genteel and sophisticated place, in spite of being so far removed from a city of any size.

"Yeah, soon as I get a few things from the hardware store," Smoke called back.

"I'll join you then."

"Good."

"What am I supposed to do while you are visiting with all your friends in Longmont's?" Sally asked.

"I figured you would want to stop by the general store," Smoke said. "You always do that, when you come to town."

"That's true."

"Then you can come on down to Longmont's. They're your friends too, and you know how Louis prides himself in keeping a place that is fit for ladies."

"All right. The general store, then Longmont's it is," Sally agreed.

In front of the general store Smoke stepped down from the buckboard, helped Sally alight, then tied the two-horse rig up to a rail. He went inside with her and looked around at the goods piled on tables and stacked in shelves. The store smelled of cured meat, flour, spices, candle wax, and coal oil. A large counter separated the proprietors from the customers, and on that counter was a roll of brown paper, and a spool of string. Peg Johnson was behind the counter, tending to another customer.

"Hello Sally, Smoke," Peg said. "I'll be with you in a moment."

"No hurry." Sally began looking through the dry goods.

"Sally, I'm going to leave the buckboard down at the hardware store while they load it. If you buy anything, just leave it here and we'll pick it up on the way out of town," Smoke suggested.

"All right. I'll see you in few minutes."

"You've been out of town, haven't you, Sally?" Smoke heard Peg ask as he was leaving. He didn't hear Sally's response, because he was already climbing onto the buckboard.

Fifteen minutes later, with his order placed, Smoke spoke to Kendall Sikes, the owner of the Sikes' Hardware Store. "Kendall, I'm going to leave my buckboard here, and if you would, please, have someone bring it down to Longmont's when you have it loaded."

"Be glad to, Smoke," Kendall replied.

On the way to Longmont's, Smoke passed a couple of the older citizens of the town, engaged in a game of checkers. There were at least five kibitzers of equal age watching the game and offering unwanted advice.

As was his custom, he entered the saloon and stepped immediately to the side, pressing his back up against the wall. He let his eyes adjust to the lower light inside while he looked for possible trouble among the patrons. He did it as a matter of habit, in every saloon he entered. In truth, it was not necessary in Louis Longmont's saloon. He was as safe there as in his own living room. But it was a habit he had cultivated, and all good habits, he believed, should be continued without an interruption in the routine.

Longmont's was truly one of the nicest establishments of its kind that Smoke had ever seen. It would have been at home in San Francisco, St. Louis, or New York. It had a long, polished mahogany bar, with a brass foot rail that Louis kept shining brightly. A cut glass mirror was behind the bar, and the artwork was truly art, not the garish nudes that were so prominent in saloons throughout the West. His collection included originals by Winslow Homer, George Catlin, and Thomas Moran.

Louis was sitting at his usual table in a corner. He was a lean, hawk-faced man, with strong, slender hands, long fingers, and carefully manicured nails. He had jet-black hair and a black pencil-thin moustache. He always wore fine suits, white shirts, and the ubiquitous ascot. Today it was a royal blue. He wore low-heeled boots, and a pistol that hung low in a tied-down holster on his right side. The pistol was nickel-plated, with ivory handles, but it wasn't just for show. Louis was snake-quick and a feared, deadly gun hand when pushed.

He was engaged in a profession that did not have a very good reputation, and there had been times when he was called upon to use his gun. Those times, he did so with deadly effectiveness. He was also a man with a very strong code of honor, as well as a belief in right and wrong. He had never hired, nor would he ever hire, his gun out for money. While he could make a deck of cards do almost anything, he had never cheated at poker. He didn't have to cheat. He was possessed of a phenomenal memory, could tell you the odds of filling any type of poker hand, and was an expert at the technique of card counting.

Louis was just past thirty. When he was a small boy, he left Louisiana and came West with his parents. They had died in a shantytown fire, leaving the boy to cope as best he could.

He had coped quite well, plying his innate intelligence, along with his willingness to take a chance, into a fortune. He owned a large ranch in Wyoming Territory, several businesses in San Francisco, and a hefty chunk of a railroad.

Though it was a mystery to many why Louis continued to stay with his saloon and restaurant in a small town, he explained it very simply. "I would miss it."

Smoke understood exactly what he was talking about.

"Smoke, *mon ami*," Louis said. "It is good to see you, as always. What will it be? Coffee, beer, wine, or whiskey?"

"It's before noon," Smoke replied. "I think a cup of coffee would be fine."

"Make it two cups," Sheriff Carson said, coming in behind Smoke.

"I just saw you drinking one cup," Smoke teased. "Now you are going to drink two more?"

"No, I meant . . ." Sheriff Carson laughed when he saw that Smoke was teasing. "I think there is a bit of leg pulling going on here."

Andre, Louis Longmont's French cook, brought

two cups of steaming coffee, and put them on the table in front of Smoke and Sheriff Carson.

"Do you have any cream and sugar back there, Andre?" Sheriff Carson asked.

"*Quelle sorte de cochon grossier detruirait du café merveilleux avec la crème et le sucre?*" Andre asked loudly and angrily, as he stormed back into the kitchen.

"What the hell did he just say?"

Longmont laughed. "Trust me, Sheriff, you don't want to know. Suffice it to say that he took umbrage with your request for cream and sugar, in a coffee that he has already declared to be marvelous."

Sally had come in during the previous exchange, and she called out from the door. "*Andre, j'aimerais une tasse de votre cafe sans cremez ou sucre.*" The French rolled easily from her tongue.

Andre kissed the tips of the four fingers of his right hand, and opened them toward Sally. "*Mme Jensen, la seule personne civiliseé dans cette terre sauvage.*"

"Why, thank you, Andre. I try to be civilized"—Sally looked at Smoke and Sheriff Carson—"though sometimes, surrounded as I am with such creatures as these, it is difficult."

Carson looked over at Smoke. "Have we just been put down?"

Smoke laughed. "Monte, you are a married man just as I am. Haven't you learned by now, never to ask such a question?"

"How is the roundup going?" Sheriff Carson ignored Smoke's question.

"We're just getting started," Smoke replied. "Cattle got scattered from here to hell and back during the winter. I've got all hands out finding them, rounding them up, as well as digging them out of sink holes."

Sally laughed. "Pearlie's favorite task," she said sarcastically.

"So, how is the law business going?" Smoke asked.

"Got a new dodger in yesterday," Sheriff Carson said. "For a man named Bill Dinkins."

"Bill Dinkins? I don't think I've ever heard of him."

"He got his name known somewhat back in Kansas," Sheriff Carson said. "Then when it got too hot for him there, he came here. Last month he and three others tried to hold up the bank in Buffalo."

"Tried to? He didn't succeed? What happened?"

"The whole town got down on 'em, that's what happened. When they came out of the bank, they ran into a hornet's nest. Half the town was armed and shootin' at them, and they were shootin' back. And here's the thing. Dinkins run out on his men. He could have gone back, helped them get remounted, then ridden on out. The shootin' wasn't that accurate, for all that there was a lot of it. All three of his men were shot down in the street, though they went down game. Dinkins ran, and now there's a nice reward out for him."

"How much money did he get from the bank?"

Sheriff Carson chuckled. "That's just it. He didn't get one red cent. Six men dead, for nothin'."

"Six men?"

"According to the witnesses—customers in the bank—Dinkins got mad when the teller refused to turn the money bag over to him, so he shot him. There were two more of the townspeople killed outside the bank, plus all three of Dinkins' men. That made it a total of six."

"How much is being offered for Dinkins?" Smoke asked.

"Right now, just five hundred dollars. Like I said, he didn't get one red cent."

"But he did kill the teller?"

"Yes. In cold blood."

"Someone like that, the reward can only go up," Smoke said.

"Yeah, I'm pretty much thinkin' that myself," Carson replied.

Smoke and Sally visited with their friends until noon. When Dr. Colton came in to have his lunch Louis insisted they all have lunch, on him.

"Not me," Sheriff Carson said, holding up his hand. "The wife will be fixin' a big lunch for me. She would be some disappointed if I didn't come home for it."

"You could eat just a little here," Louis invited, "then go home for lunch."

"Yeah, I guess I . . ." Sheriff Carson shook his head. "No, I better not. But I thank you for the invite."

"Tell us about New York, Sally," Louis said after Sheriff Carson left. "It has been so long since I was there."

"Oh, New York is wonderful. So many huge buildings, four, five, and six stories high, elevated trains whizzing all through the city, electric wires, telephone service. Surely, there is no place in the world like New York."

"You talk almost as if you would rather you and Smoke lived there," Dr. Colton said.

"Oh, no." Sally put her hand on Smoke's arm. "I am living exactly where I want to live. Remember, I came West of my own accord, and I have never regretted one moment of it."

"She met with the president of the United States," Smoke said proudly.

"The president? You met the president?"

"It isn't that big of a deal," Sally said. "He and my father were very good friends at one time."

"What do you mean, that isn't a very big deal? I think it is a huge deal," Dr. Colton said.

Laramie, Wyoming

At the remark made by the young man, all conversation in the Rocky Mountain Beer Hall ceased.

Wesley Harley was an ugly man. He was bald,

not because of age, but because some anomaly in his genetic makeup left him completely devoid of body hair—none on his head, no eyebrows or eyelashes, no mustache, and no hair on his arms, chest, or anywhere else. His face was narrow, and his skin was drawn so tight across his high cheekbones he looked almost like a skeleton.

He had been leaning against the bar, with both his hands wrapped around the beer in front of him. He turned toward the young man who had spoken to him.

"What did you say?"

"You heard what I said," the young man, barely out of the teens, said. His words were loud and precisely spoken. "I said you murdered my pa, and I intend to see you brought to justice for it."

"Do you now? And just how do you plan to do that?"

"By telling the law. I am going to the sheriff right now. I am going to tell him what you did, and I am going to tell him where to find you."

"You don't understand, do you, boy?" Harley said. "The sheriff knows where I am. Hell, all the sheriffs in the West know where I am. They just don't want no part of me."

"It ain't right," the boy said. "You murdered my pa, and I ain't goin' to let you get away with it."

"Well, now, since I done told you that the sheriff don't want nothin' to do with me, if you are lookin' for justice, seems to me the only way you goin' to get that justice is if you do it yourself. But before we get on with it, who is it I'm supposed to have kilt?"

"I don't believe this. You mean you can't even remember the name of someone you killed?"

"Sonny, I've kilt so many of 'em, they all sort of blend in. What was your pa's name? And where is it I was supposed to have kilt him?"

"His name was Conyers. Enoch Conyers," the boy said.

"Oh, yeah," Harley said. "I remember him. He was cheatin' at cards."

"My pa never cheated at anything!" the boy said resolutely.

"Yeah, I recollect now. He wasn't cheatin'. He accused me of cheatin'. I called him out on it."

"And you killed him," the boy said.

"You ought not to start somethin' you can't finish." Harley chuckled, but it was a laugh without genuine mirth. "Sort of like what you're doin' now, ain't it, boy? You've started somethin' you can't finish."

The expression on the boy's face changed from one of anger, to fear when he realized what he had gotten himself into. Then, even the fear gave way to resignation.

"Let's do it, boy," Harley said, his voice sounding almost bored.

With a defiant scream, the boy went for his gun. He had it but halfway out of the holster when Harley fired at him. The bullet hit the boy in the heart, killing him before he could even react to it.

Only one shot had been fired, and because Harley put his pistol back in his holster as quickly as he had taken it out, some in the saloon didn't even know where the shot had come from.

The sheriff held an inquest that very afternoon, and because there were enough witnesses who saw what actually happened, no charges were filed.

CHAPTER FIVE

Elco, Colorado

Frank and Travis Slater had served six months in jail for burglary, and would have gone to prison for a year, if Chance Carter hadn't paid for a good lawyer to plead their case.

"I think they're basically good boys," Carter told the judge when he was providing supporting testimony. "They just made a mistake is all, and I would hate to see their whole lives ruined because of it."

The judge had taken Carter's testimony to heart and had given lenient sentences to both of them. Now that they were out of jail they were working as hired hands for Carter. Carter's wife had died ten years ago, and Chance had raised their daughter ever since. Carrie was fifteen years old and just blossoming into womanhood.

One morning she came out to the barn carrying a milk pail. She smiled at Travis, who at nineteen, was the younger of the two brothers. Frank was twenty-two.

"Good morning, Travis." Carrie took the milking stool down from its hook.

"Pretty soon, you won't be needin' to milk that cow," Travis said.

"What do you mean?"

"Why, the way you are tittyin' up, you'll be able to give milk yourself." Travis laughed at his joke.

"That's not a very nice thing to say!" Carrie blushed at the comment.

"Sure it is," Travis said. "You think Frank an' me don't see how you come around us all the time, showin' off them titties of yours?"

"I do no such thing!" Carrie insisted. "And I don't like the way you are talking to me."

"Yeah you do. You like it a lot. Otherwise you wouldn't be showin' off like you are."

"I'm not showing off."

"You aren't? Then what did you come out here for? Did you come out here just to put a burr under my saddle?" Travis walked over to her and put his hand on her shoulder. "Or did you come out here so I could make you a woman?"

"Make me a woman? What does that mean?" Carrie asked with another laugh. "I'm already a woman."

"No, you ain't." Travis pulled her to him. "You ain't a woman until you've had a man. Like me." He pulled her to him and forced a kiss on her.

She fought against him. When he pulled his lips away, she shouted, "Pa! Pa!"

"Shut up! You want your pa to come runnin' out here?" Travis slapped her hard, and blood came from her lips.

"Pa!" she screamed again, but that was as far as she got before Travis, acting spontaneously, picked up the hammer he had been using to adjust the iron wheel rim, and hit her hard. She went down without a sound.

"Get up," Travis said. "Get up and don't be screamin' no more."

"She ain't goin' to be gettin' up," Frank said. He had been out in the corral, but was drawn back to the barn by the young girl's scream.

"Yeah she is. Get up," Travis said again.

"Travis, take a look at her. Take a good, close look at her."

Travis looked down at the young girl and saw that her eyes and mouth were open, but she was totally still. There was a very dark bruise on the side of her head where he had hit her with the hammer.

"Oh damn! Oh damn, oh damn, oh damn! Frank, I've kilt her! What am I goin' to do? I didn't mean to kill her. I was just tryin' to get her to shut up."

"Carrie!" a man's voice shouted. "What is it? What are you calling me for?"

Chance Carter, a man in his early forties, stepped into the barn and saw the body of his daughter lying on the ground. He saw Travis and Frank looking down at her.

"My God! What happened?" Chance asked in agonized shock.

"She—uh, I didn't mean—uh, I didn't think I hit her that hard," Travis said.

"You did this? You did this?" Chance asked.

"I was just funnin' with her," Travis said weakly. "Then she started screamin' and I wanted her to stop."

"You murderer!" Chance turned and started back toward the house.

"Mr. Carter, listen to me!" Travis called after him. "I didn't mean to kill her! I just wanted her to stop yelling is all! It was an accident!"

Without any reply, Chance ran into the house.

"What's he goin' to do, Frank?"

"I figure he's goin' after a gun. And I figure he's goin' to come back out and commence shootin'."

Frank took the hammer from Travis's hand, then hurried up to the big house. He stood alongside the door, with his back up against the wall, and waited until Chance Carter came back outside.

"You son of a bitch, you killed my daughter," Carter shouted, starting toward the barn with a double barrel shotgun in his hand.

So intent was Carter on extracting retribution from Travis, he didn't see Frank step out behind him. Frank brought the hammer down hard, and Chance dropped to the ground.

Frank got down on his knees beside the rancher and hit him again and again with the hammer.

He didn't stop until blood, bone, and brain matter was pouring out of the wound.

"I think you can quit now, Frank," Travis said.

Frank stood up and looked at the bloody end of the hammer. "Yeah."

"What do we do now?"

"We get our guns and get out of here," Frank said.

"How we goin' to get out of here? The only horses Mr. Carter's got is team horses. He ain't got no saddles."

In the distance they heard the whistle of a train.

"We'll take the train," Frank said.

"Like as not, it's a freight train this time of day," Travis said.

"All the better," Frank replied.

Poncha Pass, Colorado

The freight cars bumped and rattled through the night, the thunder echoing back from Poncha Pass. On the 2-4-2 locomotive the steam gushed from the drive cylinder like cannon fire as it labored mightily to negotiate the grade. But five cars back, Frank and Travis Slater, who had hopped onto the freight when they fled the Carter ranch, could hear nothing of the engine.

The car had been empty when the two brothers jumped onto the train, but just before nightfall, two other men climbed into the car.

"You think the brakeman saw us?" one of the two men asked.

"Nah. Anyway, I think it's Doodle. He's a good one. He don't ever throw you off," the other said.

In the dim light, the two new men saw Frank and Travis sitting in the forward part of the empty car, their backs braced against the front wall so no matter how much the train lurched and jerked, they were able to keep from being tossed about.

"Hello, boys," one of the newcomers said with a friendly greeting. "Been on the train long, have you?"

"Not too long," Frank answered.

"My name's Zeke, my partner here is Mickey. We know most of the riders, but I don't think we've ever run across you two before."

"No, this is our first time." Frank pointedly did not give their names.

Zeke chuckled. "Don't want to tell me your name, huh? Well, no matter. Sometimes when folks is down on their luck, they don't like to give away their names. That's fine with Mickey and me."

"How many times have you hopped a train on this line?" Frank asked.

"I'd say twenty, maybe thirty times, wouldn't you, Mickey?"

"Thirty times for sure. You might recall, one time we done it two times in the same week."

"Yeah, I do recall. So this is your first time, is it?" Zeke asked.

"Yes," Travis answered.

"Well, there's some things you need to know. If

you'll listen to me, I'll be learnin' you some of them things."

"We're listenin'," Frank said.

"The first thing is, you got to know what kind of car to hop, and you got to know how far it's goin'," Zeke said. "I mind the time Jimmy Peal . . . You remember him, don't you, Mickey?"

"I remember him well. He was a big man, maybe six feet four inches tall, or so," Mickey said.

"Yes, that's the one I'm talkin' about," Zeke said. "Well, sir, Jimmy Peal once hopped onto a car and the door got shut on him so's he couldn't get out. The car went all the way to New Orleans, it did, and when they opened it up down there, well, they found Jimmy Peal dead. He'd done starved to death."

"He died of thirst," Mickey corrected. "As big a man as he was, it would've took him a long time to starve to death. But it don't take hardly no time at all for a man to die if he don't have no water."

"We're sure goin' slow now," Travis said. "Why, I could walk faster than this."

"That's 'cause we climbin' up Poncha Pass," Zeke explained. "But we are near 'bout to the top now. You wait till we get over the top, then you'll see."

"I'll see what?"

"You'll see us speed up. The train will be goin' lickity split an' I wager you'll be a' wantin' to grab ahold of somethin' so as to be able to hang on."

The train reached the top of the pass, then

started down, gathering speed as the peaks lurched behind them in an increasingly faster rush.

"How fast you think we're a' goin' anyway?" Frank asked.

"Goin' downhill like this? I'd say thirty-five, forty miles an hour. Maybe even faster," Zeke said.

"Damn, I ain't never gone this fast before," Frank said.

"So, this is the first time you two boys ever jumped a freight, is it?" Mickey asked.

"Yeah, that's what I said," Travis answered.

"What did you jump it for?"

"What?"

"Well, I mean, you boys don't exactly have the looks of a rail bum."

"We jumped it for the same reason as you did," Frank said. "We needed to get somewhere, and we didn't have no horses."

Zeke laughed. "See, now that's the difference between you two, 'n me 'n Mickey here. You said you need to get somewhere."

Frank looked confused. "Yeah, so, what's different? We're on this train just like you are."

"No, you ain't. It ain' nothin' like Mickey 'n me," Zeke said. "That's the whole point. You said you are needin' to get somewhere. Me and Mickey, we don't need to get nowhere, on account of because we are already here."

"What do you mean, you are already here?" Travis asked. "You are on a train, goin' somewhere."

"See, that's where you don' understand men

like Mickey 'n me. We ain't goin' nowhere. We are already here," Zeke said.

"We'll ride this train for a while, then we'll ride another train, and after that, why, we'll hop on another train and ride it," Mickey said. "We ain't goin' nowhere in particular, which means we are already here."

"How do you eat?" Frank asked.

"Just like anyone else. With our mouths," Zeke replied, laughing at his joke.

"No, I mean if you are on the train all the time, how do you get food? You don't have any money," Frank said. "What do you do? Beg people for food?"

"Who says we don't have any money?" Zeke replied. "We may be gentlemen of the rails, but we aren't beggars."

"We just got through workin' for a couple weeks makin' bricks," Mickey said. "We got enough money to feed us for a month or so. Then when we run out of money, why, we'll find us some other place to work."

"You don't hardly never see nobody ridin' the rails that ain't got some money," Zeke said. "So don't go gettin' on your high horse with us."

"Well, just how much money do you have?" Frank asked.

"Seein' as I'm just learnin' you boys about the life, what with you just startin' out an' all, why, I ain't goin' take no offense to that question you just asked me. But the truth is, that ain't a question you ever want to ask anyone. How much money a man has is his own business."

"Yeah, I see," Frank said. "Sorry I asked."

"That's all right. Like I told you, you two boys is new, and you don't know no better, so I ain't takin' no offense."

The train leveled out and slowed down. Zeke got up and walked over to stand in the open door of the freight for a moment, then he came back. "Gilman is comin' up."

"What's in Gilman?" Frank asked.

"It's a new town. It has a store, a stamping mill, a café."

"Does it have a saloon?" Travis asked.

"I expect it does. I ain't never been in it though. Most of the time when we want somethin' to drink, we'll just buy a bottle. Right, Mickey?"

"Yeah. We don't go into saloons 'cause we ain't exactly what you call, social."

"Will you be gettin' off here?"

"No, we ain't got no reason to get off yet." Zeke came back to the front of the car, then sat down against the wall. Frank got up and walked over to the open door to look outside. The train had slowed considerably.

"You ever jumped off a train while it was movin'?" Frank asked.

"Yes, but you wouldn't want to do it if it was movin' any faster 'n this," Zeke said.

"How do you do it?"

"It's easy. You just jump far enough out to make certain you don't fall back under the wheels."

"And when you jump, you're goin' to tumble some," Mickey added. "So what you want to do is make sure you're facin' toward the front. Otherwise you could tumble backward and break your neck."

"Come here, Travis, have a look," Frank said.

Travis got up from his place by the front wall and walked to the door.

"How much money you think they got on 'em now?" Frank asked Travis, speaking just loudly enough for Travis to hear him.

"I don't know. Twenty, thirty dollars maybe."

"That's good enough." Pulling his pistol, Frank held it down by his side and slightly behind him as he walked back to the front of the car.

"So what did you boys decide?" Zeke asked. "You goin' to jump out of the car?" He and Mickey laughed.

"After," Frank said.

"After what?"

"After this." Frank raised the pistol and fired twice at point blank range. He hit Zeke and Mickey in the forehead, killing them instantly. Travis came up behind him.

"Why did you do that? We coulda just held 'em up."

"They knew who we were," Frank replied. "This way, they aren't likely to even be discovered for two or three days, if that. Hell, this car might wind up in San Francisco before anyone discovers them. By then we'll be so far away there won't be any way at all anyone can ever put together the fact that we was the ones who done it. You search Mickey. I'll search Zeke."

"Damn!" Travis held something up. "I bet there's over a hunnert dollars here!"

"Yeah!" Frank said with equal excitement. "There's at least that much here. Who would have thought that?"

"Come on," Travis said. "We'd better get off now."

Stepping into the open door of the freight car, the two men leaped clear of the roadbed. The jump caused them to tumble forward, in keeping with Mickey's instructions. By the time they picked themselves up, the lighted caboose of the train was rocking past them. The two men watched the car grow smaller in the distance until all they could see was the glowing red lamp that was hanging from a hook on the end of the caboose.

"What do we do now?" Travis asked.

"We follow the tracks to town."

"It's the middle of the night. There ain't goin' to be nothin' open in the middle of the night."

"We don't want anything to be open," Frank said. "When you're stealin' horses, it's best that ever'one be asleep."

Travis laughed. "Yeah."

With only moonlight to guide them, they walked along the track, following the softly gleaming rails for a mile until they reached the town. Gilman was perched on the side of a mountain, the private homes and commercial buildings clinging to the side like sprouting bushes. Taking advantage of what level land there was, two streets formed a *V* with the point pointing toward the east.

It was about two in the morning, so there was not one soul awake in the town, and the only sound that could be heard was the rustle of the wind through the limbs of the aspen trees. From the far end of town, they heard a dog barking, and Frank and Travis stopped in their tracks.

"I hope that dog is tied up," Travis said.

"I expect he is." Frank pointed. "Look over there. Do you see what I see?"

Travis looked in the direction indicated. "All I see is a lean-to."

"With a couple horses," Frank replied.

"I don't see no—" Travis stopped in mid-sentence when he saw something move in the shadows of the lean-to. "Oh, wait, yeah, I see 'em."

Moving silently through the night, the two brothers reached the lean-to where they found two horses tied to a rail, and two saddles conveniently stored on a shelf to one side. They saddled the horses, then led them out into the open, keeping a close eye on the nearby house. Travis started to mount.

"Not yet," Frank said. "Let's walk them all the way out of town first. It's quieter that way."

"Yeah," Travis said. "Yeah, good idea."

CHAPTER SIX

Sugarloaf Ranch

There had been a time in Smoke's past when he had sold all his cattle and switched over to raising horses. That had worked well for a while, because the U.S. Cavalry had provided a willing market for his stock. But with the increasing demand for beef in the East, Smoke was once more raising cattle. His ranch was the biggest in Colorado, on par with some of the largest ranches in Texas.

Although many ranchers were using Mr. Joseph Glidden's invention as a means of keeping their herds corralled, Smoke did not believe in barbed wire, or "bobbed wahr" as Pearlie, Cal, and most of his hands called it, so he let his animals run free upon the range. That freedom gave them a lot of room to roam. Sugarloaf consisted of fifty thousand acres of titled land, with an additional one hundred thousand acres of adjacent, free range land. There was ample water and grass, and ultimately the herd was fenced in by nature, with the Elk Mountain Range to the north and Grand Mesa to the west.

With over fifteen thousand head of cattle scattered over one hundred and fifty thousand acres, rounding them up would be quite an undertaking. In fact, it was a job much too large for his fulltime hands. Several additional hands had been hired for the roundup, and the operation was well underway.

The first thing was to find all the cattle carrying the Sugarloaf brand and move them into a herd. In addition, the cowboys would also have to bring in the unbranded calves that belonged to Sugarloaf. It was fairly easy to identify the calves that belonged to Sugarloaf, not only because much of the land was part of the Sugarloaf spread, but also because the newly born and unbranded calves tended to stay with their mothers—and their mothers were branded.

Gradually the far ranging cattle were brought in, and the herd grew in size. Not more than two or three riders at a time would work the assembled cattle. Too many riders cutting in and out of the herd would get the stock to milling around nervously, making them difficult to work with.

Smoke was sitting in his saddle with one leg curled across the saddle horn. He took the makings from his shirt pocket and rolled a cigarette, then using his thumbnail, snapped a match to light and held the flame to the end. He waved the match out, flipping it aside just as Pearlie came riding up.

"What did we do, give the heifers some wine, and play a little music for them?" Pearlie asked.

"What are you talking about?" Smoke blew out a stream of smoke as he asked the question.

"We got more calves this year than ever before," Pearlie said. "Our bulls must have been quite the ladies' men."

Smoke chuckled. "I guess that explains why I saw one of them with an ascot and a monocle."

Pearlie laughed. "How many head are we going to take to market this year?"

"I told the railroad people we would need at least a hundred cars."

"Four thousand head at forty dollars a head," Pearlie said. "That would be . . ."

"A hundred and sixty thousand dollars," Smoke said.

"Wow! Damn, Smoke, you must be about the richest man in Colorado."

"I am. But it doesn't have anything to do with money."

Pearlie looked confused. "I don't understand."

"Sure you do. I'm the richest man in Colorado because I have Sally as my wife, and you, Cal, Monte, Louis, and all my other friends." Smoke took in the vista with a sweep of his arm. "I wouldn't trade this place for all the money in the U.S. Treasury."

"Hey, when we goin' to eat?" Cal rode up to join them. "How come the chuck wagon ain't here yet?"

"Sally's fixing our meal today," Smoke said. "You know how she likes to take a little extra time with her cooking."

Cal smiled, and rubbed his belly. "If Sally is cooking the meal, it's worth a little delay."

"It won't be a long delay," Smoke said. "There she comes now."

The three men looked back toward the big house and saw the chuck wagon coming toward them through the emerald green fields. As it got closer, they could hear the sound of pots and pans banging about inside the wagon.

Smoke rode out to meet her, while Pearlie started toward the cowboys who were working the herd, calling them in for the meal. Sally had gone all out with a large rump of roast beef, boiled potatoes, freshly baked bread, and apple pies.

"What are you doing, Sally?" Smoke asked when the men, smelling the delicious aromas, eagerly lined up for their meal. "Don't give them this, you'll spoil them. They'll think they have to eat like this every day. Give them some beans."

A few of the men groaned.

Sally reached back into the chuck wagon and picked up a can of beans. She tossed it to Smoke. "If you want beans you eat beans. But I'm doing the cooking today and I cooked a roast beef. This is what I'm serving."

The men looked anxiously toward Smoke.

When they saw Pearlie and Cal, and even Smoke, smiling, they realized he was merely joking with them, and they laughed, then took their meal and ate with great enjoyment.

Smoke and Sally sat on the ground, leaning back against the wheel of the chuck wagon.

"I'm going into Gothic tomorrow," she said. "I wrote to Tamara and told her I would be there. I'll probably stay for a week or so, while she is getting her new restaurant set up."

"All right," Smoke said.

"I hope you don't mind, I'm taking Cal with me. He can come in handy when we start moving in the stoves, tables, and such."

"I don't mind at all," Smoke said. "As a matter of fact, I think that is probably a pretty good idea."

One of the cowboys walked up to them then, and he was rubbing his stomach. "Mr. Jensen, all the other boys has asked me to speak for 'em. We was wonderin', I mean, seein' as how good we was fed 'n all, well, it's made us all mighty sleepy. We was wonderin' if maybe we couldn't just take the rest of the day off and nap."

"What?" Smoke stood up quickly.

The cowboy laughed, then all the others laughed as well.

"You deserved that, Smoke," Pearlie said, joining in the laughter. "I mean after tellin' them they couldn't have this meal Miss Sally cooked."

Smoke laughed with them, then held up his hands. "All right, boys, we're even."

"Come on, boys, we're burnin' daylight!" Pearlie shouted. "Let's get to work!"

Toombs Trading Post was ten miles from the nearest town, surviving despite its isolation. It was located on the banks of the Grand River, which was the source of the Colorado River. Its location assured that many travelers came by. Seeing a store, hotel, restaurant, and saloon in the middle of nowhere made it a popular stop.

Its remote location also meant it was a long way from a sheriff's protection, and that was the reason the Slater brothers, Frank and Travis, chose to rob it. Standing in the store, with the bottom half of their faces covered by bandannas, they held their guns on Eli and Marcie Toombs, the proprietors. Also present in the store was Clem Perkins, an old man who had been in Colorado for over fifty years, one of the early mountain men.

Eli Toombs took all the cash from his cash drawer and dropped it in the cloth bag Travis handed him. He didn't resist. The two brothers had threatened to kill his wife if he did.

"I thank you very much for that contribution, Mr. Toombs." Travis took the bag of money, then looked over toward the old mountain man. "What have you got that we might want?"

"I ain't got a damn thing, sonny," the mountain man replied with a dismissive slur.

"Maybe I should just see about that." Travis reached toward Clem Perkins. The old mountain man grabbed his hand, raised it to his mouth, and bit the end of his finger off.

"Ahhh!" Travis screamed in pain. He shot the old man and, even after he fell, continued to shoot him until the hammer fell repeatedly on empty chambers.

"Let's go!" Frank shouted. "Let's get out of here!"

Grabbing a shirt that was for sale on one of the tables, Travis wrapped it around the end of his finger to staunch the flow of blood.

Taking advantage of the distraction, Toombs grabbed a shotgun from under the counter, but Frank saw him and before Toombs could bring his weapon to bear, Frank shot him.

When Mrs. Toombs, who was screaming in anger and fear, grabbed the gun from her husband's dead hands, Frank shot her as well.

A moment later they rode away from the store with a bag that contained forty-nine dollars and fifty-seven cents. Behind them lay the gruesome remains of their visit, the bodies of Mr. and Mrs. Toombs, and that of one of Colorado's earliest pioneers.

Risco, Colorado

Risco was a scattering of fly-blown, crumbling adobe buildings laid out around a dusty plaza. What made the town attractive to people like

Bill Dinkins, John Putnam, and Cole Parnell was its reputation as a "Robbers' Roost," or "Outlaw Haven."

The town was neither incorporated, nor listed on any map. It had no city government of any kind, including no mayor, constable, marshal, or sheriff. Visitations by law officers were strongly discouraged and there was a place in the town cemetery prominently marked LAWMAN'S PLOT. Two deputy sheriffs, one deputy U.S. marshal, and a private detective, all unwelcome visitors to the town, lay buried there.

Dinkins, Putnam, and Parnell were in the Purgatory Saloon. The three horses they had stolen from the Cañon City Livery were tied up out front. Because of the lawlessness of the town, they had absolutely no concern about riding stolen horses. It was certain nobody in town was going to challenge them over it.

Parnell recognized Frank and Travis Slater when they came in. "Well, well," he said quietly. "Last time I saw them two boys, we was in jail together back in Elco. I went to prison from there, never did find out what happened to them."

"What was they in jail for?" Dinkins asked.

"Stealin', as I recollect," Parnell said.

"We need a couple more men to make sure we pull off the job I have in mind. Do you think they would be the men for it?"

"Don't know whether they would be or not.

Don't know 'em that well. But if I was just guessin', I would say they would be all right."

"Why don't you go and invite them over?" Dinkins suggested.

"All right." Parnell finished his drink, then walked to the two bothers. "Frank and Travis Slater."

Both men whirled toward him with their hands covering the butts of their guns.

"Hold it, hold it!" Parnell held out his hands, palms open. "You ain't goin' to throw down on an old pard, are you?"

"Parnell?" Frank asked. "I thought you was in prison."

"I was," Parnell answered. "But I got let out. I guess you boys was let out too, seein' as the last time I seen the two of you, you was in jail." Smiling, he extended his hand, and each shook it. "Come on over. I've got some fellas I'd like for you to meet," he invited.

Frank and Travis followed Parnell over to the table where Dinkins and Putnam were sitting.

"Bill, Johnny, these two boys is old friends of mine," Parnell said. "Like I told you, we was in jail together back in Elco."

"Pull up a chair and join us," Dinkins invited.

The two brothers sat down.

"Before I go any further, I need to ask a question. Which side of the law are you boys on?" Dinkins asked. "What I mean is, are there any wanted posters out on you?"

"There ain't no dodgers out on us, 'cause we

ain't done nothin' to be wanted for," Travis said quickly.

"Well then, in that case, you probably wouldn't be interested in my proposal," Dinkins said. "Because what I have to suggest will put you on the wrong side of the law for sure. So, if you've got enough money that you ain't interested, well, go on back up to the bar and finish your drink."

"Wait a minute," Frank said. "What is it that you have to suggest?"

"Nothing that would interest you two, I'm sure," Dinkins said. "I mean, bein' as you ain't never done nothin' to be wanted for."

"Supposin' we had," Frank said.

"But your brother just said that you hadn't."

"Whenever a person does somethin' wrong, why he don't generally go aroun' tellin' ever'one about it. That's why Travis lied like he done."

"So, what you are sayin' is, you wouldn't be against doin' somethin' wrong, if it made you some money."

"How much money?" Frank asked.

"A lot of money," Dinkins answered.

"Where are you going to find a lot of money?" Travis asked.

"Well now, where do people keep a lot of money?" Dinkins replied.

Frank and Travis looked at each other, then smiled.

"A bank," Frank said. "You talkin' about robbin' a bank, ain't you?"

"That's where the money is," Dinkins responded. "Are you boys interested?"

"Damn right we're interested. When do we do it?"

"Soon."

CHAPTER SEVEN

Gothic, Colorado

It was four hours by buckboard from Sugarloaf to Gothic. When Sally and Cal left before dawn, there was quite a chill in the air. Their breathing, and the breathing of the horses, emitted little clouds of vapor, but the buffalo robes and sheepskin coats kept them comfortable. It had been Sally's decision to go by buckboard instead of surrey. She was sure once they started setting up the restaurant they would need some means of hauling freight around.

During their drive over from Big Rock it had warmed up considerably so they shed their coats and put them in the back, alongside Sally's suitcase and Cal's duffel. They kept the conversation light as they traveled and the time passed quickly.

The little town of Gothic had grown up in the north part of Gunnison County. It was surrounded by mountains and supported by a productive silver mine, but inexplicably bypassed by the railroad. To Sally and Cal, approaching from the south, the collection of sun-bleached and weatherworn wooden buildings were so much a part of the land that it looked almost as if the town was the result of some natural phenomenon, rather than the work of man.

Crossing the outer edge of the town they encountered a sign, erected by the Gothic City Council.

GOTHIC

POPULATION 507

Silver Capital of Colorado

Sally gave Cal a twenty dollar bill.

"What's this for, Miss Sally?"

"You'll need a place to stay while you are here. This is for your hotel and food."

"I don't think it'll cost that much."

"Well, then you'll have a little extra money left over for a beer, or perhaps a game of cards," Sally suggested. "That is, if you don't gamble too recklessly."

"Gee, thanks!" Cal said. "Don't worry none about the gamblin' part, I don't never get carried away too much."

Sally had never been to Tamara's house, but she had the address so she guided Cal to a very small structure that sat on the outskirts of town. Tamara had been watching for them, and came out front, smiling broadly as they drove up. Sally hopped down and the two women embraced, then Sally reached for her suitcase.

"I'll get that for you, Miss Sally," Cal offered.

"Don't be silly. I'm not helpless. Go get yourself a hotel room, then find a place to park the buckboard and stable the horses."

"Oh, the hotel has its own stable and wagon yard," Tamara said. "You won't have any trouble."

"Thanks." Cal snapped the reins as he urged the horses on.

"I knew you would be here about lunchtime, so I prepared lunch for us," Tamara said as they went into her house, redolent with the most enticing aromas.

"Oh, we should have held Cal here," Sally said.

"I'm sorry, we should have, shouldn't we? But I have to confess I never even thought about that. I'm afraid I made just enough for the two of us."

Although the house consisted of only one room, and was very small, the table had been covered with a white cloth, and was set with sparkling china, silver, and crystal. "Oh," Sally said. "If you set a table like this in your restaurant, you'll be drawing people from fifty miles in each direction! It is beautiful!"

"Thank you, but the presentation is only half of it. We'll have to see how it tastes."

"Let's do that right now," Sally suggested as she pulled the chair out to sit down.

Half an hour later, Sally dabbed at her lips with

the napkin. She'd eaten crispy fried asparagus, French onion soup with a toasted baguette, and a bacon and tomato sandwich with peppercorn mayonnaise. "Oh, my. Oh, my, oh, my, oh, my. Once you get your restaurant going over here, you will have to open another one in Big Rock."

"But wouldn't that upset Mr. Longmont?" Tamara asked. "I know he prides himself on his restaurant."

"And rightly so," Sally agreed. "Because it is a fine restaurant. But Louis is a gentleman, and a connoisseur. Believe me, nobody will have a greater appreciation for another fine restaurant than Louis Longmont. In fact, I would not be in the least surprised if he turned out to be one of your best customers."

"Would you like to see the building I've picked out for the restaurant?"

"I would love to."

"Do I need a coat? Or has it warmed up enough?"

"The buffalo robes and the sheepskin coat felt good on the way over here," Sally said. "But it has warmed considerably. However, I think it is still cool enough that you could use a light wrap."

A few minutes later the two women were walking down the boardwalk toward the building where Tamara intended to put her restaurant. It fronted Gothic Road, which was the main street of the town, and was well centered in the business community. The building had already been painted white and was obviously of recent construction. The door was locked, but Tamara had the key.

"Mr. Cassidy gave me the key to the building," she said as she unlocked the door. "He built it for his bakery, but decided to add on to his house and put his bakery there, instead. He has offered me a very good price on the building."

Once inside, Tamara showed where she would put all the tables, and the cashier's counter. "As you can see, the kitchen already has a built-in oven. Mr. Cassidy was going to bake bread there. I'll use it for pies, and I'll buy my bread from him. It was part of the agreement to sell the building to me."

They spent half an hour in the building, making plans for curtains, what color to paint the walls, the type of tablecloths that should be used, what pictures Tamara would want to put on the wall.

"I've made some drawings of what I think it should be if you would like to see them," she said. "They are back at the house."

They returned to Tamara's house and spent the rest of the day looking at drawings, and at swaths of material.

"I'm getting as excited about it as if I were the one doing it," Sally said.

"Well, in a very real sense, you are the one doing it," Tamara said. "You will be my full partner."

"No, I'll be a minor partner," Sally insisted. "You are the one who will be doing all the work.

Though I think I would love to come over here and help you decorate, and get everything started."

"I've never had such a friend as you," Tamara said.

"As soon as the bank opens tomorrow, we will go make all the financial arrangements," Sally promised.

Early the next morning, Bill Dinkins, John Putnam, Cole Parnell, and Frank and Travis Slater were camped in the shadow of Castle Peak, having a breakfast of coffee and jerky. Though it was late spring, the sun had not yet peeked over the mountain. At that elevation at that time of year, it was still quite cool, if not cold, and the men were huddled around the fire, reluctant to give up its warmth.

"How much money you reckon is in the bank?" Parnell asked.

"A lot," Dinkins said.

"How can there be all that much? I mean, bein' as the town is so little and all?" Putnam asked.

"Gothic is a silver mining town," Dinkins explained. "They keep a lot of money in their bank so's they can handle the silver."

"Hope it pays better 'n the last bank I hit," Parnell said. "Last bank I robbed I come up with only seventy-six dollars, 'n five years in prison."

The others laughed.

"What are you laughin' at?" Parnell asked Putnam. "You was right there in prison with me."

"Yeah, but it wasn't for no seventy-six dollars. I got more money 'n that."

"How much did you get, Putnam?" Travis asked.

"I got me a hunnert 'n seven dollars," Putnam replied, then wondered why the others laughed at him.

"I guarantee you there's more 'n seventy-six, or even a hunnert 'n seven dollars in this bank," Dinkins said. "And I don't plan on goin' to prison."

None of them had asked Dinkins about the debacle in Buffalo, and he hadn't told them. It was just as well they knew nothing about it.

In the town of Gothic, Sally, Tamara, and Cal were having breakfast in the dining room of the Silver Lode Hotel.

"Miz McKenzie, when you get your own restaurant started, why, we can eat with you whenever we come over," Cal said.

"Yes, indeed," Tamara replied. "And you can eat as my guest. There will be no charge."

"You might want to rethink that, Tamara," Sally said. "You don't have any idea how much food Calvin Woods can pack away."

"Oh, I think I will be able to manage it," Tamara replied.

"Miss Sally, are you goin' to teach Miz McKenzie how to make bear claws?"

"Tamara is quite a good cook. I'm sure she needs no instruction from me."

"Maybe so," Cal said. "But I don't think anyone can make bear claws as good as you do."

Sally laughed. "Cal, the way you and Pearlie eat bear claws, I don't think it would make any difference to either one of you, who made them."

"I don't know. Yours is—are"—he corrected himself—"awfully good."

"Very good," Sally said.

"Very good," Cal said.

"No, I was referring to the fact that you corrected yourself from is to are," Sally said. "That was very good."

"Thanks." Cal beamed under the praise.

"Sally, what time is it?" Tamara asked.

Sally had a small watch pinned to the bodice of her dress, and she pulled it away on a little retracting chain to examine the face. "It lacks fifteen minutes of nine."

"The bank opens at nine," Tamara said. "If you don't mind, I would like to get there just as soon as the bank is open."

"That's fine by me," Sally said. "The quicker we can get the business done at the bank, the quicker we can get started on putting the restaurant together."

"Good, I'm glad you see it that way too," Tamara said.

"You goin' to meet in the bank?" Cal asked.

"Yes."

"If you don't mind, I mean what with you 'n Miz McKenzie talkin' business and all, I'll probably just sort of wait around over at the mercantile store."

"I don't mind at all," Sally said.

"Hey, do you reckon Pearlie would like one of them things you poke the ends of your bandanna through, so's you can slide it up and hold the bandanna around your neck?"

Sally winced. She had long ago stopped trying to correct Cal's grammar, and was pleased and surprised when, from time to time he corrected himself, as he had earlier.

"I think he would be very pleased with it," she said.

Cal smiled broadly. "Then I aim to get him one."

Travis Slater, the youngest of the five men, slipped his canteen off the saddle horn and took a drink, wiped the back of his hand across his mouth, then recorked it and hung it back on his saddle. He looked at his hand, and at the stub of his ring finger, healed now, from having been bitten off. He was still angry about that. He had killed the son of a bitch who did it, but wished he was alive so he could kill him again.

"Damn, we been two weeks without seein' a town," Travis said. "Don't you think, maybe, we could stop at a saloon and get us a few beers afore we take care of our business?"

"Now, that would make a lot of sense, wouldn't it, Travis?" Dinkins asked. "Yeah, why don't we just go into the saloon, have us a few drinks and strike up a conversation with some of the locals? That way they are sure to have a good description of us. No, I got a better idea, why don't we see if there is one of them picture parlors in town? We could have the photographer take our pictures, then there wouldn't be no doubt as to what we looked like."

"Hell, Bill, you don't have to get so particular about it," Travis said. "I was just sayin' that a beer would be good, is all."

"How we goin' to keep from gettin' recognized anyhow, once we rob the bank?" Johnny Putnam asked.

"They ain't goin' to recognize us if we do this job right," Dinkins insisted. "If all of you do just like I tell you, we'll be into that bank, have the money and be out again afore anyone in this town even knows what hit 'em." He smiled at the others. "Then when we ride into the next town we'll be able to come in like we own the place. All the beer we can drink, women, gamblin' money. Hell, we'll be king of the roost."

"Have any of you ever know'd anyone to get hisself two whores at the same time?" Travis asked.

Parnell laughed. "Two whores? What the hell would you do with two whores at the same time? Hell, Travis, I'm not sure you'd even know what to do with one whore. You ain't never even been with a whore yet, have you?"

"Why, sure I have, lots of times," Travis insisted.

"Where did you have a whore?"

"I had me one oncet when I was in Denver."

"Ha! One time in Denver. Yeah, that sounds like lots of times," Parnell said

"That's only 'cause I don't never have enough money for whores," Travis said.

"Well, you just do what I tell you to today, and you'll have all the money you need . . . even enough for two whores at the same time if you think you can handle that," Dinkins promised. "Now, let's get on with it. You boys, check your pistols."

The men pulled their pistols and checked the cylinders to see that all the chambers were properly charged. Then they slipped their guns back into their holsters.

"Ready?" Dinkins asked.

"I'm ready," Travis replied.

The others nodded.

CHAPTER EIGHT

When Tamara and Sally went into the bank, they walked over to one side, where a low rail separated the lobby from a small office. The owner of the bank, a man named Kurt Flowers, was sitting at a desk. He was tall and distinguished looking, with silver hair, blue eyes, and a silver Vandyke beard.

"Mr. Flowers, I wonder if we could speak with you for a moment?" Tamara asked.

"Of course you can," Flowers answered with a smile. There were no other chairs in the office area so he didn't invite them in. Instead, he stepped through a little gate, then over to stand by the small, wood-burning stove. "What can I do for you?"

"This is my friend, Sally Jensen," Tamara introduced. "You may know of her husband, Smoke Jensen."

Flowers' smile broadened. "Indeed I do know

of him. Tell me, Mrs. Jensen, what brings you to our fair city?"

"Business," Sally said. "Tamara intends to start a new restaurant here, and I want to help her."

"A new restaurant? What a wonderful idea." Flowers chuckled. "Of course the Silver Lode Hotel will probably not welcome it, at least, not initially, as it will be competition for their restaurant. But they will come around to it. Any new business helps the town grow and maintain a level of prosperity, and that accrues to the benefit of us all. Where do you plan to put your restaurant?"

"I intend to buy the building Mr. Cassidy built. You know, the one that was going to be used for a bakery? He decided to enlarge his house and put the bakery there instead."

"Ah, yes, I'm sure, under the circumstances, you will get a very good price on the building."

"Tell me, Mr. Flowers, you have your fingers on the pulse of business in this town. Do you think two thousand dollars will be enough to buy the building, equipment, and get the restaurant started?"

"Yes, ma'am, I think two thousand dollars would be more than enough money," Flowers replied.

"I have two thousand dollars in cash," Sally said. "I would like to open an account for the restaurant and fill out whatever paperwork is necessary for Tamara to be able to access the account."

The banker smiled. "Yes ma'am, Mrs. Jensen,

we can open an account for Mrs. McKenzie right now. How is Mr. Jensen doing? I haven't seen him in a while."

"He's doing fine, thank you. He's back at Sugarloaf, taking care of things. We are right in the middle of the spring roundup."

"Sugarloaf is a fine ranch," Flowers said. "In fact, it's as fine a ranch as there is in all of Colorado."

"Thank you," Sally said with a broad smile. "We certainly like it."

Half an hour earlier, Dinkins, Putnam, Parnell, Frank, and Travis separated about half a mile outside of town.

"I'll go in first, alone," Dinkins said. "Johnny, you and Cole come in a couple minutes later, from the north end of town. Frank, you and Travis come in from the south end. That way we won't be arousin' any suspicion."

"Where will we meet up?" Frank asked.

"In front of the bank."

"Won't that cause some suspicion?"

"By that time it'll be too late for 'em to do anything about it. The bank opens at nine, I think it lacks about twenty minutes of nine now. I'd like to get there as soon after it opens as we can. Johnny, you get the rest of you started on time."

"All right," Putnam said. "We'll be there on time."

* * *

Half an hour later five riders, all wearing long, tan-colored dusters, and strangers to everyone in town, had what seemed like an incidental meeting in front of the Miners' Bank. Dinkins, Putnam, Parnell, and Frank Slater dismounted and handed their reins to Travis. He remained in the saddle and kept his eyes open on the street. Dinkins looked up and down the street once, taking notice of the fact that nobody seemed to be paying any attention to them. Then he and the other men pulled their kerchiefs up over the bottom half of their faces, and, with their guns drawn, pushed open the door.

Cal Wood was two blocks down the street at the mercantile store. He had been standing at the counter, paying for a kerchief slide and a stick of peppermint candy when the five men rode into town, so he didn't notice them, nor did he see them pull the kerchiefs up over the bottom half of their faces and go into the bank with their guns drawn. When he walked back up to the front of the store, sucking on the candy stick he looked through the big front window though and saw only one man in front of the bank—mounted, and holding the reins of four other horses. That did arouse his curiosity.

"Mr. Wood?" the proprietor of the store called.

"Yes?" Cal turned back toward him.

"Your change."

Cal smiled. "Oh, yes, I nearly forgot that. Thanks."

Sally, Tamara, Kurt Flowers, and Burt Martin, the bank teller, were the only people in the bank when Dinkins and the others went in. Because of the masks on their faces and the guns in their hands, everyone in the bank knew immediately what was going on.

"You three! Get your hands up and stay back there against the wall!" Dinkins shouted to Sally, Tamara, and Flowers. "If I see any one of you move, I'll shoot."

The three complied with the orders.

Cole Parnell hopped over the railing to go behind the teller cage, then held his sack out toward the teller. "Put all your money into this sack," he growled.

Trembling, the teller emptied his cash drawer.

"Hey, Dinkins, there ain't that much here," Parnell called.

"Parnell, you dumb son of a bitch! You just give 'em my name!" Dinkins growled. "Get the rest out of the safe."

"I can't open the safe till ten o'clock," the teller protested.

"What the hell do you mean you can't open the safe till ten o'clock? You work here, don't you?" Dinkins asked.

"Ye-yes," the teller stuttered. "But there's a time lock on the safe. It can't be opened till ten o'clock."

Dinkins stepped up to the teller and put the muzzle of his pistol one inch from the teller's head. "Open the damn safe or I'll blow your brains out."

"Please, he's telling the truth!" Flowers shouted from his position by the wall.

Dinkins looked toward him. "Who the hell are you?"

"My name is Kurt Flowers. I own this bank."

"You own it, do you?"

"Yes."

Dinkins turned his gun toward Flowers. "Then I'm pointin' my gun at the wrong man. You open the safe."

"I can't open the safe. Mr. Martin is telling the truth. There is a time lock on it. Nobody can open it until ten o'clock."

"Why the hell would you do something like that?"

"Isn't it obvious, Mr. Dinkins?" Sally asked. "It is to keep polecats like you from being able to rob the bank."

Dinkins saw the money in Sally's hand, and smiled. "Well now. If I can't rob the bank, I'll just rob you. Hand the money over, missy."

"If you want it, you grub around on the floor for it, like the rat you are." Surprising Dinkins, Sally threw the money up in the air, one hundred individual, twenty-dollar bills. They fluttered down, scattering all over the floor.

"You bitch!" Dinkins shouted, pulling the trigger.

Tamara screamed as Sally grabbed her stomach where the bullet hit. Blood oozed through her fingers and she staggered back against the wall, then fell.

Suddenly the front door opened and Travis, who didn't have the bottom half of his face masked, stuck his head in. "Come on quick! Folks heard that shot! We got to get out of here!"

"Open the damn safe!" Dinkins shouted, pointing his pistol toward Flowers and cocking it.

"I told you, I can't!"

"I don't believe you!" Dinkins shouted, and he pulled the trigger a second time. Flowers went down with a hole in his temple.

"There's folks comin' toward the bank!" Travis shouted. "We gotta go now!"

"Come on, let's get out of here!" Dinkins ordered.

With the sack of money he'd taken from the teller's tray, Parnell vaulted back over the teller's counter.

Hearing the two gunshots, Cal ran out of the mercantile with his pistol in his hand. He saw the men run out of the bank, and leap onto their horses. Someone across the street from the bank fired at the five riders with a shotgun. The charge of double-aught buckshot missed the robbers, but it did hit the front window of the bank, bringing it down with a loud crash. One of the robbers shot back at the man with the shotgun and he went down. The five bank robbers galloped down the street, away from Cal. Cal shot at them, and saw one of the riders tumble from the saddle. None of the other four paid any attention to the one who went down.

Cal fired a second time, but they were out of range, and his shot did nothing but help chase them on, as they sped out of town. There had been several citizens on the street and sidewalks when the shooting erupted, but most watched in openmouthed shock as the men who had just robbed their bank galloped away. Either none of them were armed, or none of them wished to be a hero, for, other than Cal and the one attempt with a shotgun, no one made any effort to stop them.

The route out of town took the outlaws right by the sheriff's office. At the far end of the street a man stepped off the boardwalk and into the street. A flash of sunlight revealed the star fastened to his vest.

"It's the sheriff!" Dinkins shouted. He shot at him and the sheriff grabbed his shoulder, then staggered back a step. Dinkins shot a second time, as did the other three who were with him, and the sheriff went down under the fusillade of bullets.

Out of town, the four men pushed their horses hard to put as much distance between them and the town as they could.

"Is anyone comin' after us?" Dinkins shouted.

Travis, who was bringing up the rear, looked over his shoulder at the receding town. He saw no riders. "No. They ain't no one mounted. 'Cept for Putnam, we got away clean!" He laughed out loud, whooping into the wind. "We got away clean!"

CHAPTER NINE

Cal ran into the bank with his pistol drawn. The bank teller raised a shotgun to his shoulder and aimed at Cal.

"Mr. Martin, no!" Tamara shouted. "He's with me!"

Martin lowered the shotgun.

Distracted by the shotgun, Cal had not seen Sally. Looking over toward the wall, he saw her and the bank owner, lying on the floor. "Miss Sally!" Cal moved quickly to her side, then knelt down beside her.

"How is Mr. Flowers?" Sally asked, her voice weak.

Cal looked toward Flowers and saw that he was dead. But before he could respond to Sally, she passed out.

"We need a doctor!" Cal said. "Is there a doctor in this town?"

"Yes," Tamara said. "His office is down the street, just over the hardware store!"

Cal didn't have to go all the way down to the doctor's office. The doctor was across the street looking at the man who had fired the shotgun.

"How's the sheriff?" one of those gathered around the doctor said.

"He's dead." The doctor looked at the man on the ground and shook his head. "Poor Mr. Deckert is too."

"What about the outlaw?"

"I don't know. I haven't checked on him yet."

"Doctor, quick!" Cal called. "There's a woman in the bank who's been shot and is still alive!"

"A woman was shot?" one of the people in the crowd said. "You mean those no count sons of bitches shot a woman?"

"The outlaw can wait. Where is the woman?" the doctor asked, carrying his bag and starting toward Cal.

"She's in the bank, on the floor. The owner of the bank, he's there too, but he's dead."

"That's three," someone said. "Three, they kilt. And like as not, the woman is goin' to die too."

"No!" Cal shouted angrily. "Miss Sally is not going to die! Do you hear me? She is not going to die!"

When Cal and the doctor stepped into the bank, Tamara was on her knees beside Sally. Tamara had taken off her petticoat and was holding it in a wad over the wound. The petticoat was already soaked with blood.

"Very good, Mrs. McKenzie," the doctor said.

"You are doing exactly the right thing by stopping the bleeding like that. Let me look at the wound."

The doctor removed the blood soaked petti-coat and looked at the wound. The blood coming from the bullet hole was very dark in color, and it was coming out in a slow, but steady flow. "Good. The bleeding is venous instead of arterial."

He put his hand under Sally's back, felt around, then frowned. "The bullet is still inside. It's going to have to come out."

"Is she going to live, Doc?" Cal asked anxiously.

"I don't know. We need to get her to my office." Several people had come into the bank.

"How is she, Dr. Gunther?" one of the towns-people asked.

"She's in bad shape," Dr. Gunther said. "Paul, run across the street, get a blanket from the mer-cantile. Tell C.D. I'll pay for it later. We need it to carry her to my office."

Within a few minutes Paul returned with a blanket. Dr. Gunther put a man at each corner, one of them being Cal, then instructed them to pick her up. A cavalcade of bystanders followed them to the doctor's office, which could only be reached by going up a set of stairs along the side of the hardware store building.

Dr. Gunther turned toward them.

"All of you stay down here. The only people al-lowed up are the four who are carrying her, then they are going to have to leave as well."

"I'm not leavin' her, Dr. Gunther," Cal said resolutely.

"All right, you can stay."

"I intend to stay as well," Tamara said.

"Yes, I want you to stay. I will need you. You can act as my nurse. But no one else."

The four men, holding the blanket in such a way as to keep Sally as level as possible, climbed the stairs until they reached the top. Maneuvering her through the door, they took Sally's still unconscious form into the office, and laid her on the examination table.

Dr. Gunther took two clean sheets and a pair of scissors from a cabinet. "Mrs. McKenzie. I want you to strip her naked. You will probably have to cut her clothes off. Then place these two sheets over her, one across the top of her body and one across the bottom. But leave the wound exposed so I can examine it."

"You're going to take all her clothes off?" Cal asked in alarm.

"I have to. But these bed sheets will preserve her modesty."

"I ain't goin' to watch this," Cal said.

Dr. Gunther chuckled. "I don't intend for you to. You and I will wait over there until it is done. Mrs. McKenzie, please do it as quickly as you can."

"What am I going to tell Smoke?" Cal asked as he paced back and forth.

"Smoke?"

"Smoke Jensen. He's Sally's husband."

"Oh, Lord," Dr. Gunther said. "I've never met

Mr. Smoke Jensen, but I have certainly heard of him. And this is his wife, you say?"

"Yes, sir. You gotta keep her alive, Doctor. I come over here with her. I'm responsible for her. I shoulda gone into the bank with her, but instead I was all the way down to the other end of the street in the store, buying a stick of candy. I shoulda been in the bank with her."

"What is your name?" Dr. Gunther asked.

"It's Cal. Cal Wood. I work for Smoke and Miss Sally back at Sugarloaf."

"Look at it this way, Cal. If you had been in there, you might have been killed as well. Then for sure you could have done nothing for her."

"Doctor Gunther, she is ready," Tamara called from the other side of the room.

Cal and Dr. Gunther returned to the table. Sally was lying on her back, her eyes closed, her head turned to one side. A bed sheet covered her shoulders and breasts. A second bed sheet covered her legs and lower abdomen. There was only about a six inch area of her belly exposed. The bullet wound, an ugly black hole, was about an inch and a half to the left, and on line with her belly button.

Dr. Gunther used warm salt water to wash away the blood, so only the dark red, almost black hole marred the smooth, white skin. Then, leaning down, he began sniffing.

"What are you doing?" Cal asked.

"If the bullet hit any of the vital organs inside, I should be able to smell it." The doctor got his nose so close to the bullet hole it was almost touching her skin, and he sniffed again. "That's good." He rose up.

"What did you smell?"

"Nothing. That's why I say it is good." Gunther got a bulb syringe and began using it to aspirate blood from the wound. After that, he bathed the wound in warm salt water. He took a clean cloth from a cupboard, poured a bit of chloroform onto it, and handed the cloth to Tamara.

"I am going to have to probe for the bullet. If she awakens during the procedure, hold this over her nose and mouth for a count of three. Only until the count of three, mind you. Then take it away. Holding it there any longer could be dangerous."

"All right," Tamara said, taking the strong smelling cloth from him.

For the next step in the procedure Dr. Gunther used a Nélaton probe, which was a long probe with a tiny porcelain bulb on the end. After first pouring alcohol over the end of the probe, he stuck it into the wound, then followed the trajectory of the bullet until he hit something hard.

"I found something."

"The bullet?" Tamara asked.

"Either the bullet or bone. We'll know in just a moment." Gunther withdrew the Nélaton probe and examined the porcelain tip. "Yes, there it is." He pointed to a little gray smudge on the tip. "You see that? That's lead from the bullet."

After having found the bullet he picked up a pair of long legged forceps and pushed them into the wound. Sally began to regain consciousness.

"The chloroform," Dr. Gunther said quickly.

Tamara applied the chloroform cloth to Sally's nose and mouth, and counted to three. When she pulled it away, Sally was unconscious again.

"Good." Dr. Gunther pushed the forceps into the wound until he encountered the bullet. Moving slowly and delicately, he probed around, then he pulled the bullet out and dropped it into a pan of water that was sitting near the operating table. Little bubbles of blood formed a string of red beads from the bullet to the surface of the water.

Gunther walked over to a glass front cabinet, opened the door, then took out a small, brown bottle. "I'm glad she is still unconscious," he said, as he pulled the stopper from the bottle.

"Why is that?" Cal sked.

"I need to disinfect the wound." Gunther held up the bottle. "This is iodine, and it will burn like the blazes." After pouring iodine on the wound, he took strips of gauze bandage and wrapped them around her.

"What happens now?" Cal said.

"I will keep her here overnight, then we need to find a place for her to go while she recuperates."

"Can I take her back home?"

Dr. Gunther shook his head. "No, I'm afraid not. The trip would be far too dangerous for her."

"She can stay with me, Doctor," Tamara said.

"That would be good. You could keep an eye on her, and I can check in several times a day," Dr. Gunther said.

"Doc, I need to send a telegram to Smoke," Cal said. "What should I tell him?"

"Tell him that Mrs. Jensen was seriously wounded, but that the outlook is hopeful."

Sugarloaf Ranch

Pearlie was trying to wrestle a calf down so it could be branded, but the calf was fighting him and Pearlie lost his balance. He fell and the calf fell on top of him.

Smoke started laughing, and he laughed so hard he had to hold on to his sides. "Pearlie, you've got that backwards, haven't you? You are supposed to throw the calf! He's not supposed to throw you!" Smoke hooted, unable to stop the laughing.

"Get off me, calf." Pearlie pushed the animal to one side, and stood up, brushing the dirt off his clothes. Looking past Smoke, he saw a rider approaching. "Someone is comin'."

Smoke looked around too. "That's young Eb Kyle, isn't it? Delivers telegrams for Will Winsted?"

"I believe it is," Pearly said. "He must be lookin' for directions."

Smoke started toward Kyle, the smile still on his face. But when he saw the expression on Kyle's face, he felt a quick twinge of worry and the smile disappeared.

"Kyle, what is it?" Smoke asked. "Do you have a telegram for me?"

"Yes, sir, Mr. Jensen, I'm afraid I do," Kyle said. "And I'm terrible sorry to be the one what has to deliver it."

"Give it to me." Smoke held his hand out impatiently. He tore open the envelope, then removed the telegram.

MISS SALLY HAS BEEN SHOT SHE IS
AWFUL BAD HURT BUT DOCTOR SAYS
THERE IS HOPE
CAL

"Smoke, what is it?" Pearlie asked.

Smoke handed the telegram to him and looked at Kyle. "When did you receive this?" he asked.

"It took me just under half an hour to ride out here," Kyle said. "Mr. Winsted, he give it to me just as quick as it come in, and he wrote it down."

Smoke started toward the barn. "Pearlie, fill my canteen, bring me my pistol and my other hat," he called back over his shoulder.

"We're goin' over there?"

"Not we, *I. I'm* going," Smoke said. "We're still in the middle of a roundup. I need you to stay here and watch after things."

"Smoke, come on. I can't just sit here, wonderin' what's goin' on," Pearlie insisted.

"You aren't going to have to wonder. I'll keep you posted. I'll send you a telegram every day."

"You promise?"

"I promise. Now get my gear together while I'm saddling my horse. Oh, and give Kyle a dollar."

"Wait there, Kyle," Pearlie said as he hurried into the house to respond to Smoke's requests.

"I will, thank you," Kyle said. "I'm awful sorry I'm the one had to bring this message."

CHAPTER TEN

Gothic

It took Smoke just over two hours to make the ride, which was about as fast as he could go without crippling his horse. As he rode into the town, he saw a man's body in an open coffin, standing up in front of the feed and seed store. A sign was propped against him.

KILLED IN A BANK ROBBERY
Do you know this man?

So, there was a bank robbery. That has to be how Sally was hurt. But how did she get involved?

"Smoke!" a familiar voice shouted.

Looking toward the hardware store, Smoke saw Cal come running toward him.

"I knew you would come!" Cal said. "I've been keepin' an eye out for you ever since I sent the telegram."

"How is she?" Smoke asked.

"It ain't good."

"Damn it, Cal, is she alive?" he literally shouted.

"Oh, yes, yes, she's alive. I'm sorry, didn't mean to scare you none."

"Where is she?"

"She's over here." Cal pointed toward the hardware store.

"She's in a hardware store?"

"What? Oh, no, no, I mean, she's in the doctor's office. His office is just over the hardware store. You get to it by goin' up those steps on the side of the building there. He's at . . ."

Cal didn't finish his sentence, because Smoke slapped his legs against the side of his horse, galloping the final fifty yards. Swinging down from his horse he made a quick tie of the reins to the hitching post, then clambered up the external stairway, taking the steps two at a time. When he reached the little stoop up top, he jerked the door open, then pushed inside without knocking. He saw Sally on the table, and the doctor and Tamara Gooding standing alongside, looking down at her.

"Hey! What do you mean barging in here like this?" Dr. Gunther scolded.

"He's Sally's husband," Tamara said quickly.

"I'm Smoke Jensen. Sorry about breaking in like that."

"No, no, that's quite all right, Mr. Jensen," Dr. Gunther said. "I'm sorry I spoke so harshly."

"How is she?"

"I won't lie to you, Mr. Jensen. She was shot through the lower abdomen, and the wound is quite serious."

"Is the bullet still inside?"

"No, I got it out. As far as I can tell, it did not hit any of her vitals."

"Can I talk to her?"

"She has been in and out of consciousness ever since she was shot," Dr. Gunther said. "Even when she is conscious, she isn't very communicative. I'm sorry."

"Doctor, give it to me straight. Is she going to live?"

"I wish I could tell you with one hundred percent assurance that she is going to live. Unfortunately, I can't promise you that. After I removed the bullet, I irrigated the abdomen with a saline solution until all the effluent was clear, then I made generous use of an antiseptic, in this case, iodine. If I were making a bet, I would say her chances are better than fifty-fifty that she is going to live."

"Fifty-fifty? You can't do any better than that?" Smoke asked.

"I'm sorry. I want to give you and Mrs. Jensen hope. I believe hope is an important part of the healing process. But I don't want to give you false hope."

"How many people have you seen who are gut-shot, and survive?" Smoke asked.

"Quite a few. Those that die, generally do so

because of pathogenic infection, or a condition of shock."

"She's a fighter, Smoke. You know that better than anyone," Cal said. "I'm bettin' that if there is any chance at all, Miss Sally is going to come through this."

Smoke had not heard Cal come up behind him, but he wasn't surprised to see his young friend, at hand. Smoke nodded his head. "You've got that right, Cal. If ever there was a fighter, it would be Sally."

Smoke turned back toward Dr. Gunther. "So, what do we do now? Can I take her home? I'll hire the finest coach I can find."

"No, no, not yet," Dr. Gunther insisted. "Mrs. McKenzie has agreed to let your wife stay with her until it is safe enough for her to travel. In the meantime, she will be much better off here."

Smoke turned to Tamara. "Thank you for agreeing to look after her."

"Oh, don't be silly, Smoke. Sally is a very dear friend. Of course I will look after her. Oh, just a minute, I have something for you."

Tamara walked over to her handbag, opened it, and took out a packet of money. "This is the two thousand dollars Sally was going to invest in my restaurant."

"You still plan to build the restaurant, don't you?"

"Yes."

"Then keep the money. That is why Sally came over here in the first place."

"I know, and I feel so guilty about that. If she

hadn't come over to see me, she wouldn't have been in the bank to get shot."

Smoke took Tamara's hand in his. "These things happen. Don't blame yourself. You had nothing to do with what happened."

"I tell myself that," Tamara replied. "But I'm having a hard time convincing myself."

"Put it out of your mind." Smoke sighed. "If I'm going to stay here for a while, I need to find a place to spend the night here in town."

"I'm stayin' over to the hotel," Cal said. "Come on with me. I know there are some empty rooms there."

"I don't want to leave."

"Trust me, Mr. Jensen. Right now, she doesn't even know you are here," Dr. Gunther said. "You will do neither yourself nor her any good by staying here. When she comes to, and if she is communicative, I will come get you."

"By the way, Doc," Cal said. "You don't need to worry none about the outlaw that got shot. He's dead. They've got him propped up in a coffin down at the feed store."

"I'm sorry to say I had forgotten all about him," Dr. Gunther said. "Was he killed instantly?"

"He probably was," Cal said. "But the truth is, I would've told you that anyway just to make sure you was taking care of Miss Sally."

"I would not have abandoned Mrs. Jensen to tend to the outlaw," Dr. Gunther said. "But I am a doctor, and honor bound to treat everyone, even those who we might consider undesirable."

"Yes, sir, I understand," Cal said. "But when I shot the son of a bitch, I hit him right in the back of the head. Not that I am that good of a shot, mind you. It just so happens, that is where I hit him."

"As I say, I am a doctor. But I also have a strong sense of justice. Those people killed three of our citizens and wounded Mrs. Jensen. I feel no sense of remorse that one of the outlaws was killed in the process."

Purple Peak

Twenty miles west by northwest of Gothic, Dinkins and the others stopped in the shadow of Purple Peak Mountain, which was significant. When they rode out of Gothic, they were going east, then rode in a great circle. It was late afternoon by the time they actually reached the mountain.

"Parnell, climb up a ways and make certain there ain't no one a' followin' us," Dinkins said. "If you don't see anyone, we'll stay here for the night."

"We got 'ny thing to eat?" Travis asked. "I'm hungry."

"Got some bacon and hard tack," Dinkins said. "And coffee."

"Ain't all that much of a meal, but it's better 'n nothin'," Travis said.

Parnell climbed about three hundred feet up the side of the mountain and looked back along the trail over which they had just come, then came back down to report to the others. "I could see ten miles or more back. And I didn't see nobody."

"Like as not there won't be nobody comin' after us," Dinkins said. "I'm pretty sure we kilt the sheriff as we was leavin' town, so there wouldn't be nobody to organize a posse."

"Yeah, and even iffen they did put one together, like as not they'd be lookin' for us goin' east," Travis said.

"Anybody see what happened to Putnam?" Parnell asked.

"He was ridin' alongside me," Frank said. "One minute he was there 'n the next minute he wasn't. I reckon he got shot."

"You and him was pards, wasn't you?" Travis asked Parnell.

"I never know'd him till I met him in prison," Parnell said. "But we was pards in there, as much as you can be pards in prison."

"How much money did we get?" Frank asked.

"I don't know," Dinkins said. "Whatever it is, we would've got a lot more if we had been able to get into the safe."

"You reckon they was tellin' the truth?" Travis asked. "You reckon there really is such a thing as a time lock? I ain't never heard of such a thing before."

"I heard folks talkin' about it in prison," Parnell said. "But this here is the first time I ever run into one."

As the others were discussing the time lock,

Dinkins emptied the bag of cash they had managed to get from the cashier's drawer.

"How much?" Frank asked.

"Two hundred and eleven dollars," Dinkins said. He gave fifty dollars to the other three, and kept sixty one dollars for himself.

"That ain't much for what we went through," Travis said. "Hell, me 'n Frank got damn near that much money just robbin' a store."

"We didn't go through nothin'," Dinkins said. "Except for Putnam, who was kilt, there wasn't none of us hit, and there ain't nobody chasin' us."

Travis started gathering some firewood, and a few minutes later they had a fire going. They fried bacon, then cooked four pieces of hard tack in the bacon grease. They also made a pot of coffee.

"So what do we do next?" Parnell asked.

"I know what I'm goin' to do next," Frank said. "I think me 'n Travis will find us another store. There ain't as many shootin' at you when you rob a store, as there is when you rob a bank. And you wind up with damn near as much money."

"I didn't know this bank had a time lock," Dinkins said. "I'll make sure with the next one."

"The next one?" Frank asked. "You plannin' on robbin' another bank?"

"Why not? We've got our gang together, don't we?"

"Yeah, but we lost one."

"We'll get another man."

"Where?"

"Don't worry. I've already asked him to join us."

"Do you know him? Can we trust him?" Parnell asked.

"And can he hold up his end?" Travis asked.

"Yeah," Dinkins answered. "I know him, we can trust him, and he can hold up his end."

Parnell stretched and yawned. "I don't know about you fellas, but I aim to get me a little shut-eye."

Parnell got the saddle blanket from under his saddle, spread it out, then lay down using his saddle as a pillow. He covered himself with the coat he had been issued by the prison.

"Hey, Dinkins. Next time we steal a horse, what do you say we steal one that already has a bedroll?"

The others laughed at Parnell's observation, then, like Parnell, they bedded down for the night.

CHAPTER ELEVEN

Gothic

Smoke remained in the doctor's office for the rest of the day, hoping Sally would regain consciousness. She did wake up a few times, but was so groggy she was incommunicative, just as Dr. Gunther said she would be.

Finally, as darkness fell, Smoke checked in at the Silver Lode Hotel, then went to the Silver Nugget Saloon. He and Cal took a beer to a table in the back. There was a buzz of excitement and anger in the saloon. Friends of the three men who were killed were airing their anger and their sympathy for the widows of Mr. Flowers, the banker, Mr. Deckert, the owner of the tobacco store who had tried, with a shotgun, to stop the outlaws, and Sheriff Tyson.

"What about the lady that was shot?" one of the men asked. "Has anyone heard how she is doin'?"

Cal started to answer, but Smoke put his hand out on Cal's arm. "I don't want to visit with anyone," he said quietly.

"I hear she's still alive," someone else said. "She's up in the doc's office now."

"I hope she pulls through all right. I mean it's bad enough to kill the three men. But it just ain't right to shoot a woman. No matter how you look at it."

"You know about Nicole, don't you?" Smoke continued in a quiet voice.

"Yes, I know about her. She was your first wife, and I know she was murdered."

"I cannot let that happen again, Cal. God help me, it just can't happen again."

Cal had never seen Smoke this distraught. The thought of this strong man, the strongest man he had ever known, the man he respected and admired more than any other, being in such a state of despair, frightened him. He put his hand on Smoke's shoulder.

"Smoke, I probably wouldn't even be alive if it hadn't been for Miss Sally. You know that better than anybody. Here I was, a dumb kid, and I actually tried to hold her up. Instead of shooting me, like she could have, or turning me over to the law, like she should have, she took me out to Sugarloaf, fed me the first good meal I had eaten in weeks, then offered me a home. I'm telling you, right now, that I know, as sure as God made little green apples, that Miss Sally is going to pull through this. I know she is."

Smoke looked into the earnest and determined face of his young cowboy, then managed a smile. "I know it too, Cal."

Cal nodded, pleased that his declaration seemed to have made some inroad into Smoke's melancholy.

"Tell me about the people who did this," Smoke said.

"Well sir, like you seen, one of 'em is dead," Cal said. "I shot him as they was riding out of town. I fired a second time, but they was too far away, and to tell the truth, I was damn lucky to hit the first one."

"Do we know who they are?"

"Mr. Martin, the bank teller, and Mrs. McKenzie, heard some of the names as they was talking to each other. The leader was someone named Dinkins. There was also someone named Parnell. That's all we know."

"Hey!" a man said loudly, just coming into the saloon and addressing all therein. "We just found out who the dead bank robber is!"

"Who?" half a dozen voices called.

"His name is John Putnam. He just got out of prison no more than a month ago," the man with the news said.

"How do you know this, Chris?"

"Sheriff Carson come into town and he recognized him," Chris said.

Smoke and Cal looked at each other.

"Monte is here?" Smoke asked.

"I guess so, from the way that fella was talkin'," Cal said. "But I ain't seen him yet."

"Let's see if we can find him," Smoke suggested. "Where do you think he might be?"

"My guess would be the sheriff's office. Seeing as the local sheriff was one of the ones killed, I expect Monte has set up a temporary office there."

The two men left the saloon, then walked down the street, dark except for the little squares of dim yellow light spilling through the windows of the occupied buildings. When they reached the sheriff's office, they saw a black bow on the door of the office, put there in memory of the slain Sheriff Tyson. When they went inside they saw Sheriff Carson standing behind a desk, looking at an array of wanted posters which were spread out before him. Standing beside Sheriff Carson was the man who had been deputy to Tyson.

"Hello, Monte," Smoke said as he and Cal stepped into the room.

Sheriff Carson looked up. "How is Sally?"

Smoke shook his head. "Not good, but she is still alive, and fighting it."

"Do you know Thad Malcolm? He was Sheriff Tyson's deputy. Thad, this is Smoke Jensen."

Malcolm extended his hand. "We've never met, but I've heard a lot about you. All good," he added hastily. Then the smile left his face. "I'm awful sorry about your wife, Mr. Jensen. I sure hope she pulls through all right."

"Thank you, Deputy Malcolm."

"Smoke, I've identified three of the people who did this." Sheriff Carson pointed to the posters on his desk. "John Putnam. He's the one that you killed, Cal." Carson pointed to one of the other posters. "This is Cole Parnell. Putnam and Parnell were serving time together in the state prison at Cañon City. They were both released last month."

Sheriff Carson picked up another wanted poster, and showed it to Smoke. "This august gentlemen, and believe me, I use that term in the most contemptuous way, is one William Dinkins. According to Mr. Martin and Mrs. McKenzie, Dinkins is the one who killed Mr. Flowers and shot Sally. But, shooting unarmed people in a bank isn't something new to him. Two months ago, he killed a teller in a botched bank holdup in Buffalo. Last year, Dinkins led a gang of outlaws who robbed the Tucumcari, New Mexico, bank and he shot a twelve-year-old boy who was holding his hands in the air. He is a real prince of a fellow," Sheriff Carson added sarcastically.

"I'm going to get him, Monte," Smoke said. "He shot my wife, and whether Sally lives or dies, I'm going to get Dinkins."

A young man stepped into the sheriff's office. "Excuse me, Sheriff. Do you know where I might find Mr. Smoke Jensen?"

"I'm Smoke Jensen." Apprehension was apparent in his voice.

"Mr. Jensen, Doctor Gunther sent me to find you. He said to tell you Mrs. Jensen is awake and is asking about you."

"Thank you!" Smoke practically shouted the words as he was already on his way almost before the boy could finish his report.

Smoke ran down the street to the doctor's office and, as he had before, took the steps up the side of the hardware store two at a time. He barged into the office, again without knocking, but it didn't disturb Dr. Gunther, who was expecting him.

"She is conscious," Dr. Gunther said.

Smoke hurried to Sally's side. "I thought I taught you to duck," he said, taking her hand in his.

Sally smiled. "Smoke, what are you doing here?"

"What am I doing here? Did you think I would stay at the ranch, once I learned you had been shot?"

"I've been shot?"

"You don't remember?"

"Oh, yes," Sally said, her voice weak. "I'd nearly forgotten that."

Smoke chuckled. "You're quite a woman, Sally, if you can be shot and nearly forget it."

"Oh! The two thousand dollars! I threw it! I don't know what happened to it."

"Tamara has it."

"I'm glad."

Smoke raised Sally's hand to his lips and kissed it.

"Is that the best you can do?" she asked. "That's the way you greet some old lady at a party."

"I don't want to do anything that will hurt you."

"I'm not made out of glass."

Smiling, Smoke leaned over to kiss her on her forehead, but when she pursed her lips, he knew she wanted a real kiss, so he obliged her.

"Maybe if the other folks would leave, I could climb up on the table beside you," Smoke suggested.

Sally laughed out loud, then winced in pain and put her hand to her wound.

"Oh, Sally, I'm sorry," Smoke apologized.

"Don't be ridiculous. That was a perfectly outrageous thing for you to say." She smiled. "And I wouldn't have it any other way."

Laramie

The saloon was relatively quiet, with only a couple tables full. A bar girl, finding the pickings slim, was leaning against the wall next to the piano, talking to the bald headed piano player. Wes Harley stood alone at the far end of the bar, nursing a drink. Four at a table were playing cards.

A couple cowboys came into the saloon, laughing and talking, brushing the dust from their clothes. When they noticed Harley, and the hairless skull that was his head, they stopped in mid-conversation to stare at him. He looked back with an unblinking stare of his own.

"What'll it be, gents?" the bartender asked.

The cowboys continued to stare.

"You boys just goin' to stand there and gawk? Or are you going to order?"

"Oh," one of them said. "Uh, two beers."

"Two beers it is," the bartender replied. He turned to draw the beers. As soon as he put the beers in front of the two young men, they picked them up and held them to their lips, drinking with Adams apple bobbing swallows, until all the beer was gone. With a mighty sigh of satisfaction, they put the glasses back down and swiped the backs of their hands across their lips.

"One more," one of the boys said.

"You boys have quite a thirst on you," the bartender said. "Been ridin' long, have you?"

"Yes, sir, we have," the taller of the two answered. "We've been on the trail for nearly three weeks. Come up from Texas, we did."

"Did you now?" The bartender put two new beers in front of them. "That's a long ride. What brings you to Laramie?"

"We're lookin' to get on with a ranch up here."

"Texas," Harley hissed. He continued to stare into his glass as he spoke, not bothering to look over at the two young cowboys.

"You got somethin' against Texas, mister?" one of the young men challenged.

"You rode a long way for nothin'," Harley said.

"If I was you, I'd turn around and head back. There ain't no self-respectin' rancher from Wyoming goin' to hire trash from Texas." He continued to stare into his glass.

"Mister, I don't appreciate bad talk about Texas." The young man's level of irritation rose.

"You don't have to talk bad about Texas," Harley said. "All you have to do is mention the name. That's bad enough."

"Danny, leave it be," the other boy said.

"The hell I will," Danny said. "You don't want any part of this, Andy, you just stand aside. But I don't figure on lettin' this hairless son of a bitch talk bad about Texas and not do nothin' about it."

"Tell you what," Andy said. "Looks to me like we're just gettin' off on the wrong foot here. If we're goin' to work up here, we can't be makin' enemies the first day. Bartender, give our new friend here a beer, on me."

"Mr. Harley?" the bartender asked uneasily. "Do you want another beer?"

"Not if some Texas trash bought it," Harley replied.

"What is it with you, mister?" Danny asked angrily. "Here my pard is tryin' to be real friendly with you, and you're actin' like that. You know what? Somebody needs to take you down a notch or two. And I might just be that somebody."

"Danny, come on, we don't want no trouble on the first day we are in town, do we?"

Danny continued to stare at the skull face of

Harley, but Harley showed no expression of any kind, no anger, fear, or anxiety. Danny was a little surprised how the man could be so confrontational, and yet show no expression. Perhaps with no hair, and his skin drawn so tight across the bones of his face, it might be that the man could not show expression even if he wanted to.

"It's too late for that, sonny boy," Harley asked. "You done stepped into it. You got more trouble than you can handle."

"More than I can handle?" Danny said angrily. "I'll show you how much I can handle. I'm about to whip you like a rented mule!" He put up his fists.

Harley turned toward the two young men and showed his first expression. He smiled, though it was a smile without mirth.

"You don't understand, do you, boy?"

"Oh, I understand all right. I understand that I'm going to leave you with a broken nose, black eyes, and a fat lip. As ugly as you are, that can only improve your looks." Danny laughed at his own joke.

"Uh-uh," Harley said. "If we're going to fight, it's going to be for real." He stepped away from the bar, flipped his jacket back, exposing a pistol which he wore low, and kicked out, in the way of a gunfighter.

"Mr. Harley, there is no need for this now," the bartender said. "I'm sure these boys would apologize to you if you asked them for it."

"Aplogize? Apologize to this . . . walking

scarecrow? Why the hell should we apologize?" Danny asked.

"Cowboy, don't you know who this is?" the bartender asked, his voice reflecting his shock. "This is Wes Harley."

"Wes Harley? Is that name supposed to mean something?" Danny asked.

"Oh, God in heaven, you don't know do you?" the bartender said.

"Don't know what?"

"Who Wes Harley is," the bartender said.

"I expect you're talkin' about this skull-faced piece of cow dung here," Danny said.

"Danny, come on, let's go," Andy said. "I don't have a good feelin' about this. This ain't worth one of you dyin' over."

"It ain't goin' to be one of us, sonny," Harley said. "It's goin' to be the two of you."

"You're crazy, mister," Andy said. "We just come in here for a drink. We're goin' to leave now and just pretend none of this happened."

"It's too late," Harley said.

"We ain't drawin' on you," Andy said.

"Oh, I think you will," Harley said. "The fiddler is already playin' his tune, the dance has started, and here we are, the three of us, standin' out on the dance floor."

"Mister, you are crazy," Andy said. "We ain't goin' to get into no gunfight with you."

"Yeah, you are," Harley said, his voice a quiet sigh.

Andy turned to the others in the saloon. "Do

you people see what's going on here? Are you goin' to let this happen?"

"It ain't our fight, boy," one of the others said.

"Danny?" Andy's voice broke in fear. "We can't do this."

"Looks to me like we don't have no choice," Danny replied.

Danny started his draw and seeing that, Andy drew as well.

With a smile that made his face look even more skeletal, Harley drew, the gun appearing in his hand as if by magic. Danny was so shocked at the speed of the draw that he hesitated for an instant. Had he not hesitated, he might have had a chance, but Harley got two shots off so fast it sounded as if it were only one. Danny pulled the trigger on his pistol, but the bullet went into the floor. Andy didn't even get a shot off.

Harley was calmly sipping his whiskey by the time one of the sheriff's deputies arrived.

"I might have known it would be you," the deputy said.

"They drew first."

"I'm sure they did. Just as I'm sure you goaded them into it," the deputy said.

"I might have teased them a bit about bein' from Texas," Harley said. "Didn't know they was goin' to take it so hard."

The deputy stepped over to look down at the two young cowboys.

"Damn, Harley, they're just kids. Who are you going after next? Grade school kids?"

"Won't be any of your concern who it is, Deputy. I got a telegram today, offerin' me a job."

"Somewhere else, I hope."

"Yeah, somewhere else," Harley said.

CHAPTER TWELVE

Gothic

Sally was in New York City, sitting on the windowsill of the third floor of one of the Greek revival row houses on the north side of Washington Square. The apartment belonged to her Aunt Mildred, and Sally had come to New York to spend a couple weeks with her. It was late March, a cold and gray day with steely sunlight that illuminated, but did not warm the city. Spring had already begun, but the pedestrians walking on the sidewalk below wore heavy coats and scarves. From this elevation they were a never ending flow of black figures, rather like a stream of ants on the march.

She heard the distant rumble of an El train and the clatter of an omnibus, and wondered about so many people on the move. Who were they? Where were they going? What lay ahead of them?

What lay ahead for her?

She had already made the decision for her own future, and had announced it to her family with great passion *and intensity. She was going West. She was going West to teach school, and to see some of the country she had only read about.*

Her parents were completely opposed to the idea, and sent her to New York on a visit so Aunt Mildred could "talk some sense in to her."

To Sally's surprise and relief, Aunt Mildred did nothing to try and dissuade her. In fact, she disclosed the secret that she had once had a strong desire to move to San Francisco, to see what was on the other side of the country.

So, without Aunt Mildred to dissuade her she was left to her own thought and reason. Was she making a mistake? Should she go West? Or should she stay safe, comfortable, and stable in Vermont, where her father was wealthy, and a "respectable" marriage would occur some day, with an "acceptable" man who was a moneyed member of society?

If only she knew what was the right thing to do.

"You are making the right decision," Smoke said. "Come West. Marry me. We will grow old together, and you will have all the comfort, love, and security you will ever want. And you will have something else. You will have excitement, not the dull future Vermont holds for you."

"I will come, Smoke," Sally said. "I will come West and I will marry you."

Sally woke up, and for a moment, had no idea where she was. Was she at her aunt's apartment in

New York? No, that's not possible. Smoke isn't someone in a dream. Smoke is real.

But where is Smoke?

She reached over to touch him, but he wasn't there. As she tried to raise up to look for him, a sudden ache in her side brought her back down sharply to lie on her back on the hard surface of the examination table. She moved her hands around her, feeling the edges.

Yes, an examination table.

But where was Smoke? She vaguely remembered talking to him earlier.

"Mrs. Jensen, try not to move," a soft, calming, and reassuring voice said.

"Who are you?" Sally asked. "Where am I?"

"I am Doctor Gunther. You are in my office."

"Why?"

"You have been shot. Remember?"

Sally was quiet for a moment. "Yes. I remember. Where is Smoke?"

"He is staying in the hotel across the street. He will be back here first thing in the morning, but I can get him for you now, if you wish."

"Am I dying? If I am dying I want to tell him good-bye."

"You are not dying."

"Then let him sleep," Sally said. "I am sure he is worried about me. I am sure he isn't getting much sleep."

"You need some sleep as well," Dr. Gunther

said. "Do you want me to give you something to make you sleep?"

"No. I will be all right."

"I'll be right here if you need me." Dr. Gunther's words fell on deaf ears. Sally had already drifted off to sleep again.

The next morning Sally was strong enough to be moved from the doctor's office to Tamara's small house on the edge of town. She was put on a stretcher and carried two blocks to Tamara's one room cabin.

Smoke and Cal walked beside the stretcher with her, all the way. And, somewhat embarrassing to Sally, so did much of the town.

"How is she doing?" someone called.

"We're prayin' for you, Miz Jensen," another shouted.

When they reached Tamara's cabin the stretcher bearers, two young men hired by Smoke for the job, took her inside and put her on the bed.

There could not be a greater contrast between Sally's fine house at Sugarloaf—a two-story edifice with five bedrooms, a living room, parlor, dining room, and kitchen—and Tamara's tiny abode. The house was one room, with a bed, a table and two chairs, a cooking/heating stove, and a small settee. There was also a cot, where Tamara said she would be sleeping during Sally's convalescence.

Dr. Gunther had walked down with his patient as well, and as Sally was moved gently, from the litter to the bed, he put the back of his hand on her forehead. He looked over at Tamara.

"I'm going to leave you a thermometer so you can take her temperature from time to time. There are two things we need to look out for. Shock and infection."

"How do I look for them?" Tamara asked.

"If there is a change in her alertness, if she starts having dizzy spells, quick, shallow breathing, or clammy skin, those would be signs of shock. I think she is past that danger, but one should always be careful."

"What do I do if she has shock?"

"If you think she is going into shock, lift her legs so that they are higher than her head. And keep her warm."

"All right."

"There may be a greater danger of infection, so I want you to look out for it as well. Her wound will probably start suppurating, or draining. If the liquid that comes out is clear, there's no problem. That is to be expected. But if it looks like pus, or has an odor, or if you see little red streaks on the skin, leading away from the wound, that would indicate infection. Then I want you to take her temperature. If it is over 101 degrees, that is absolute evidence that her wound has become infected."

"And if that happens?"

"Treat the wound with iodine," Dr. Gunther

said. "In fact, if you keep the wound treated, I think the likelihood of infection will be remote. I will leave you two bottles, along with the thermometer."

"Thank you," Tamara said.

Smoke sent Cal back to Sugarloaf to help Pearlie with the spring roundup. Over the next week, he developed a routine. Every morning he walked down to Tamara's house to have breakfast with Sally and her friend. He would sit beside Sally's bed, talking to her, sometimes reading to her while she was awake, remaining quiet as she slept. At night, he slept in the hotel room.

On the third day Sally developed an infection. At first, it was just some red lines, radiating out from the wound. Then her temperature rose to 102. Dr. Gunther was called. He cleaned and disinfected the wound, and kept a wet cloth on her face.

For two days, Sally hovered between life and death. Smoke stayed in the little house with her, talking to her, reassuring her when she was conscious, that everything was going to be all right. But was it?

During Sally's periods of unconsciousness, Smoke slept fitfully.

A violent thunderstorm struck the valley, scattering the herd of breeding horses, and sending the milk cow off.

"I've got to get the horses back," Smoke told Nicole. "We've got to have them for breeding stock. But I hate to leave you and the baby alone."

Nicole laughed away his fears. "Don't worry about me. Remember, I'm a pretty good shot."

"I might be gone for several days."

"Honey"—Nicole touched his face—"it was the hand of Providence that brought us that cow. Lord knows how it got here. But you've got to get it back for the baby." She pressed a bundle of food on him. "I'll be packing while you're finding the herd—and the cow." She laughed. "You always look so serious when you are milking."

"I never did like to milk, even when I was a boy, back in Missouri."

Smoke left reluctantly, knowing he had no choice. As he rode away on his horse, Seven, he stopped once, turning in his saddle to look back at his wife, holding their son in her arms. The sun sparkled off her hair, casting a halo of light around the woman and baby. Smoke lifted a hand in good-bye.

Nicole waved at him, then turned and walked back into the cabin.[1]

That was the last time he ever saw her alive.

"Don't worry about Sally, my darling," Nicole said. "She will be all right."

"Nicole!" Smoke said, startled to see his dead first wife. "You know about Sally?"

"Of course I know about Sally. And so does our son, Arthur. We love her, as we love you."

"But you are . . . I mean . . ."

[1] *The Last Mountain Man—The Legend Is Born*

"*You can say it. I am dead. Though, here, we laugh at that word. You are never more alive than you are when you are here.*"

"*What are you doing here? Why have you come now? I mean, after all this time?*"

"*I've had no need to come before now,*" Nicole said. "*I know how worried you are about Sally. I could not stand by and see you suffer so. I had to come tell you that it will be all right. Sally will not die.*"

"*Nicole, I . . .*"

When Smoke awakened from his troubled sleep, he realized he was holding both his arms out in front of him. It was dark in the little house, the only light being the soft, silver splash of moonlight, spilling in through the window. He could hear the soft breathing of Sally from the bed, and Tamara from her cot.

He got up from the settee and walked quietly over to the bed. Reaching down, he put the back of his hand on Sally's forehead. Where it had been hot for the last three days, it was now cool. Her fever had broken and the infection was stopped.

"You're going to live," Smoke said aloud. "Nicole was right. You are going to live."

"Hmm?" Sally stirred, then woke up. Her face and eyes gleamed in the moonlight. She smiled. "Smoke"—she held up her hand—"what a pleasant surprise. Have you been here long?"

"Not too long," Smoke replied. "How do you feel?"

"I feel fine." She touched the wound. "Ha. It doesn't even hurt anymore."

"Good."

"Smoke, tomorrow, I would like to go back to Sugarloaf."

"We'll see what the doctor says."

"Let me reword that. Tomorrow, I am going back to Sugarloaf."

Smoke laughed. "With that attitude, I'm pretty sure you will."

Sally looked up at Smoke. "Were you thinking about Nicole?"

"What?" Smoke asked, startled by the question.

"Nicole was killed. I know how you grieved over her. Were you afraid that was going to happen to you again?"

"I gave it some thought," Smoke admitted.

"You needn't have worried," Sally said. "Nicole came to visit me. She told me that everything was going to be all right."

"What do you mean Nicole came to visit you?"

"She was here tonight. I was talking to her, just before you woke me up. Oh." Sally chuckled. "I guess what I meant to say was I dreamed about her tonight. You loved her very much, didn't you?"

"Yes, but . . ."

Sally held up her hand. "You don't need any buts. She was your wife. Don't you know that your capacity to love is one of the things I love most about you?"

Smoke picked up Sally's hand and kissed it.

She giggled. "There you go again, kissing my hand like I'm some grand dame in the queen's court. You can do better than that."

Smoke leaned down and kissed her full on the mouth.

A telegram brought Pearlie over from Big Rock. Doctor Gunther had given Sally permission to go home, provided she not be jostled about too much. When Pearlie arrived he was driving a grand carriage.

"Hello, Miss Sally." Pearlie smiled down at her from the driver's seat of the carriage.

"Hello, Pearlie." Sally took in the carriage with a sweep of her hand. "My, what an elegant carriage! Wherever did you get such a thing?"

"Ain't she a beaut, though? The seats inside is all red velvet, and if you get cold, well all you got to do is close the windows. This belongs to the governor."

"The governor?"

"Yes, ma'am," Pearlie said proudly. "The governor had the carriage brought to Big Rock, 'cause he wanted Elmer Baker to touch up the gold trim for him." Pearlie pointed to the side of the coach. "He done a real good job, too, didn't he? Look at how that gold is shinin'."

At that moment, one of the doors opened, and Dr. Colton—the doctor from Big Rock—stepped down.

"Dr. Colton!" Sally said in surprise. "What are you doing here?"

"I got a telegram from Smoke," Dr. Colton replied. "He told me you were coming home today, and asked if I didn't think it would be a pretty good idea if I came along to ride back with you."

Sally looked at her husband. "Smoke, you know I'm fine. Why did you bother him like that?"

"Believe me, Sally, it is no bother," Dr. Colton replied. "I consider it an honor. In fact, Louis Longmont thought about closing his saloon and coming over with me."

"Oh, well I'm glad he didn't do that. Otherwise, I would have every beer drinker in Big Rock angry with me."

Dr. Colton laughed. "I see you still have your sense of humor about you. That's a good sign. That's a very good sign." He helped Sally into the carriage, then sat across from her.

Smoke tied Seven on behind the carriage, then climbed into it to sit beside Sally. As Pearlie drove down the main street, people stared in amazement at the fine coach, wondering what it was doing there. Smoke waved at them with the back of his hand.

"Smoke, what on earth are you doing?" Sally asked.

"I am waving at the little people from this fine carriage."

She laughed hard, then winced with pain and put her hand over her wound.

"Sally, are you all right?" Smoke asked in concern.

"I'm fine," Sally replied. "Just quit making me laugh out loud like that. It hurts." She paused and tilted her head. "On the other hand, make me laugh out loud all you want. I need the laughter, and I don't care whether it hurts or not."

CHAPTER THIRTEEN

Sugarloaf Ranch

Sally was sitting in a rocking chair on the front porch of the house. Smoke, Pearlie, and Cal were hovering around her, offering to bring coffee or tea, whichever she might want, a shawl, a footstool, something to read, something to eat.

"For crying out loud," Sally finally said with a laugh. "Don't any of you have something else to do? What about the spring roundup? We do have a ranch to run, you know."

"Yes ma'am. Right now seems like most of the work is findin' cows and calves that's got themselves bogged down in mud holes here and there," Cal said.

"But we've brung in some hands for that," Pearlie said.

"And we've got calves to brand," Cal added.

"You're turning all that over to temporary help?" Sally asked.

"No ma'am, we're goin' to be out there. Some-one needs to be ram roddin' it."

"By someone, you mean you?"

"Yes, ma'am, I reckon so," Pearlie answered. "That is, me and Cal."

"Let me ask you this. Do you plan to actually participate in the roundup? Or is it your inten-tion to spend all the time here, on the porch?"

"Oh, no ma'am, we ain't goin' to be spendin' all our time here on the porch. Fact is, we're goin' right now," Pearlie said. "We was just wantin' to make sure that if there was somethin' we could do for you, why we would be here to do it, is all."

"Going to work would be doing something for me," Sally said.

"Yes, ma'am." Pearlie glanced over at Cal. "What are you standin' around for? We got work to do. We can't spend the whole day up here, just hangin' around on the porch."

"I'm goin', I'm goin'," Cal said, hurrying down the porch steps. "What I'm wonderin' is when you are goin' to get to work."

The two young cowboys continued their argu-ing all the way out to the barn.

"You were a little hard on them, weren't you, Sally?" Smoke asked with a chuckle, after Pearlie and Cal left.

"Well come on, Smoke, you saw them. Tiptoe-ing around me, trying to wait on me, like I was an invalid or something."

"You are an invalid."

"I'm not an invalid. I'm recovering from a gunshot wound," Sally said. "You've had to recover from a few, I recall."

"Yes, I have."

"That's a temporary thing. Besides, they need to keep themselves busy doing something on the ranch, so they won't be worrying so much about me. Especially Cal, bless his heart. He feels personally responsible for what happened."

"Cal feels responsible?"

"Yes."

"Now what could possibly make him feel responsible?"

"You know how he is, Smoke. He thinks he let me down because he wasn't in the bank with me when it happened."

"That's foolish. No one expected him to spend every moment with you."

"Of course it is foolish. But try telling him that."

Smoke walked over to the edge of the porch and stood, looking out. It was still early morning and the rising sun had painted the clouds in brilliant crimson, sending its rays to turn to gold the sheer walls of the cliffs that protected Sugarloaf from the most severe winter blasts. The creek that watered his stock was glistening silver, the trees, vividly green, and in the clefts, rays of sunlight burned away the blue shadows.

"Are you enjoying the view?" Sally asked. "It is a beautiful view, I admit. But I have a feeling you are trying to come up with a way to tell me."

"Tell you what?" Smoke replied.

"Tell me that you are going after them."

Smoke turned toward her. "I have to do it, Sally. You know I have to do it."

"If you remember, Smoke, that's how I met you. You were coming after the men who had killed Nicole. I know you have to do it. And I know it would be useless for me to try and stop you."

Smoke smiled, then walked over and leaned down to kiss his wife. "The only thing is, I'm concerned about leaving you here."

"Don't be concerned. I'm going to be fine. Besides, I have Pearlie and Cal here to watch over me. What more could you ask for?"

"I'm going into town. I need to visit with Sheriff Carson for a bit. I'll come back here before I leave."

Sally started to stand. "I'll fix a little something for you to take with you."

"No you don't. You stay right there in that chair, and don't even try to get up unless Cal or Pearlie are here to help you."

"I don't know if you think I am three years old or ninety years old," Sally replied in frustration.

"Neither. I think you are wounded."

Big Rock

Dr. Colton laughed when Smoke told him that Sally had wanted to fix something for him to have on the trail. "She would do something like that. For anyone else with a wound that severe, they would be soliciting all the sympathy and care they could get. For Sally, it is naught but a temporary inconvenience."

Smoke and Dr. Colton were in Longmont's Saloon. Louis, the dark-eyed Frenchman who owned the saloon, was sitting at the table with them.

"In France, we have a saying," Louis said. *"Pour un seul sang, je vais extraire. Ma vengeance sera sévère."*

"That sounds just real pretty, Louis," Dr. Colton said. "What does it mean?"

"For one blood, I shall extract two," Louis translated. "My revenge shall be severe."

At that moment Sheriff Carson came in. He smiled when he saw Smoke. "I got it. It just came in by telegraph a few moments ago."

"Thanks, Monte," Smoke replied.

"You got what?" Louis asked.

"I sent a telegram to Phillip Wilcox in Denver. He is the U.S. marshal for Colorado. He has sent authorization to make Smoke a deputy U.S. marshal. That way, Smoke can go after the murderers and thieves who shot Sally, with universal authority."

Sheriff Carson held up a badge. "I keep a couple deputy U.S. marshal badges in the office for just such a thing. Hold up your right hand."

Smoke repeated the oath as administered by Sheriff Carson. "As a deputy United States marshal, I, Kirby Jensen, do solemnly swear that I will support and defend the Constitution of the United States against all enemies, foreign and domestic; that I will bear true faith and allegiance to the same; that I take this obligation freely, without any mental reservation or purpose of evasion; and that I will well and faithfully discharge the duties of the office on which I am about to enter. So help me God."

"Congratulations," Sheriff Carson said as he pinned the badge onto Smoke's shirt. "You are now an officer of the law."

Mrs. Smoke Jensen Recovering

Mrs. Jensen has returned to her residence at Sugarloaf and is said to be recuperating in a marvelous fashion. All who know this wonderful lady are mouthing prayers of relief for the ongoing recovery.

While visiting in Gothic one week previous, Mrs. Jensen was in the Miner's Bank when a band of brigands attempted to rob that institution. Encountering unexpected resistance due to the installation of a time lock safe, the bank robbers, said to be led by Bill Dinkins, gave vent to their frustration.

Dinkins fired his pistol twice inside the bank, one ball striking the bank owner, Mr. Kurt Flowers, with deadly effect. The second ball struck Mrs. Jensen, wounding her grievously. Before leaving Gothic, the brigands murdered two more of the town's finest citizens, including Mr. Deckert, a merchant, and Sheriff Tyson. Both men were killed instantly.

Escape was not without some penalty however, as Mr. Calvin Woods, an employee of Mr. Smoke Jensen, who was present in the town at the time, having escorted

Mrs. Jensen there, took the fleeing bandits under fire. He killed John Putnam with what the citizens of the town say was a shot of extreme range and magnificent skill.

As to the location of the remaining bank robbers, nothing is known. Smoke Jensen has been appointed a deputy United States marshal, and it is said that he will pursue the evildoers to the very gates of hell if need be.

Were the editor of this newspaper afforded the opportunity to speak with Bill Dinkins and the evildoers who accompany him, he would feel the obligation to issue a warning. Smoke Jensen is not only a man of steely nerve, dogged determination, and deadly skills with firearms, he is also cloaked in the armor of righteousness. He has, in the course of his life, dispatched many a bad man to stand before that final judge of all mankind.

To Mr. Dinkins, and all who ride with you in your nefarious transgressions, I issue this warning. Beware, for truth and justice, when pursed by a man such as Smoke Jensen, will triumph.

Gunnison, Colorado

Like many other towns in the county, Gunnison began its life because of the silver that was dug out of the nearby mountains. When the silver played out, the town survived because a railroad served the area ranchers. Like many Western towns, it was divided into two sections, a rough collection of saloons and shanties, and legitimate businesses and homes. The Hard Rock Saloon was in the rougher section of town. Inside, occupying a table at the back, sat Bill Dinkins, Cole Parnell, Travis Slater, and his brother Frank.

Parnell had been reading the newspaper, and he slapped it down on the table with an angry snarl. "Son of a bitch, they know who we are."

"Who knows who we are?" Dinkins asked.

"The law knows who we are." Parnell pointed to the paper. "It says right there, that the Bill Dinkins' gang held up the bank and killed the bank president, some merchant, and the sheriff."

"Don't forget the woman," Frank said. "Dinkins kilt her, too."

"She ain't dead," Parnell said.

"How do you know she ain't dead?" Travis asked.

"Hell. 'Cause it says right here in the newspaper," Parnell said. "It says she is recuperatin' just fine."

"Then that's prob'ly how they found out who we was," Travis said. "She prob'ly told the law ever'thing."

"That ain't the bad thing," Parnell said.

"What is the bad thing?" Travis asked.

"This ain't just any woman that you shot." Parnell looked directly at Dinkins. "Maybe you don't know it, but the woman you shot is married to Mr. Smoke Jensen."

"Smoke Jensen?" Dinkins replied. "That ain't good."

"Damn right, it ain't good," Parnell said. "Accordin' to this here newspaper, he's done got hisself deputized, and he aims to come after us."

"Deputized? Hell, that don't mean nothin'. All we got to do is leave the county, and he can't come for us."

"Uh-uh. That won't work. He's been deputized a United States marshal, and that means he can go anywhere he wants," Parnell said.

"Yeah, well if he does come after us, he just may be bitin' off more than he can chaw," Dinkins said. "I've sent word for someone to join us."

"What do we need someone else for?" Travis asked.

"We lost Putnam, didn't we? I figure on replacing him."

"I know'd Putnam when we was in prison together," Parnell said. "It's goin' to take a good man to replace him."

"The man I've got comin' is worth five Putnams," Dinkins said.

"Who would that be?" Frank asked.

"You'll see when he gets here," Dinkins said mysteriously.

"When will that be?" Travis asked.

Dinkins twisted around in his chair and looked up at the clock. "The train gets here at two. We got less than an hour to wait now, I reckon."

* * *

He stood on the platform for just a minute, looking around. Behind him the train was a symphony of sound, from the bubbling water in the boiler, to the venting of steam, to the snapping and popping of heated journals and bearings. Nobody came to meet him, but he wasn't expecting anyone. A child who saw him was frightened by his skull-like head, and turned his face into his mother's skirt and clutched it about him.

Harley waited on the platform until his horse was led down the ramp from the cattle car, then walked down to claim him.

"Yes, sir, here is your mount, as fresh as he was when he boarded the train." The groom held the horse's reins in one hand, while his other hand was palm up for the expected tip.

Harley ignored the groom's palm and, without a sound, mounted, and rode away. It took but a minute to ride from the depot to the saloon where he dismounted and tied his horse to the hitch rail. He glanced up and down the street as if making certain there was no potential threat, then pushed his way through the swinging bat wing doors.

He was wearing a gun strapped low on his right hip, and once inside, he stepped away from the door so he wasn't back lighted. He paused for a moment. Only when his eyes were fully adjusted to the dimmer light, did he walk over to the bar.

"You know who that is?" Dinkins whispered to the others.

"Can't say as I do," Parnell said.

"That is Wes Harley. I reckon you've heard of him, ain't you?

"I've heard of 'im," Travis said. "He's a—"

"He's a gunfighter," Dinkins interrupted, intending to keep control of the conversation.

"He's supposed to be fast," Travis said.

"He's not just supposed to be fast, he *is* fast," Dinkins said.

"I don't believe that is him," Parnell said.

"What makes you say that?"

"Well think about it. What would someone like that be doin' here?"

"He's here 'cause I asked him to be here," Dinkins said.

"What?"

"He's the one I was telling you about. He's the one I asked to join us. He'll be with us when we hit the bank in Crystal."

"You really think we need someone like that to hold up the bank in that little town?" Parnell asked.

"If people like Smoke Jensen are going to start coming after us, it would be good to have someone like Harley on our side," Dinkins said.

Harley stepped up to the bar and slapped a coin down.

"Whiskey," he grunted. "The good stuff."

"Oh, sorry, mister, but you are just a little too late for any of our good stuff. That miner down there at the other end of the bar just bought our last bottle of blended whiskey. But I think you'll find our trade liquor ain't that bad."

Harley turned to look at the young miner, who had just poured himself a glass from the bottle. "Mister, I'll be askin' you to sell that bottle to me."

The miner shook his head. "Friend, I been bustin' up hard rock all week, just a' thinkin' about comin' in here for a good bottle of whiskey. I aim to keep it for myself."

Harley put some money on the bar and slid it toward the cowboy.

"Mister, don't you hear good?" the miner asked. "I told you, I ain't sellin' my whiskey."

"Either pick up the money, or go for your gun," Harley said.

"What?"

"I said, pull your gun or give me the bottle."

"I ain't even wearin' a gun. What the hell are you talkin' about?"

"You." Harley looked toward Travis Slater. "You're wearin' a gun. Give it to the miner there."

"All right." Travis pulled his pistol from his holster by thumb and forefinger, carried it over to the miner, and held it out toward him.

The miner held up his hands, as if pushing Travis away. "I don't want your gun."

"Put it on the bar, then back out of the way," Harley said.

Travis did as Harley directed.

"You're armed now," Harley said. "Pick it up."

"Mister, are you serious?" The miner's voice was high-pitched and cracking with fear. "You really aimin' to throw down on me over a bottle of whiskey?"

"For God's sake, give him the bottle, boy," the bartender said.

"I paid for this bottle, and there ain't nobody goin' to buffalo me into givin' it up. I don't know who you are, mister, but I ain't givin' you my bottle, and I ain't goin' to pick up this pistol."

Harley pulled his gun and fired. Pink mist sprayed from the miner's earlobe and he slapped his hand up to the side of his head with a howl of pain. By the time the smoke cleared, the pistol was back in Harley's holster.

"Give me the bottle," Harley ordered.

With his left hand still pressed against his ear, the miner shoved the bottle down the bar with his right. "Here. Take the goddamn bottle." He reached for the money.

"Uh-uh. That ain't your money now. You didn't take it when I give you the chance."

The miner stared at Harley through terror-stricken eyes. Keeping his hand pressed against the side of his head, he rushed out of the saloon.

Harley picked up the bottle. Carrying it and Travis's pistol with him, he walked over to join Dinkins and the others at his table. "I thank you for the loan of the pistol." He held the gun across the table. Raising the bottle to his lips, he took a couple swallows, then wiped his mouth with the back of his hand and looked over at Dinkins. He smiled. "Hello, Little Brother."

"Brother?" Frank Slater said. "You two are brothers?"

"Yeah." Dinkins reached over to shake hands with Harley.

"How come you ain't got the same last name?"

"We got the same mama, but different daddies," Dinkins said.

Harley took another swallow from the bottle. "We think."

"You think?" Parnell asked, clearly confused by the strange answer. "What do you mean, you think? Do you have different daddies or not?"

"Mama was a whore," Dinkins said. "She didn't always keep track of the men she slept with."

"When you sent for me, you said you had somethin' in mind," Harley said. "What is it?"

"Banks," Dinkins replied. "Startin' with one over in Crystal, tomorrow."

"Banks?" Parnell asked.

"You didn't think we was goin' to do only that one in Gothic, then quit, did you?" Dinkins asked.

"Yeah, well, I didn't know. I mean the first one sure didn't turn out well now, did it?" Parnell said.

CHAPTER FOURTEEN

Elco

Smoke had been on the trail for two days, but so far he had no leads on where the bandits were, or even where they were going. He saw a small town rising ahead of him. He hadn't happened on the town by accident. He knew it was there, and he knew, too, that the men he was looking for would be in a town somewhere. Because towns were few and relatively far between, he was prepared to search every town until he found them.

As he approached the town Smoke decided to get a haircut. He had to find someone talkative enough to engage in conversation if he was going to find out any information. He didn't know anyone more talkative than a barber. He wasn't in desperate need of a haircut, but he could use one.

Emerson Bates had his chair tipped back against the rip-sawed boards that made up the false-front of Wong's Laundry. He liked sitting there, because he lusted after the Chinaman's two daughters. Of course, he had never been able to act on his lust. They were not whores, and he could not get them to show any interest in him. At the moment, his feet were wrapped around the front legs of the chair and his hat was pulled down low over his eyes. The sun was almost dead overhead so there were no shadows on the street. It was the hottest time of the day which meant most citizens stayed out of the sun as much as they could.

Bates was a deputy sheriff and the only one out in the noonday sun. The other deputies and the sheriff were in the saloon drinking beer and playing cards.

Bates heard the hollow, clumping sounds of a single rider and looked toward the south to see a horseman coming into town. Tipping his chair forward Bates stood up and watched as the rider came farther into town. Just across the street from the Chinese laundry, the rider pulled up, then dismounted in front of Max's Barbershop.

As Smoke was tying his horse off at the hitching rail, the barber stepped out through the door of his shop. "Yes, sir." He smiled at his potential customer as he stood with a damp towel draped across his shoulder. "Would you be wanting a haircut and a shave?"

"Just a shave," Smoke answered. "From the sign outside, you would be Max, I take it?"

"Yes, sir, Max Gibbs is the name, and this shop, such as it is, is all mine. And you would be?"

"Smoke Jensen."

"Smoke Jensen! My, what a privilege it will be to

serve you, Mr. Jensen. Yes, sir, I have read about you." Max stepped back into his shop and invited Smoke in with the motion of his arm. "Please, step inside."

The barber shop was very small, just barely large enough to accommodate the barber chair and a small, leather covered settee where customers could wait their turn.

"You'll be wantin' to wash some of the trail dust off your face, I expect," Max said. "There's a wash basin on that table there. Help yourself. That comes with the price of the haircut and shave."

"Thanks," Smoke said as he took advantage of the barber's offer. "How much is a shave?"

"Shave and a haircut is two bits," the barber answered. "But seein' as you are just getting' a shave, it will only be a dime."

"Tell you what. I only want the shave, but suppose I pay you for both anyway." Smoke flipped the barber a quarter.

"Thank you, sir! Here, have a seat."

Smoke took his seat in the single chair.

"You just passing through, are you, Mr. Jensen?" Max picked up a cup and brush and began working up a lather.

"Yes. I came through Gothic a couple days ago. I guess you heard about what happened over there. I'm talking about the bank robbery."

"Oh, indeed we have heard about it over here. It was in the newspa—" Max stopped in midsentence. "Oh, my, the lady who was shot. That was your wife, wasn't it?"

"Yes."

"How is she, if I may ask?"

"Thank you for asking. She is much better."

"Well, thank God for that," Max said.

"I have," Smoke replied.

"You know, to those of us over here, that bank robbery and the shooting was particular upsetting, considerin' the Slater brothers."

"Slater brothers?"

"Travis and Frank Slater. They used to live here. They was our neighbors, you might say. And now they are riding with Dinkins. I don't tell you that as a point of pride, by the way. The truth is, them two boys never was no good. They was working for Chance Carter, a rancher just south of town. Mr. Carter had him a fifteen-year-old daughter, prettiest little girl you ever seen. Well, one day Mr. Carter an' his daughter both turned up dead, and the Slater brothers both turned up missin'."

"So you are saying that the Slater brothers killed Mr. Carter?" Smoke asked.

"Yes, sir, I reckon I am sayin' that. Of course, we don't none of us have no proof or nothin' like that. But Frank and Travis Slater never was no count a-tall. Mr. Carter turned up dead, and them two no accounts turned up missin'."

Smoke nodded. This was a good stop. Max had just supplied him with the last names of two people who were with Dinkins.

Max stretched the chair out, used a brush to apply the lather, then a straight razor to shave him. When that was done, he wrapped warm wet towels around Smoke's face.

Bates had been waiting for just that moment. He walked into the shop. "Plannin' on stayin' in our town long?"

Smoke's face was wrapped in the towels, but not his eyes. "I just stopped in for a shave. And that's about done, I expect. Wouldn't you say so, Max?"

"Yes, sir, just another moment to relax your face is all, I would say," Max replied.

Smoke noticed a twinge of fear in the barber's voice, but had no idea why.

"Yes, well, here's the thing, mister," Bates said. "We got law in this town. And we don't take to strangers comin' in and breakin' the law."

"Have I broken the law by getting a shave?" Smoke asked.

"It ain't the shave I'm talkin' about."

"I see. And you enforce the law, do you?"

"I do indeed," Bates said. "Do you see this star? That means I'm a deputy sheriff."

"Your mama must be real proud," Smoke said calmly.

Bates blinked a few times at the response. This wasn't going the way he had planned. "The point is, mister, I am a deputy. And bein' as I'm a deputy, well, sir, that means I can collect taxes when they're due. And right now, you owe this here town two dollars in taxes."

"Why is that?"

"It's to pay for the protection we give you while you are here in town," Bates said.

"I'll protect myself."

"Mister"—Bates' voice reflected his growing anger and frustration—"you ain't payin' much attention to me, are you? Now I'm goin' to say it real slow so's maybe even someone as dumb as you can understand. You owe the city of Elco two dollars, and I aim to collect it."

"I told you, deputy, I don't live here, I don't plan to live here, and I don't need your protection."

"Bates, there ain't no call for you to come in here and be talkin' to my customer like this," Max said. "He told you, he's just passin' through. Now why don't you just go away and leave us alone?"

"Stay out of this, Max," Bates said coldly. "Unless you want to get hurt."

With Bates' attention diverted by the barber, Smoke pulled the apron off.

When Bates looked back toward him he saw that Smoke was holding a pistol. "What the hell?" Bates said with a gasp. "You're pulling a gun on an officer of the law?"

"Maybe you didn't notice." Smoke jerked the thumb of his left hand toward his badge. "I'm also an officer of the law, a deputy United States marshal. And like I said, I don't need your protection."

"Oh. You should have told me you was a lawman like me. Of course, bein' as you are a lawman, why, there ain't no tax due. Sort of a professional courtesy, you might say."

"I accept your courtesy." Smoke got out of the chair, put his pistol back in the holster, then turned to reach for his hat, which was on the hat rack in the corner of the little room.

"Marshal, look out!" Max suddenly shouted.

Smoke spun around, drawing his pistol as he did so. He saw Bates standing in the doorway with his own gun drawn.

Seeing Smoke's rapid reaction to Max's warning, the expression on Bate's face changed from one of triumph, to one of shock. He thumbed back the hammer on his pistol, but it was too late. Smoke fired, and the bullet tore through Bates' heart, leaving a quarter-sized exit hole just beside his left shoulder blade.

Hearing the shot, several people came running toward the barbershop.

Smoke noticed some of the men had stars pinned to their vest or shirt, but he had no idea which one was the sheriff.

"Who did this?" one of the men demanded. From the authoritative tone of his voice, Smoke realized the man had just answered his question.

"I did," Smoke said.

"Mister, you are under arrest."

"I don't think so."

"What do you mean, you don't think so? Mister, you just killed one of my deputies!"

"Bates drew first, Sheriff Cooper," Max said. "In fact, he was goin' to shoot Marshal Jensen in the back."

"Marshal?" the sheriff asked. "What kind of marshal?"

"I'm a deputy United States marshal."

"Why would Bates try to shoot you in the back?"

"Bates was tryin' to make Marshal Smoke Jensen pay him two dollars for tax," Max said.

The expression on Sheriff Cooper's face changed dramatically. "Did the barber just call you Smoke Jensen?"

"Yes."

"Well, uh, Marshal Jensen, I don't know exactly what sort of scheme Deputy Bates was trying to run, but I assure you, we don't collect a tax from people who are just passing through our fair city."

"I didn't think you would," Smoke said. He turned to Max. "Thank you for the shave."

"Hastings," Sheriff Cooper said, speaking to one of his deputies. "Get Gustafson up here to take care of this body."

"Yes, sir," Hastings answered.

"Sheriff Cooper, I wonder if you could tell me anything about the Slater brothers?" Smoke realized he had an advantage over the sheriff. He was positive Cooper not only knew Bates was shaking down strangers for tax money, but that he was probably behind it. Whereas Cooper might be reticent to talk about the Slater brothers under ordinary circumstances, he would welcome the discussion as a diversion from his own crooked dealings.

Cooper had photographs of Travis and Frank Slater. "These here pictures was took by Fred Dysart. He runs the picture shop here." Cooper handed the first photograph to Smoke. "This one is Frank Slater. He is the oldest."

Frank had a high forehead, thin hair, beady eyes, and a handlebar mustache.

Cooper gave Smoke the second photograph. "And this one is Travis."

Travis had his head tilted to one side. He was clean shaven, and his hair was neatly combed.

Smoke studied the pictures for a couple of minutes, then handed them back.

"Marshal Jensen, about Bates and the tax," Sheriff Cooper said. "We are collecting taxes as a way of raising money, but I don't know why he tried to shoot you. I ain't never authorized nothin' like that."

"You reap what you sow," Smoke said.

"Yeah, well, I think we've raised enough money now, I'm probably going to stop it."

"Alvin Marsh, the state attorney general, is a friend of mine," Smoke said. "I'm sure that when he sends some of his people down here to have a look around, he will appreciate that you have stopped taxing strangers."

Crystal, Colorado

The Crystal River, a fast flowing stream that broke white over the rocks, set up a roar that could be heard, twenty-four hours a day, all over the town of Crystal. It was impossible for the streets to run parallel, or at right angles to each other. The result was a swath, cut by the river through the pass, along which a couple roads had been fashioned. On either side of the roads the buildings stood as if hanging on to the side of the mountain.

An industrious town, supported by the silver that was extracted from two producing mines, the citizens were sure that someday Crystal would be one of the largest communities in Colorado, if not in the entire West.

Thaddeus Walker, Raleigh Jones, and Emerson Teasdale were having breakfast together at Wilson's Café. Businessmen, they were vocal advocates of the town, and so convinced of its future they were about to engage in a new venture. They were going to build a hydroelectric plant on the Crystal River. Bringing Crystal into the modern age of electricity would, they believed, not only bring about growth, but insure it would survive far into the future, even if the silver played out.

They had calculated it would cost ten thousand dollars to build the plant, and they were putting in two thousand dollars each. As soon as the bank opened, they were going to present their plan to the loan officer at the Bank of Crystal, to secure the rest of the money.

A year earlier Thaddeus had visited his brother in Appleton, Wisconsin, where the first hydroelectric generator had been put in use. He convinced Jones and Teasdale they could not only put in an electric power plant in Crystal, they could sell "electric subscriptions" for enough money to pay them back for their investment, then continue to make money for years to come.

It had not been a hard sale. Jones, who owned the dairy, and Teasdale, a partner with Walker in a silver mine, were entrepreneurial enough to see the benefits. They walked into the bank to take the final steps to bring it about.

Unfortunately, Walker, Jones, and Teasdale were not the only entrepreneurs with an eye on Crystal. There were five others who also saw Crystal as the key to a financial windfall, though their entrepreneurial experiment was criminal in its intent. Dinkins, Harley, Parnell, and the two Slater brothers rode down the street to the bank. Leaving Travis and Parnell to hold the horses, Dinkins, Harley, and Frank lifted bandannas to cover the bottom of their faces as they rushed in through the door. There were three customers inside the bank.

"You three!" Dinkins shouted. "Down on the floor!"

Frightened by the masked gunmen who had just entered the bank, the three customers did as they were told.

"You," Dinkins said, pointing his pistol at the teller. "Listen real careful to what I am goin' to say. I want you to empty your cash drawer, then I want you to go over to that safe, open it up, and give me all the money in there. If you tell me you can't open it, I am going to shoot you dead. Now, do you understand me?"

The teller, who was shaking visibly, nodded.

."Let me hear you say that you understand what I just told you," Dinkins said.

"I-I understand," the bank teller said, barely able to choke the words out.

"Good for you." Dinkins handed a cloth bag to the teller. "Now, empty your cash drawer into this bag, then go over there, open the safe, and empty it as well."

With his hands shaking so badly he could scarcely hold on to the money, the bank teller did as he was instructed. When the cash drawer was emptied, he moved over to the big safe and opened it rather easily. Taking bound packets of money from the safe, he dropped them into the cloth bag.

As he handed the bag of money to Dinkins, there was a loud commotion outside the bank.

"Don't go in there!" a voice shouted. Dinkins recognized it as Parnell's voice.

"What do you mean, don't go in there? What the hell is going on here?" another voice yelled gruffly.

A gunshot followed.

As Dinkins, Harley, and Frank Slater started toward the front door, distracted by the gunshot outside, Thaddeus Walker pulled his gun. He fired, but missed. Harley spun around, and in three quick shots, killed all three of the bank customers.

"Let's go," Dinkins called.

Outside, the man Parnell had frightened off by a gunshot was running down the street, away from the bank. The citizens of Crystal, who but a moment earlier had been going about their daily commerce, watched as five horseman galloped out of town, firing their pistols indiscriminately. Most dived to the ground as the bullets flew, but a man stepped out of the gun store, and raising a rifle to his shoulder, fired.

One of the galloping horses went down, leaving an outlaw without a horse. He yelled at those galloping away, but they didn't come back for him. Turning, he saw at least a dozen men running toward him, all of them armed. He threw up his hands. "Don't shoot, don't shoot!" he shouted. "I give up!"

"Get a rope!" one of the men shouted. "We'll string the son of a bitch up right here, and right now!"

"No!" called a man wearing a badge. "We ain't goin' to have no lynchin's in this town. We're goin' to try this man legal!"

There were several groans, and the outlaw nodded. "Thanks, Sheriff."

"Then we'll hang you," the sheriff concluded.

The groans changed to cheers.

CHAPTER FIFTEEN

"*Oyez, oyez, oyez,* this here court is about to convene, the honorable Judge Thurman Norton presiding," the sheriff called. "All stand!"

Sheriff John Dennis was acting as bailiff of the court, and because court was being held in the saloon, he pointed toward the bartender. "Dooley, you make dead certain you don't serve no liquor durin' this trial, 'cause if you do, I'll put whoever bought the drink, and you, in jail."

"I ain't plannin' on servin' no liquor, Sheriff." The bartender pointed to a sign that was on the mirror behind the bar. "As you can see, I got the place posted CLOSED, and I ain't served a drop for the last half hour."

During the discussion between the sheriff and Dooley, the honorable Thurman Norton came out of the back room of the saloon and took a seat at his "bench," which was the best table in the saloon. The table sat upon a raised platform which had been built just for that purpose. The saloon was the largest, most substantial building in Crystal, and the easiest place to empanel a jury, for it was always crowded. It was easy for the judge to round up twelve sober men, good and true. If it was sometimes difficult to find twelve sober men, the judge could stretch the definition of sobriety thin enough to meet the needs of the court. The "good and true," however, had to be taken upon faith.

"You may be seated," Judge Norton said.

There was a rustle of clothing and a scrape of chairs as the gallery, which consisted of nearly half the town, took their seats. Though respectable women rarely saw the inside of the saloon, many were present, for by court decree, at the moment, it was not a saloon, it was a courtroom. Out of deference to the ladies, the more objectionable artwork—meaning the nude paintings of women—had been covered.

"Is the prisoner present?"

"I've got the guilty son of a bitch right here, Judge," the deputy sheriff said. His remarks generated laughter, and Judge Norton let it be known by the glare in his eyes that he did not appreciate it.

The saloon grew quiet.

"Is the accused represented by counsel?"

"I'm his lawyer, Your Honor," a man sitting to the right of Cole Parnell said. The lawyer, who was short and chubby, was wearing a suit and cravat. "Daniel Gilman."

"Is counsel for the state present?"

"I am, Your Honor. Michael Thomas." The

prosecutor was tall and thin, with a prominent Adam's apple. Like Gilman, he was wearing a suit.

"Voir dire having been completed, are both counselors satisfied with the jury as it now sits?"

"I am, Your Honor," Gilman said.

"As am I," Thomas added.

"Very well, Mr. Prosecutor, you may make your case," the judge said.

Thomas was so tall that as he stood, it looked like he was unfolding. He walked over to the side of the saloon where the twelve jurors sat. "Gentlemen of the jury, it is a simple case to present. There will be no need for flowery language or lengthy discourse. The simple truth will be all that is necessary to convict. This outlaw"—he pointed to Parnell—"and four of his cohorts robbed the bank. The money they took belonged to you, and to everyone else in this town who had their money on deposit, with the reasonable expectation that it would be safe.

"And, in robbing the bank, they committed murder, not once, but three times, cutting short the lives of Thaddeus Walker, Raleigh Jones, and Emerson Teasdale. Husbands and fathers, they were all good and upstanding citizens of our community. These three men committed no wrongdoing. They were merely in the bank, conducting business, when Cole Parnell and his partners in crime entered the bank and, in but the wink of an eye, dispatched the souls of all three to eternity."

Thomas called as his witness the bank teller, whose name was Clyde Bailey. After the teller was sworn in, Thomas began to question him. "Tell the court, in your own words, what happened yesterday."

"Four masked men came into the bank, all four holding guns," Bailey said. "They made Mr. Walker, Mr. Jones, and Mr. Teasdale lie down on the floor, then they commenced to take all the money from my cashier's drawer, then all the money from the safe. As they was leavin', well, Mr. Walker, he shot at them. And that man"—Bailey pointed to Parnell—"turned and shot all three of them. Then they ran out of the bank."

"Objection, Your Honor," Gilman said. "If all four men were masked, how does he know which one did the shooting?"

"Sustained."

"How much money did the robbers get?" Thomas asked his witness.

"They got nearly six thousand dollars."

"Six thousand dollars? Is that the total amount of money in the bank?"

Bailey smiled. "No, sir. All the robbers did was clean out our daily working safe. They had no idea that we keep most of the money in a vault in the back of the bank."

"I have no further questions of this witness," Thomas said.

"Cross, Mr. Gilman?" the judge asked.

Gilman stood, but he didn't approach the witness. "You said my client is the one who shot those three men, but the truth is, you don't know who did the shooting, do you?"

"No sir, I guess not."

"And if, as you say, all four men were masked, you can't even testify, with certainty, that Mr. Parnell was one of those who entered the bank, can you?"

"When they was all ridin' away, this fella's horse was shot," Bailey said. "And they captured him. That proves he was one of the ones in the bank."

Gilman held up his hand. "You are conjecturing now. Listen carefully to my question. Can you testify, with certainty, that Mr. Parnell was one of the four in the bank?"

"Yes, sir. He was wearin' the same clothes then he's wearin' now."

"You mean his blue shirt?" Gilman turned toward the gallery. "Like the blue shirt Mr. Engle is wearing?" He pointed to one of the men in the jury. "Or the blue shirt Mr. Puckett is wearing? Or the blue shirt Sheriff Dennis is wearing?"

A buzz went through the courtroom, for Gilman had pointed to three men who were wearing a shirt identical to the one being worn by the prisoner. "Should we consider any of those three men, suspects?"

"No," the witness replied in a small voice.

"No further questions, Your Honor."

"Redirect, Mr. Thomas?"

"No redirect, Your Honor."

Thomas then called Frank Tanner, the man who shot the horse Parnell had been riding. Tanner testified that he had heard shots in the bank, and concerned, had grabbed a rifle, then went outside just in time to see the men exiting the bank, mount their horses, and ride away.

"Do you here testify that the man on trial is one of those who ran from the bank?" Thoams asked.

"Yes."

"How can you be sure?"

"Because I had my eyes on him from the moment he left the bank, until I shot his horse."

"No further questions."

"Mr. Gilman?" the judge asked.

"Mr. Tanner, as they were leaving, did you have it in mind to kill the horse Parnell was riding?"

"No sir, I had it in mind to kill the bank robber, only I missed and hit his horse."

"So, your eyesight isn't all that good, is it? What I mean is, we are supposed to accept your story that you had Mr. Parnell in sight all along, but, with poor eyesight, you might have been wrong."

"There ain't nothin' a-tall wrong with my eyesight," Tanner replied, bristling at the question.

"No further questions, Your Honor."

Thomas called two other witnesses who testified they had heard the shots and seen the men run from the bank. They also testified they had no doubt Parnell was one of the four. Thomas also said he could call a dozen more witnesses, but their testimony would be redundant as Parnell's participation in the robbery had been proven beyond the shadow of a doubt.

Gilman had no witnesses for the defense, deciding it would not serve Parnell well to testify.

"Summation, Mr. Gilman," Judge Norton said.

"Gentlemen of the jury, what we have here is circumstantial. Mr. Bailey was the only witness to the actual murder and robbery, and in his own words, all the perpetrators were masked. He claimed to identify my defendant by the fact that he is wearing a blue shirt. But that could have been any one of three men in here, including a member of the jury and the sheriff. Since he cannot, with certainty, place my client in the bank at the time of the robbery, it is absolutely impossible for him to say that Parnell is the one who shot the three customers. Remember, in our system of government, you have to know beyond the shadow of a doubt that someone is guilty, before you find for the prosecution."

In Thomas's closing, he pointed out that there were enough eyewitnesses who heard the shots, saw the robbers leave the bank, then saw one of the robbers unhorsed—the unhorsed rider being Parnell—that there could be no doubt of his guilt.

"As to who actually fired the shots that took the lives of Mr. Walker, Mr. Jones, and Mr. Teasdale? That is immaterial. The law clearly states that if someone dies as the result of a felony in which you are participating, you are guilty of murder. It does not matter whether you are the one who pulled the trigger or not."

The trial took less than an hour. The jury's deliberation lasted only fifteen minutes. At five minutes after eleven o'clock in the morning, the jury sent word they had reached a verdict, thus causing court to be reconvened—meaning court was called to order again, as no one had left the saloon.

When the jury filed back in, Judge Norton adjusted the glasses on the end of his nose, then cleared his throat. "Would the foreman of the jury please stand?"

Mr. White, the druggist, stood.

"Mr. Foreman, I have been informed that the jury has reached a verdict. Is that true?"

"It is true, Your Honor."

"Would you publish the verdict, please?"

White looked confused. "Publish, Judge?"

"Tell the court the verdict," Judge Norton explained.

"Oh, yeah. Uh, I mean, yes sir. We the jury find the defendant guilty of bank robbery and guilty of murder in the first degree."

"Thank you, Mr. Foreman and gentlemen of the jury. This jury is dismissed, though you may remain in place during the sentencing phase."

Mr. White sat back down.

"Would the bailiff please bring the prisoner before the bench?"

Sheriff Dennis, who had been leaning against the piano with his arms folded across his chest, spit a quid of tobacco into the brass spittoon, then walked over to Parnell. "Get up. Present yourself before the judge."

Parnell was not only handcuffed, his legs were shackled together. With the assistance of the deputy sheriff and Mr. Gilman, Parnell stood, then shuffled over to stand in front of the judge.

Judge Norton took off his glasses and polished them as he studied the prisoner standing before him. Finally he put them back on and stared pointedly at Parnell.

"Cole Parnell, you have been tried before a jury of your peers and found guilty. Before this court passes sentence, have you anything to say?"

"Yes, Your Honor. I admit I was one of the men who robbed the bank, but I wasn't the one who shot them three men. If you want to know who it was that done that, it was Wes Harley. Wes Harley did the shootin', and that is a fact."

The gallery reacted to that, for it was the first time Wes Harley's name had been mentioned.

"Wes Harley! He was here?" someone asked.

"Wes Harley, in our town."

"I never thought Wes Harley would do a thing like that."

Judge Norton pounded his gavel. "Order! I will have order now, or I will empty this courtroom."

The gallery grew quiet.

Norton glared at Parnell. "Mr. Parnell, by your admission to being one of the robbers, you have just confirmed the jury's finding. For as Mr. Thomas pointed out, your very participation in the crime, during which someone was killed, makes you guilty of murder, whether you did the actual killing or not."

"I didn't know there was any such law," Parnell said.

"Ignorance of the law does not excuse you from its consequences. Cole Parnell, there are three families in this town who are, today, without the family head. Husbands and fathers, Thaddeus Walker, Raleigh Jones, and Emerson Teasdale leave a hole in our community and especially in their families, that cannot be filled because of the most evil deed performed by you and your cohorts in this dastardly crime. Therefore, Mr. Parnell, it is the sentence of this court that you be taken from this place and put in jail long enough to await your execution. At a time to be fixed by the sheriff, you are to be taken from jail and transported to a place where you will be hanged."

Pittsburg, Colorado

After leaving Elco, Smoke rode to Pittsburg, where he sent a telegram to Big Rock to check on Sally. He figured it would take at least an hour and a half to get a response. Kyle would have to deliver the telegram to Sugarloaf, then ride back with the answer. He had a leisurely lunch in the café, then walked back to the telegraph office.

"Yes, sir, Deputy," the telegrapher said when he saw Smoke come in. "I've got your message right here."

Anxiously, Smoke opened the envelope to read the message, then he laughed out loud.

I WANT YOU TO FIRE BOTH PEARLIE AND
CAL THEY WON'T LET ME DO A THING I
TRIED TO BRIBE THEM BY TELLING THEM
I WOULD BAKE SOME BEAR SIGNS FOR
THEM BUT EVEN THAT DIDN'T WORK
BE CAREFUL AND COME HOME SOON
I LOVE YOU
SALLY

Picking up a pencil and a form, Smoke wrote out the telegram he wanted to send back to Sally.

I HAVE NO INTENTION OF FIRING PEARLIE
OR CAL IN FACT I AM GOING TO GIVE
BOTH OF THEM A BONUS THEY ARE
DOING EXACTLY AS I ASKED THEM TO DO
I LOVE YOU TOO
SMOKE

While Smoke was reading his telegram, and writing his response, a new telegram came in. The telegrapher, his green visor in place, sat at the desk of the machine, writing quickly.

"It looks like they are going to hang him tomorrow," the telegrapher said.

"Hang who?" Smoke asked, made curious by the telegrapher's strange comment.

"There was a bank robbery over in Crystal," the telegrapher said. "Three bank customers were killed."

Smoke's immediate reaction was that it was exactly like the bank robbery in Gothic. It had to be the same people.

"Do they know who did it?"

"Well, they know the one they caught, the one they're going to hang tomorrow."

"Who is it? What is his name?"

"Parnell. Cole Parnell. He was tried and convicted a couple days ago. I guess they held off on hangin' him until they could get the gallows built, 'cause it looks like they're goin' to be hangin' him tomorrow."

Cole Parnell, Smoke knew, was one of the men who had robbed the bank in Gothic, which meant he was one of the men who shot Sally.

"Send this for me," Smoke said, handing the telegrapher his reply to Sally. "And thanks for the information about the bank robbery."

Leaving the telegraph office, Smoke walked down to the livery to get Seven. He intended to ride over to Crystal.

CHAPTER SIXTEEN

Crystal

When Smoke rode into the little town the next day the street was crowded with men, women, and children. Vendors were doing a brisk business as they worked the crowds selling everything from sandwiches, to beer, to candy.

"Tommy, where are you going?" a mother called to her son.

"I'm goin' to climb up to the loft of the livery. I'll bet there's a real good spot to watch it from there," Tommy answered.

"You'll do no such thing. You are going to stay right here with Maggie. You hold her hand."

"Why?"

"Because she is your little sister, that's why. And she might wander off."

"It ain't fair that I'm gettin' punished for somethin' she might do." Reluctantly Tommy reached down and grabbed the little girl's hand.

Riding farther into town, Smoke passed a medicine wagon. The tailgate of the wagon was down, and a man was standing on it, playing a banjo. He was quite good, and his efforts were being watched and appreciated by a fairly substantial crowd of men and women. Finishing his song to a polite applause, he put the banjo down. "Now that I have your attention, folks, let me tell you about this wonderful elixir."

"Play us another tune," someone called from the crowd. "You're pretty good on that thing. How did you learn?"

"I didn't learn," the medicine man replied. "I never took a lesson in my life."

"Then how is it you can play so well?"

The medicine man held up a bottle of his elixir. "I took one bottle of this, picked up the banjo, and discovered to my surprise that I could play it."

The crowd laughed.

"I ain't never heard such a lie," another said.

"Let's put it to a test." The medicine man pointed to the man who had asked him how he learned to play the banjo. "Would you come up here on the stage for a moment?"

"No, I ain't one for standin' up in front of other folks."

"It will only be for a moment, and to prove a point. Folks, give him a hand."

The others applauded, and the man climbed awkwardly onto the little stage formed by the tailgate of the medicine wagon.

"Here, play this banjo for me." The medicine man handed him the banjo.

"I can't play that thing."

"Try."

The man plucked a few strings, making a discordant sound.

"I don't want to hurt your feelings, sir, but let me ask the crowd. If I said that sounded like a heifer with her foot caught in a wire fence, would you agree with me?"

"Yeah, that's exactly what it sounded like," someone from the crowd shouted, and they all laughed.

"Drink this," the medicine man said, holding out the bottle of his elixir.

The man drank the whole bottle, then handed the empty bottle back.

"How do you feel?"

"I feel pretty good," the man said. "My back was a' hurtin' when I clumb up here, but it ain't a' hurtin' no more."

"Try to play the banjo again."

"So's you can have fun by pointin' out how bad I am?" the man asked.

"Trust me. Just give it a try."

The man raised up the banjo, plucked a few strings, sounding as discordant as before. Then, suddenly he began playing "Ole Dan Tucker," dancing around as he did so.

"Give me some of that!" someone shouted from the crowd, and Smoke, who had stopped to watch the show, smiled as he rode on away from the wagon.

Finding an empty hitching rail, he dismounted, then tied Seven to the rail. As he did so, a young, freckle-faced boy walked over to him, holding up a stiffened piece of card.

"Mister, you want to buy this here official program what was put out by the town of Crystal?" the boy asked. "It only costs a nickel, and you'll be able to keep it for a long time as a souvenir."

"A nickel, huh?" Smoke took a coin from his pocket. "Well, I reckon I can see my way clear to spending a nickel. But tell me, what is it a souvenir of?"

"Why, it's a souvenir of the hangin' of course," the boy said. "You mean you didn't know nothin' 'bout the hangin' we're fixin' to have here?"

"I'm afraid I didn't," Smoke replied. "Is that what all this is? Are all these people here to see a hanging?"

"Yes, sir, that's what this is. This fella Parnell that we're fixin' to hang, him and four others it was that robbed the bank and got away with over six thousand dollars, they say. Only it ain't the bank robbin' he's gettin' hung for. What the robbers done is, they kilt Mr. Walker, Mr. Jones, and Mr. Teasdale, all of 'em bein' customers in the bank when it was bein' robbed."

Although Smoke had told the boy he knew nothing about the hanging, that was a lie. He was there, not only because of the hanging, but specifically because Parnell was the name of the man being led to the gallows.

"Yes, sir, it's goin' to be a jim-dandy of a hangin' all right," the boy said. "I can't hardly wait to see it."

"Have you ever seen a hanging, boy?" Smoke asked.

"No sir, not for real. That's 'cause we ain't never had no legal hangin' here before. But last summer, a fella by the name of Kelso was found hangin' from a tree downtown, and I seen that afore they cut him down. Onliest thing is, they don't nobody know whether he kilt hisself, or whether someone else kilt him."

"Trust me, son," Smoke said. "A hanging isn't a good thing to watch."

"Yes, sir, well, I reckon I'm goin' to watch this one, though. And the hangin' is all legal and proper. He was tried and ever'thing, and found guilty. You can read all about it in the program." The boy turned and started toward another part of the crowd. "Program!" he shouted. "Get your souvenir program here!"

Smoke read the program.

LEGAL HANGING!

OF THE BANK ROBBER

COLE PARNELL

TO TAKE PLACE IN THE TOWN OF

CRYSTAL, COLORADO

ON THE 21ST INSTANT

SCHEDULE OF EVENTS:

ADDRESS BY MAYOR KINCAID

SONGS BY METHODIST CHURCH CHOIR

PRISONER VISITATION ON THE GALLOWS BY

FATHER LESTER D. OWENS

OF ST. PAUL'S EPISCOPAL CHURCH

READING OF WARRANT OF EXECUTION BY

SHERIFF JOHN C. DENNIS

LAST WORDS BEFORE HIS EXECUTION BY

COLE PARNELL

HANGING!

Smoke looked around until he saw the jail, then walked to it. A deputy stood just outside the front door. He held out his hand to stop Smoke. "Can't nobody go in till after the hangin'."

"I'm a deputy United States marshal investigating a murder," Smoke said. "I need to talk to your prisoner before they hang him."

"I don't care who you are. Sheriff Dennis told

me not to let anyone in and that's just what I'm doin'."

"Is the sheriff inside?"

"Yeah."

"Let's see what he says." Smoke started toward the door.

"I done told you what he said." The deputy went for his gun.

Smoke had his own pistol out so quickly the deputy was startled. He stopped, midway through his draw and offered no resistance as Smoke reached out to take his pistol from him.

"What do you say we talk to the sheriff now?" Smoke suggested.

They went inside. The sheriff was standing alongside his desk, looking down at an older man, who was filling out some papers.

"Here, what is this?" the sheriff asked. "Scooter, I told you to keep everyone out till after the hangin'."

"Don't blame Scooter, Sheriff Dennis. I forced the issue." Smoke still held both pistols in his hands and seeing that, the sheriff put his hands up.

"What do you want, mister?"

Smoke put his pistol back in his holster, then handed the deputy's gun back to him. "It's like I told your deputy. I'm a deputy United States marshal, and I'm investigating a case. I need to talk to your prisoner before you hang him."

"Did you have to come in with your gun drawn?"

"Uh, Sheriff, I drawed on him first," Scooter said.

"I see. Well, Deputy . . . what's your name?"

"Jensen. Kirby Jensen, but most folks call me Smoke."

The irritated expression on the sheriff's face disappeared, replaced by a broad smile. "Smoke Jensen? *The* Smoke Jensen."

"That's *the* Smoke Jensen, all right, John," the older man said. "It's been a long time, Smoke. How are you doing? And how is your beautiful wife, Sally?"

"Hello, Judge Norton," Smoke replied. "Sally was shot. And the polecat you have here, and the others who were with him when he robbed the bank, are the ones who shot her."

The smile left the judge's face. "Oh, Smoke, I'm so sorry. Is she—I mean did he . . . ?"

"She's going to be all right. But they killed three others in the same bank robbery."

"Yes, they killed three here as well," Judge Norton said. "I was just signing the warrant authorizing the execution."

"Is Parnell in the back?"

"Yes, you can go on back there to talk to him if you want."

Smoke started toward the door that led into the back, then stopped, pulled his pistol from the holster, and walked over to lay it down on the corner of the desk. "You forgot to ask me for that."

"Yeah, I, uh—wasn't sure how you would handle it," the sheriff said.

When Smoke went into the back of the building he saw that, though there were four cells, only one was occupied. The occupant of that cell was sitting on a cot, holding his head in his hands.

"Parnell?"

He looked up. "Who wants to know?"

"My name is Jensen. Smoke Jensen."

"I'll be damned. You're the husband of the woman Dinkins shot, ain't you?"

"Dinkins is the one who shot her?"

"Yeah, Dinkins shot her. He also shot the man that said he owned the bank."

"What about Mr. Deckert? And the sheriff? Who shot them?"

"Truth to tell, there ain't no way of knowin' who it was shot them, seein' as we was all shootin' while we was leavin' the bank."

"Where are they now, Parnell?"

"You think you can come in here and just ask me to tell you where my friends are and expect me to tell you?"

"Your friends?"

"Damn right, they are my friends."

"I understand that as you were riding away after the bank robbery here, your horse got shot."

"Yeah. You think I would be here iffen I had had me a horse to ride?"

"Did any of your friends come back for you?"

"No."

"Do you think any of them care now, that you are about to be hanged?"

"I-I don't know," Parnell admitted.

"Parnell, you don't owe them anything," Smoke

said. "And in another hour or so it won't make any difference to you one way or another. As a matter of fact, nothing will make any difference to you. So, as one of your last acts, you may as well do the right thing and tell me where they are."

Parnell was quiet for a moment. "To tell the truth, Jensen, I don't exactly know where they are. But I know that Dinkins was plannin' on hittin' just about ever' bank he could. The plan was to get a lot of money, then we was goin' to divide it up an' we was all to go off on our own. All except the Slater brothers, that is. I figure they'll probably still stay together."

"I was told that five men robbed the bank here. But Putnam was killed back in Gothic, so that left only four," Smoke said.

"Yeah, that's right. And four is how many of us there was until Harley joined us."

"Harley? Would that be Wesley Harley?"

"Yeah, do you know him?"

"I know of him."

"I bet you didn't know that he is Bill Dinkins' brother, though."

"No, I didn't know that."

"I figure most people don't know that, seein' as they got different last names and all. Harley is the one who kilt all three of the people in this bank holdup."

"Why did he shoot them?"

"One of them took a shot at us as we was leavin'

the bank, and Harley, he just spun around and shot all three of them. He's fast with a gun."

"So I've been told," Smoke said.

"He's damn fast. He may even be faster 'n you."

The door to the front of the building opened then, and Sheriff Dennis came through. "It's time, Parnell."

"Yeah."

"Turn your back to the bars, then put your hands behind you."

Parnell did as he was directed. "Is there a crowd of folks to see my send off?"

"It's going to be a show, all right," the sheriff said.

"Jensen?" Parnell called. "I'm sorry your woman got shot. Was she kilt?"

"No. She's going to be all right."

"I'm glad about that. Listen, I'll tell you somethin' else. You think you are just goin' after Dinkins, Harley, and the Slater brothers, don't you?"

"You mean there are others in the gang?"

"No, not exactly. But, ever since that newspaper article come out, saying that you was comin' after us? Well, it spooked Dinkins somethin' fierce. So, what he has done is, he has put up a thousand dollar reward to anyone who kills you."

"How has he done that?"

"How? He's just let it be known, that's all. Folks like us, we got our own way of spreadin' the news around. I'll guarantee you there ain't an outlaw in Colorado, Wyoming, or Arizona that don't know it's worth a thousand dollars to kill you. They'll be comin' after you from ever'where."

"Thanks for telling me that," Smoke said.

"So, seein' as I told you that, I want you to do me a favor, will you? Sort of like a last wish from a dyin' man?"

"What?"

"I want you to stick around and watch me hang."

CHAPTER SEVENTEEN

Lamp of our feet, whereby we trace
our path when wont to stray;
stream from the fount of heavenly grace,
brook by the traveler's way.

The members of the First Methodist Church Choir had formed four half circles just in front of the gallows, and they were already singing when Smoke went back outside. The crowd of spectators filled the street from side to side, so Smoke found a place across the street from the gallows in front of Haussler's Apothecary. Standing on the front porch and leaning against a roof support post, he had a pretty good view of the gallows, which, for the moment, was empty.

The choir finished their song and Smoke checked the program he had bought from the boy. He saw that the choir was singing, which meant the mayor had already spoken, and he was thankful for small pleasures. He had already missed the mayor's speech.

"Here he comes!" someone shouted, and a buzz of excitement passed through the crowd.

"Hey, Parnell!" someone shouted. "How does it feel to know you're going to have supper in hell tonight?"

"It will probably be better than the supper I had in jail last night," Parnell responded.

Some, but not all, of the crowd laughed at the remark.

"You think gettin' hung is funny, do you boy? We'll see who is laughin' half an hour from now."

Parnell did not respond to the taunt. His face was without expression of any kind.

He was led up the thirteen steps to the gallows, and carefully positioned over the trap door. His arms were then tied to his sides, and his legs were tied together. Sheriff Daniels stepped to the front of the gallows, cleared his throat, and read the warrant which stated that Cole Parnell, having been found guilty in a legally constituted court of law, was hereby sentenced to death by means of hanging.

"You've got it coming to you, you horrid person!" a woman shouted. "My husband was a good man, a father of three children, and you took him away from us!" She broke down in racking sobs.

There were a few other taunts, jibes, and sneering verbal attacks, but they quieted when a tall, very thin man, dressed all in black but with a bright white collar, started up the thirteen steps to the platform. He stepped over and whispered something to the prisoner. Parnell shook his head, and the priest spoke a second time. Parnell nodded in the affirmative.

With that, the priest walked away from Parnell, and opening the little black book he was carrying, began reading the prayer *Prayers for Persons under Sentence of Death* from the *Episcopal Book of Common Prayer.*

"Dearly beloved, it hath pleased Almighty God, in his justice to bring you under the sentence and condemnation of the law. You are shortly to suffer death in such a manner, that others, warned by your example, may be the more afraid to offend; and we pray God, that you may make such use of your punishments in this world, that your soul may be saved in the world to come."

As the priest droned on, Smoke looked into the faces of the crowd, seeing in them a mixture of morbid fascination, naive curiosity, fear, and even some pity.

When the priest was finished, Parnell was invited to give his final words.

"Boys," Parnell said. "This is really going to teach me a lesson."

There was a scattering of nervous laughter through the crowd, then the sheriff stepped back to Parnell and offered him a hood. When he declined, Sheriff Dennis fitted the noose around Parnell's neck. Stepping away from the trap door, he looked over at the hangman, who was standing by the trip lever. The sheriff nodded.

As the lever was thrown and the trap door fell

open, the sound of the mechanism was drowned out by the sounds from the crowd, a mixture of shouts of excitement and wails of compassion. Parnell fell through the trapdoor, was jerked up short, then turned one half turn to the left as he hung there, already dead.

A child, who had been brought to the hanging, began to cry. Finding her in the crowd, Smoke saw that it was Maggie, the little girl he had seen when he first rode into town.

He wondered what kind of parent would bring a child to an execution. He had no problem with them hanging Parnell. If he had encountered him on the trail, he would have shot him himself. But he didn't like the idea of it being turned into a carnival.

He stayed in town for about four more hours, long enough to exchange telegrams with Sally.

I AM STILL ON THE MEND PEARLIE AND
CAL ARE PLEADING WITH ME TO LET THEM
COME JOIN YOU PLEASE BE CAREFUL
LOVE SALLY

By the time Smoke left town the crowd had dispersed, and only a handful of the most morbidly curious remained standing by the gallows, looking up at the figure who was still hanging there with a stretched neck and bulging eyes. Most of them, Smoke noticed, were young boys, probably between twelve and fourteen.

"You think he can see us?" one of the boys asked.

"Nah, he can't see us."

"But look at him. His eyes is bugged way open and he's starin' right down here at us."

"He's dead, stupid. Dead men can't see you. Dead men can't do nothin'."

"He's lookin' at us from hell."

"He ain't lookin' at us from nowhere a-tall."

"It's kinda scary, ain't it?"

"Nah, it don't scare me none."

Smoke smiled as he rode by, because even the boy who proudly proclaimed that he wasn't frightened belied that claim by the expression in his voice.

Parlin, Colorado

It was late afternoon by the time Smoke reached the town that did not exist prior to the arrival of the railroad. As a railroad town, it was growing so quickly it had already surpassed many of the older, more established towns that had been missed by the railroad. On the south side of the tracks lay the holding pens and feeder lots for cattle the area ranchers brought to ship to the slaughter houses in Kansas City and Chicago.

The town proper was north of the tracks. Earl Avenue, the main street, ran at right angles to the tracks in a mostly unsuccessful attempt to get away from the smell and the flies of the holding pens. The town, built by merchants and businessmen, boasted a bank, three lawyers, a doctor, a thriving newspaper, a hotel, restaurant, playhouse, and four saloons.

The stores and business buildings had not yet had time to become weather-worn, and stood proudly along either side of the street with board-walks connecting one to the next so that, even in the worst weather, pedestrians did not have to walk in the mud of the street. Behind those were private homes where the townspeople lived. Most of the houses had vegetable gardens, but the tomatoes, corn, carrots, beans, lettuce, and cab-bage plants were nothing but late spring green.

A train sat at the Parlin Depot and its presence had drawn several people to the station to watch its arrival and departure. Because there were so many people at the depot, the main street of town was relatively empty as Smoke rode in. Though it wasn't yet dark, the lamplighter was al-ready making his rounds, to provide some illumi-nation once darkness fell.

Smoke stopped at the Silver Spur Saloon, not only for a beer to cut the trail dust, but also on the chance that he could pick up some news about Dinkins and the other men he was look-ing for.

Because of his longtime friendship with Louis Longmont, Smoke had the tendency to gauge all saloons by Longmont's. Nearly all the saloons he had ever seen came in lacking, but the Silver Spur missed it by a mile. Even in the nighttime, Long-mont's was well lit. In this place, all the chimneys of the lanterns were soot-covered, so the light was dingy and filtered through drifting smoke.

The place smelled of whiskey, stale beer, and

sour tobacco. A long bar was on the left, with dirty towels hanging on hooks about every five feet along its front. The large mirror behind the bar, like everything else about the saloon, was so dirty Smoke could scarcely see any images in it. What he could see was distorted by imperfections in the glass.

Against the back wall, near the foot of the stairs, a cigar-scarred, beer-stained upright piano was being played by a bald-headed musician, while out on the floor of the saloon, nearly all the tables were filled. A half dozen or so bar gals were flitting about and a few card games were in progress, but for the most part the patrons were just drinking and talking.

"What can I get for you?" the bartender asked.

"Beer," Smoke said. "And a recommendation for some place to eat."

"We got food here," the bartender offered.

"No, I have a hankerin' for a real sit-down restaurant," Smoke replied.

"Kind of a high falutin fella, ain't you?"

"No, I just like clean food," Smoke replied.

The bartender took a mug down, then held it under the spigot as he drew a glass of beer. "You might try the Parlin Diner. Folks talk high about it."

"Thanks." Smoke paid for the beer. Without turning away from the bar, he drank his beer and listened to the conversation going on all around him.

"Hung him, they did."

"What was it? A lynchin'?"

"Weren't no such thing. They had a trial and ever'thing."

"When did it happen?"

"Today. Over in Cyrstal. He was one of 'em that robbed the bank there a few days back. When they was all ridin' out of town, well, someone shot this fella's horse. He was left without a ride and the rest of the outlaws just left him behind."

"One less person for 'em to have to divide up the money with, I reckon."

"How'd you find out about it?"

"I was down to the newspaper office when they brung in the telegram to Mr. Denton, tellin' about it. It'll be in tomorrow's paper."

Smoke listened a little longer, hoping to get some information that would be useful to him, but he heard none. He finished his beer, then walked down the street until he found the Parlin Diner. After a supper of roast beef and home-made noodles, he took Seven to the livery to be put up for the night.

"Fine looking animal," the liveryman said.

"He is a good horse."

"You'll be wantin' to feed an animal like this oats, I'm sure."

Smoke chuckled. "And here, I thought you were just telling me how good a horse Seven is. Turns out all you want to do is sell me some oats."

"Oh, no, sir, no sir, not at all, sir!" the livery-man said. "This truly is a fine horse."

"Never mind. I would have bought oats for him anyway."

"I'm sure you would, sir, for an animal like this."

Smoke laughed again. He knew the liveryman didn't even realize what he was doing. "I need a hotel for the night. Any suggestions?"

"That depends. You want a hotel for sleepin'? Or for somethin' else?"

"Sleeping," Smoke said.

"Then that would be the Homestead Hotel. It's up toward the depot, on the left-hand side of the street."

The lobby of the Homestead Hotel was well appointed with overstuffed sofas and chairs, a rose-colored carpet, and several brass spittoons. A few strategically placed lanterns provided light, if not brightness.

The lobby was quiet and empty, except for the desk clerk who sat in a chair behind the sign-in desk, reading a newspaper. The clerk looked up as Smoke stepped up to the desk.

"Do you have a room that overlooks the street?"

"We do indeed, sir."

"Good."

Smoke signed the register and the clerk turned it around to read the name before he reached for a key. "Smoke Jensen? My, what an honor, sir, to have you stay in our hotel."

"Thanks." The number of newspaper articles and even books that had been written about Smoke Jensen made him one of the best known men in Colorado, if not throughout the entire West. Sometimes being well-known was advantageous, sometimes it was annoying, and sometimes it was just a little embarrassing.

The clerk turned toward a board filled with keys hanging from hooks, and took one down. "Your key, sir. You are in room two-twelve. Go upstairs, turn back toward the street, and it will be the last room on the right."

Smoke nodded and started toward the stairs.

"Enjoy your stay, Mr. Jensen!" the clerk called loudly.

Rufus Barlow was sitting in the lobby, reading the newspaper when he heard the desk clerk call out to Smoke Jensen. Barlow watched Smoke go up the stairs, then walked over to the front desk. "Who was that fella that just checked in?"

"Why, that was Mr. Smoke Jensen," the clerk said proudly. "Staying right here, in our hotel."

"You don't say."

"I do say. You want to see the register, where he signed in?"

The clerk turned the register toward him, and Barlow read it, then smiled.

"How about that," Barlow said. "That's somethin', ain't it."

"Mr. Barlow, may I ask what you are doing here?" The desk clerk suddenly realized who he was talking to. "You never do anything except come into our lobby, read our newspapers, and drink our coffee. I have told you that the lobby and the coffee are for paying guests, not derelict bums. Now if you don't leave, I will summon the sheriff."

"I'm goin', I'm goin'," Barlow said, hurrying out of the hotel.

Like the lobby, the hotel room was nicely furnished. More spacious than most hotel rooms, it had a bed, a settee, a chest of drawers, and a chifferobe. A porcelain pitcher and bowl sat on a dry sink. Smoke poured water into the bowl, took off his shirt, washed, then turned the covers down to crawl into bed. Since starting on his quest to find the people who shot Sally, it would be the first time he had slept in a real bed and this one felt particularly comfortable.

In Blakely's Saloon, which was halfway up Earl Avenue on the east side of the street, Rufus Barlow sat nursing his beer as he discussed a plan with his partner, a plan that both knew could either make a lot of money for them, or get them killed. Barlow's partner was a man named Murdock Felton, but he had been called Slim for so long that even he had almost forgotten his real name. He fingered his mustache fitfully.

"Are you sure that the fella stayin' in the Homestead is really Smoke Jensen?" Felton asked. "Or is it just Waycox shootin' off his mouth?"

Waycox was Jeremy Waycox, the desk clerk at the hotel.

"It's Smoke Jensen all right. I seen the register where he signed in."

"Might have been someone just sayin' that's who he is," Felton suggested.

"No, I seen him go up the stairs. It's Jensen all right. I seen him one time in Colorado Springs. I didn't recognize him right off, 'cause it's been a long time, but he's damn near big as a bear, so it ain't like you could miss him."

"That don't sound to me like the kind of fella you would get into a fight with," Felton said. "Yet that's exactly what you're wantin' us to do."

"It ain't goin' to be no fistfight," Barlow said. "This here fight is goin' to be fought with guns."

"That's even worse. They say he's as quick as lightnin' with 'is gun."

Barlow smiled. "Yeah, he is, and that's somethin' I'd be worryin' about iffen this was goin' to be a fair fight. Only it ain't goin' to be what you would call a fair fight. The plan I got laid out is foolproof."

"There ain't nothin' foolproof," Slim replied. "Most especial when it comes to dealin' with someone like Smoke Jensen. That man ain't even human."

"What do you mean, he ain't human? He's human just like ever'body else is, and if you shoot him, he'll die, just like ever'one," Barlow insisted.

"Then how come he ain't already dead? You got 'ny idea how many folks have tried to kill 'im?"

"Yeah, well, they just didn't go about it right, is all. We'll do it right."

Slim drummed his fingers on the table for a moment as he thought about what Barlow was saying. "How much money is it again?"

"There's a thousand dollars in it, Slim. Five hundred for each of us."

"That's a lot of money."

"You're damn right, that's a lot of money."

"All right." Slim finally agreed. "I'll go along with your plan."

The next morning a slight breeze filled the muslin curtains and lifted them out over the wide-planked floor of Smoke's hotel room. Smoke moved to the window and looked out over the town, which was just beginning to awaken. Water was being heated behind the laundry and boxes were being stacked behind the grocery store. A team of four big horses pulled a heavily loaded freight wagon down the main street.

From the restaurant, and maybe even from half a dozen private homes, Smoke could smell bacon frying. His stomach growled, reminding him that he was hungry. He splashed some water in the basin, washed his face and hands, then put on his shirt and hat and went downstairs. There were a couple people in the lobby, one napping in a chair, the other reading a newspaper. Neither paid any attention to Smoke as he left the hotel.

The morning sun was bright, but not yet hot. The sky was clear and the air was crisp. As he walked toward the café he heard sounds of commerce; the ringing of a blacksmith's hammer, a carpenter's saw, and the rattle of working wagons. That was quite different from the night sounds of clanking liquor bottles, off-key piano, laughter, and boisterous conversations. How different the tone and tent of a town at work in the morning was from the same town in the play of evening.

CHAPTER EIGHTEEN

Sugarloaf Ranch

As the ramrod of Sugarloaf, Pearlie's duties were greatly increased during Smoke's absence. He had to supervise all the hands, including the extras who had been put on for the spring roundup. Cattle that had wandered away during the winter had to be found and brought back into the herd, and calves produced during that time had to be branded.

He was laying out the irons with the slash SJ brand, when Cal came into the barn with a worried look on his face.

"What is it, Cal?" Pearlie asked.

"She ain't got up."

"Who ain't got up? What are you talkin' about?"

"Miss Sally. She ain't got up yet this mornin'."

"Maybe she's just tired and is sleepin' in," Pearlie suggested.

"No, it ain't that," Cal said. "It's somethin' bad. I just know it is."

"What makes you think that?"

"'Cause, I stood outside her bedroom door and I called out to her. I called loud too, loud enough to wake her up if all she is doin' is sleepin'. But she didn't answer me. I'm worried, Pearlie. I'm awful worried."

"All right. Let's go see if we can wake her up."

"Pearlie, you don't think she's dead, do you?" Cal asked anxiously as they walked quickly from the barn to the big house.

"No, she was feelin' real good last night. You know that."

"Yeah, and that's what is got me worried. I mean, if she was feelin' all that good last night, how come it is that she ain't woke up yet this mornin'?"

"You worry too much," Pearlie said.

The two men entered the big house, then walked down the hallway to the bedroom that Smoke and Sally shared. Pearlie knocked on the door.

"Miss Sally? Miss Sally, it's Pearlie. It's late mornin', now. You want somethin'? Would you like for us to bring you a cup of coffee?"

The two men waited outside the door for Sally's answer, but no answer was forthcoming.

"Miss Sally, are you all right?" Pearlie called. "Me 'n Cal is gettin' a little worried here. I mean, not hearin' nothin' from you and all. Would make us feel a lot better if you would answer us."

There was still no answer.

"Oh, she's dead, Pearlie. She's dead, I just know it," Cal said. "We was left to look after her, and we didn't do our job."

Pearlie tried the door, and finding it unlocked, pushed it open.

"You ain't goin' into her bedroom, are you?" Cal asked, aghast at the idea.

"Why not?" Pearlie replied. "If she's dead, it won't matter none. And if she is alive, then somethin' is obvious wrong and she needs us."

"Yeah," Cal answered. "Yeah, I guess you are right."

The two walked into the bedroom. Sally was lying on her back, covered to her shoulders, with her head turned to one side on her pillow. Pearlie put his hand down in front of her nose. "She's alive. I can feel her breathin'."

"Miss Sally? Miss Sally, wake up," Cal said. "You're scarin' us somethin' fierce. Please wake up."

Sally's eyes opened, but there was a glazed look in them, as if she didn't quite know where she was, or what was going on.

Pearlie touched her forehead, then jerked his hand back.

"What is it?" Cal asked.

"Her skin is hot."

"She's got a fever. I remember Doctor Gunther tellin' us that if she got a fever, we was to come get him right away, 'cause that would mean somethin' bad was happenin'."

Pearlie turned away from the bed and started out of the bedroom.

"Where are you goin'?" Cal asked.

"I'm going after Dr. Colton. And I'm going to send a telegram to Smoke."

"How do we even know where he is?"

"Before he left he made a list of what towns he was goin' to, and when he would get there," Pearlie said. "I'm goin' to send the telegram to three towns, the one he was just at, the one he is supposed to be at now, and the next town on his list. He is sure to be in one of those three places."

"What should I do?" Cal asked.

"I don't know. I'm not sure what should be done. But I reckon that if you kept a dampened cloth on her forehead that might help some. And if it don't help, it's for sure goin' to make her feel better, I would think."

"Yeah, good idea. I'll get a pan of water," Cal said. "And I'll be right here when you get back with the doctor."

It took Pearlie less than half an hour to get to town from the ranch. He found Dr. Colton sitting around the cracker barrel in the general store, talking with half a dozen citizens of the town. Dr. Colton smiled when he looked up, but seeing the expression on Pearlie's face, the smile left.

"What is it, Pearlie? What is wrong?"

"It's Miss Sally, Dr. Colton. She's took much worse. You got to come quick."

Dr. Colton got up so fast his chair tipped over

behind him, the commotion causing others in the store to look over to see what was going on.

"I'll be there as quickly as I can get my medical bag, and my surrey hitched up."

"You get your bag and whatever else you need," Pearlie said. "I'll hook up your surrey. Then I'm goin' to have to send a telegram to Smoke."

Parlin

It was just after lunch when Smoke went into the saloon.

"I see you are back," the bartender said when Smoke stepped up to the bar. "I reckon the beer you got here last night didn't kill you."

"I reckon not," Smoke said.

"You want another one?"

"Yes, please." Smoke put a coin on the bar as the bartender turned to draw a draft for him.

There were very few customers in the saloon at that hour, but Barlow and Slim were sitting at a table in the far back corner of the saloon, waiting for the opportunity to put their plan in motion. When Smoke came into the saloon, Barlow reached over to touch Slim on the shoulder. "That's him."

"You sure?"

"Yeah, I'm sure. You see anyone else that big around here?"

"All right. How are we going to do this?"

"Just like we talked about it last night," Barlow said. "You go up there and brace him. While you're callin' him out, he won't be payin' no attention to me. I'll shoot him when he starts to draw on you."

"Why am I the one who has to brace him?" Slim asked. "This is your idea. Why don't you do it?"

"I'm a better shot than you are, that's why. Iffen I was to be the one to brace him, you might miss. Then where would we be?"

"They say he's awful fast. What if you don't get your gun out in time?"

"My gun is already goin' to be out," Barlow said. "You want your share of the thousand dollars or not?"

"Why don't we just wait outside, say, behind a buildin' or somethin', and shoot him when he walks by?"

"If we do somethin' like that, we could get hung for murder. But this way we can pass it off as a fight."

Slim had a glass of whiskey in front of him, and he tossed it down, then reached over for Barlow's whiskey, and drank it down as well.

"Are you ready now?" Barlow asked.

"Yeah." Slim took a deep breath, stood up, then walked up to the bar, standing at the opposite end from Smoke. Smoke was leaning forward with both arms on the bar, his hands wrapped around a beer mug.

"Hey, you!" Slim called out. "Smoke Jensen! That is your name, ain't it? Smoke Jensen?"

Like many men who live on the edge, Smoke had developed an awareness of danger that could not be explained by any of the other senses. He had felt, rather than heard, the two men talking about him, and he knew they were going to try to kill him. He just didn't know when, where, or how. Now it was playing out.

Smoke turned toward Slim. "Mister, you think you're going to collect that thousand dollar reward that Dinkins has out on me?" Smoke asked the question as calmly as if he were inquiring as to the time.

That frightened Slim the most—the quiet and completely unruffled demeanor of the man.

"I-I don't know what you are talking about," Slim said.

"Oh, sure you do," Smoke said. "Bill Dinkins, the man who shot my wife and has murdered at least six people in the last month, has put out a one thousand dollar reward to anyone who would kill me. And here you are, about to make a grab for that money. That's right, isn't it?"

Slim licked his lips, but didn't say anthing.

"How is this supposed to work?" Smoke asked. "Are you supposed to get my attention while your friend over there at the table shoots me?"

"Barlow, he knows!" Slim shouted.

"Slim, you fool! Shut up!" Barlow shouted, firing at Smoke even as he was shouting at Slim.

Smoke's sense of awareness kicked in, and he stepped back just before Barlow fired. The bullet from Barlow's pistol slammed into the bar right where Smoke had been but a second earlier.

He returned fire, his bullet catching the would-be assailant in his throat, knocking him onto the table behind him. The table turned over, dumping

Barlow to the floor. Unaware of that, Smoke had already turned his attention back to Slim.

Slim fired at Smoke, his bullet crashing into the beer mug Smoke had just put down. Smoke returned fire and Slim dropped his pistol, then clasped his hand over his wound. The blood pooled up behind his hand, then spilled over as his eyes rolled up in his head and he fell.

Smoke stood his ground, holding a smoking pistol as he looked around the room. He didn't think there was any more danger, but he wasn't prepared to turn his back on it, just yet. There were only four other people in the saloon, three men and one bar girl. The men's faces all reflected surprise and even a little excitement over what they had just witnessed. The woman's face showed surprise and fear.

Smoke put the pistol away just as he heard the fall of running footsteps outside. A man wearing a badge burst into the saloon. "Someone want to tell me what happened here?"

"These two men tried to kill me," Smoke said. "They shot first and missed. I shot back and didn't miss."

"So, you are telling me that two of them shot first, but you still managed to kill them?"

"He's tellin' it true, Deputy Burns," the bartender said.

"Absolutely true," one of the other men said.

"You others agree?"

"Deputy, Mr. Barlow started shooting first. For no reason at all that I could see," the bar girl said.

"Then Mr. Jensen shot back, and it was while Mr. Jensen was shooting at Mr. Barlow, that Slim started shooting. So Mr. Jensen turned around and shot him too."

"Jensen?" the deputy asked. "Are you Smoke Jensen?"

"Yes."

"Mr. Jensen, the telegrapher is looking for you. He stopped by the marshal's office about ten minutes ago, askin' if we knew where you were."

Smoke didn't even bother to answer the deputy. He took off on a dead run toward the railroad depot.

"Don't worry none about this!" the deputy called to him. "Ain't goin' to be no charges!"

Smoke did not stop running when he went inside the depot. He ran through the waiting room, and to the back corner where there was a Western Union sign.

"My, you seem to be in quite a hurry," the telegrapher said. "Is what you have to say that important?"

"I'm Smoke Jensen. Do you have a telegram for me?"

"Oh, yes, Mr. Jensen. Just a moment." The telegrapher leafed through some of the messages he had on the counter in front of him, then came up with what he was looking for. "Here it is."

SMOKE CAN YOU COME HOME QUICK MISS
SALLY IS TOOK SOME WORSE
PEARLIE

"Any reply, Mr. Jensen?" the telegrapher asked.

Hastily, Smoke wrote out an answer, then left it and the money on the counter in front of the telegrapher. He didn't bother to wait for his change.

I AM COMING NOW

Luckily, both Parlin and Big Rock were on the railroad, which meant Smoke could be back home much faster than if he returned by horseback. But the next train wasn't due for four more hours, then it would be three hours on the train until he reached Big Rock.

Pittsburg

The printer took the first impression off his press and looked at it.

WANTED

FOR MURDER

SMOKE JENSEN

$5,000 REWARD

DEAD OR ALIVE

to be paid by
Sheriff of La Plata County

"You sure I'm not going to get into trouble for this?" the printer asked.

"Get in trouble for what?" Dinkins replied.

"You know for what. I don't believe for one minute that Smoke Jensen is wanted for murder."

"What difference does it make to you whether he is wanted or not? How much would you normally get for printing five hundred of these things?"

"Five dollars," the printer admitted.

"I'm giving you one hundred dollars," Dinkins said. "Seems to me like anyone getting one hundred dollars for a five-dollar job would not be all that anxious to look a gift horse in the mouth."

"What are you going to do with these posters?"

"That's none of your concern," Dinkins answered.

"Just don't tell anyone where you got them," the printer said as he accepted five twenty-dollar bills.

With the five hundred wanted posters in hand, Dinkins rode back out of town where the others were camping. He had not told them why he was going into town so they were curious when he returned.

"We've got some work to do," Dinkins said as he opened the package containing the posters. He pulled one out and held it up to show to the others. "We are going to plaster these posters all over the place."

"Whoa, we can't pay no five thousand dollars just to have Jensen kilt," Travis Slater said. "I thought you said we was only goin' to pay one thousand dollars."

"Yeah, but that's before I got the idea of having the state pay for it," Dinkins replied.

"What do you mean? Is Jensen wanted for murder?"

"Not as far as I know," Dinkins said.

"But that's what this poster says."

Dinkins chuckled. "Yeah, don't it?"

"But if he ain't wanted for murder, and somebody kills him and brings him in, there won't be no money paid at all."

"There you go, Travis. You're smarter than I thought you were," Dinkins said.

"Ha! Good idea, Little Brother," Harley said. "There are bounty hunters all over the state who will shoot first, and ask questions second."

"Let's get these things posted," Dinkins said, dividing them up and passing them out to the others.

CHAPTER NINETEEN

On the train from Parlin to Big Rock

Nervously, Smoke paced up and down in the train, going from the front car to the rear car, two or three times during the trip. What, exactly, did Pearlie mean when he said she was "took some worse?"

Finally he forced himself to sit down and stare through the window at the passing countryside. Smoke watched a coyote spring up, then run for several yards, easily keeping pace with the train. In the distance he saw antelope grazing and once he saw a big horn sheep, standing on a precipice, looking out over the world.

After three hours on the train, Smoke started seeing countryside that was familiar to him. Recognizing that they were getting close to Big Rock, he got more anxious.

What would he find when he got home?

When the train ground to a stop ten minutes

later, Smoke was the first one off. He hurried up to the stock car and was standing impatiently as the railroad liveryman slid open the door.

"Hurry, man, hurry," Smoke said.

"I have to wait until they bring the ramp."

"No you don't. Seven!" Smoke called. He whistled. "Seven, come down boy!"

Seven, who was already saddled, appeared in the doorway.

"Come on down, boy," Smoke called.

Seven measured the distance, then jumped, landing easily. Before the liveryman could even comment, Smoke mounted and, slapping his legs against the side of his horse, left the depot at a gallop. Though Smoke wanted to gallop all the way, he knew Seven could not sustain a gallop for more than a mile or two. But he could maintain a rapid trot, if given a few walks, for fifteen miles or so. He had only eight miles to go, so he slowed Seven from a gallop, to a brisk trot. It took him less than half an hour to reach Sugarloaf.

As he rode into the front yard he saw Dr. Colton's surrey parked out front. He didn't know if that was a good sign or a bad sign. He told himself it was a good sign. If the doctor was there, that meant that Sally was still alive.

Smoke urged Seven into a gallop for the last one hundred yards, then leaped from the saddle directly onto the front porch. Leaving Seven breathing hard and sweating, Smoke dashed into the house. He hated to do that to his horse, but the foremost thing on his mind was the condition of his wife.

"Sally!" he called as he stepped into the long, wide hallway that ran from the front door to the rear door, and basically divided the house into two sections.

He saw Dr. Colton stepping out of the bedroom.

"How is she?" The inflection in Smoke's voice and the expression on his face disclosed his concern.

"She is still alive," Dr. Colton said.

"Still alive? Good Lord, man, is that all you can tell me? That she is still alive?"

"Smoke, you don't know how thankful I am to tell you that," Dr. Colton said.

"But, what happened? I thought she was getting better. I thought everything was fine."

"She got an infection," Dr. Colton said. "That's one of the biggest dangers in wounds like this. If a person isn't killed instantly, and if they don't die of shock, then the only danger left facing them is infection. And infection can occur at almost any time. To tell the truth, I thought we were out of the woods with Sally. But a new infection set in last night."

"What can we do about it?"

"I've got a poultice of honey and lard applied over the wound. And I've given her a solution of aloe, mixed with some wine. All we can do now is wait."

"Wait for what?"

"Until the fever breaks or . . . ," Dr. Colton let the sentence drag out.

"Or what?"

"Or it doesn't break."

"And what happens if the fever doesn't break?"

"You know what will happen if we can't beat it, Smoke," Dr. Colton said. "There's no sense in dwelling on it. Let's just think positive, all right?"

"Yeah," Smoke said. "Yeah, I'm sorry."

"It's quite all right. It's only natural for you to be worried."

"Can I see her now?"

"Yes, of course."

"Is she awake?"

"She was a moment ago. I expect she is still awake. She knew you were coming back, so she has been anxiously awaiting you."

When Smoke stepped into the bedroom, he happened to glance through the window and saw Cal leading Seven to the barn. Cal was a good man, and he would see to it that Seven would get a rubdown, food, and water. Smoke's concern was with Sally.

Crossing over to the bed he stood looking down at his wife. Her hair was tousled and her eyes were closed, but he thought she was every bit as beautiful as she was the first time he ever saw her. In her state of distress, he knew that he loved her more than he would ever be able to express by word or deed.

He had never felt more helpless in his life. She was suffering so and there was nothing, not one thing, he could do for her. Bending over, he kissed her on the forehead, noticing how hot it felt.

Sally opened her eyes. "Is that the best you can do?"

Smoke smiled at her. "Seems to me like you asked that question before."

"Did it do me any good to ask it?"

Smoke kissed her again, on the lips. Seeing that a chair had been pulled up alongside her bed, he sat down, then reached out and took her hand. "How are you feeling?"

"I don't think I would be up to a brisk horse-back ride," she said.

"Really? Damn, and I had just such a thing planned, too. I thought we might go up to your secret overlook and have a picnic."

Sally smiled. "You don't know about my secret overlook."

Smoke snapped his fingers. "That's right, I don't. How could I know? It's a secret."

"I'm sorry that you had to come back, Smoke. I know finding those men is important to you."

"Don't be silly. Nothing is as important to me as you are. And whether I find those men now, or later, I will find them."

They were quiet for a moment, with Smoke sitting beside her, holding her hand as she lay in bed, taking shallow breaths.

"Smoke?"

"Yes, love?"

"I'm glad you came home. I stayed awake for you, you know."

"Yes, I know."

"But I think I'm going to sleep now."

Smoke lifted her hand to his lips and kissed it.

Sally managed a smile. "I told you, I'm not some grand dame in the queen's court."

"Any court in the world would be glad to have you as the grandest of their grand dames," Smoke said.

"Why, Smoke, sometimes you really can be downright romantic," Sally replied.

He sat there until her breathing became more regular, then quietly left the bedroom and walked up to the parlor. It was getting dark, and three lanterns burned brightly to push away the darkness. Dr. Colton was still there, and Pearlie and Cal had also come into the house.

"I put Seven away," Cal said.

"Yes, I saw you through the window. Thanks, Cal."

"I wish I could do more. I wish I could . . . ," Cal choked up and quit talking.

"I know you do."

"It's my fault, Smoke. It's all my fault."

"Don't be ridiculous, Cal. Sally's having a hard enough time fighting this, she doesn't need your guilt to contend with as well. Especially when you don't have anything to feel guilty about."

"That's what I've been telling him as well," Pearlie said. "There wasn't nothin' he coulda done, even if he had been there. 'Cept maybe get 'em both kilt."

Cal hung his head and Smoke reached up to

squeeze his shoulder. Then he looked over at Dr. Colton. "All right, Doc, give it to me straight. What are her chances?"

"I don't like to roll dice with people's lives," Dr. Colton said. "Like I told you before, let's keep a positive attitude."

"Yeah, well, I had a positive attitude when I left. I thought the worst was over. Then I got the telegram from Pearlie. How did it happen? How did she go from mending, to—well—to this?"

"According to man named Louis Pasteur, infections like this are caused by bacteria."

"What is bacteria?" Cal asked.

"They are little organisms, so small that the only way you can see them is by looking through a microscope," Dr. Colton said. "We don't know exactly where they come from, but sometimes, not all the time, mind you, but sometimes they can get into a body, either through a sore, or the mouth, or the nose, and when they do, it upsets the natural order of things."

"And you think that's what Miss Sally has? She has the bacteria?" Cal asked.

Dr. Colton drew a breath as if to explain it further, but thought better of it. "Yeah. For the time being you can say that she has the bacteria."

"How do we get rid of it for her?" Smoke asked.

"That is the big question, isn't it? Fortunately, the human body seems quite capable of fighting off the bacteria on its on, at least most of the time. And aloe, as well as honey and lard also do a pretty job."

"Good enough?"

"We can only hope and pray that it is good enough," Dr. Colton said. "It's good that you are here, Smoke. Tonight is critical. If the fever breaks tonight, then she will have beaten it. And having you here with her, helps. I am convinced of that."

The doctor went over to the hat rack and retrieved his bowler. "I'm going to go back into town. I will come back out first thing tomorrow."

"Thanks, Doc." Smoke walked out to the front porch with him, then watched as he climbed into his surrey and drove off.

When Smoke came back into the house, Cal greeted him with a cup of coffee. "I figure it's going to be a long night."

"Yeah, thanks. I think you are right." Smoke took the coffee and sat in the leather chair near the window, looking out at the stars, the moon, and the castellated escarpment that guarded the north end of his property. The window was open and he could smell his cattle and horses, and hear the sounds of the night creatures—the howl of a distant coyote, the whicker of a horse, the thrum of frogs, and the hum of insects. Sugarloaf was as fine a ranch as there was in all of Colorado, and it had made Smoke a rich man, though he wasn't a person who thought often of that.

Big Heart Creek, which provided water for his stock and kept his land green, played out before him, glistening like molten silver in the moonlight. From his perspective, it was as if the creek was running, not south toward the West Elk Mountains, but into the yesteryears of his life. Smoke Jensen had come a long way from Kirby Jensen, the sixteen-year-old boy who, during the Civil War had worked the southwestern Missouri farm like a man, doing all he could to keep himself alive during that terrible time. It was necessary that he do all the work because his older brother, Luke, had gone to war with his father. Luke got himself killed, his mother had died, and his sister ran off with a peddler, later to become a soiled dove.

It seemed like there was never enough food then, and he was always hungry. But even as a sixteen-year-old boy he was tough. The work had hardened his muscles and sharpened his mind. When his father came back from the war, there was nothing to keep either one of them in Missouri, so Kirby and his father came west. Not too long after that, he lost his father, but gained a lifelong friend, an old mountain man called Preacher. He also picked up a new name. Kirby Jensen became Smoke Jensen.

He didn't know if he was dreaming or remembering his past, it just seemed to flow effortlessly through his mind so that he was no longer aware of time or place—until he smelled bacon frying.

Opening his eyes he saw that Pearlie and Cal were still in the parlor, and both were asleep. Curious, he walked toward the back of the house and saw a splash of light spilling into the hall from the kitchen. Putting his hand on the handle of his pistol, he moved quickly, but quietly to the kitchen door and looked in.

Sally was standing over the stove frying bacon!

"Sally!"

She jumped. "Goodness gracious, Smoke, you scared me to death. You ought to know better than to come up on a person like that."

"What are you doing?"

"What does it look like I'm doing? It's been twenty-four hours since I had anything to eat, and I'm starving to death."

"But you should be in bed."

"Oh, poo. Come here. Put your hand on my forehead. You can see that I don't have a fever."

"I—" Smoke started, but that is as far as he got.

"I'm making biscuits too. They ought to be out in a moment. I know it will be an early breakfast for you, but I would like for you to join me."

It wasn't until then that Smoke realized that he'd had no supper, so it was quite a while since he had eaten as well.

"I hope you made enough for me 'n Cal," Pearlie said, appearing in the door of the kitchen then.

"I did. I knew you two wouldn't turn away from a meal, no matter what time it might be served," Sally said. "But, I'm sorry to say, no bear claws."

"That's all right. Fresh biscuits is near 'bout as good."

"Pearlie, I'm going to remind you of that, next time you start pestering Sally for my bear claws," Smoke remarked.

"*Your* bear claws?" Sally smiled. "You think I make those just for you?"

"Come here." Smoke put his arms around her, pulling her close to him. "I'm so happy right now, I don't care if you ever make them again."

"Oh, Lord, Smoke, don't say that!" Pearlie said. Smoke laughed out loud.

CHAPTER TWENTY

Risco

By the time Dinkins, Harley, and the two Slater brothers reached the town of Risco, they had put out all five hundred reward posters on Smoke Jensen. By making the reward as high as five thousand dollars, Dinkins knew that not only every bounty hunter in the country, but even those who had never considered such a thing, would be after Smoke to get the reward money. No one would question the authenticity of the poster until it was too late—until they showed up with the body of Smoke Jensen to collect the reward. Then, like as not, they would be charged with murder.

Dinkins laughed at that last thought. He did not like bounty hunters, posse members, or anyone who represented authority. The idea of some bounty hunter or vigilante facing a murder charge, tickled him.

Shortly after their arrival, Dinkins and the others took rooms in the brothel. Located across the alley behind the saloon, it was a row of six small houses, all connected so that each little crib shared a wall with the crib next to it. Dinkins woke up the morning after their arrival with a ravenous hunger and a raging need to urinate. The soiled dove he had chosen the night before was still asleep beside him. She had the bedcover askew, exposing one enormous, blue-veined breast. One leg dangled over the edge of the bed. She was snoring loudly and a bit of spittle drooled from her vibrating lips. She didn't wake up when Dinkins crawled over her to get out of bed to get to his clothes, and he was just as glad. Just how drunk was he, to have chosen someone like this, last night?

"Wes," he called. "Big brother, are you still here?"

"Yeah, I'm here. No need to be wakin' the dead," Harley called from the room next door, his voice heard easily through the thin walls.

There was an outhouse twenty feet behind the brothel, but Dinkins would have had to go out the single, front door, then walk all the way around to the back. Not willing to do that, he decided to go against the wall.

Just as he stepped up to the wall, Harley came in through the door. He joined Dinkins in peeing on the wall. "What do you want?"

Dinkins shook himself, then put it away. "Let's have breakfast and talk about our next job."

"Our next job? Damn, Bill, we just pulled off a

job. Don't you think we ought to hole up for a while and enjoy the money?"

"Tell me, when you are playing cards, and you get a winning streak going, do you quit?"

"No."

"We hit the bank in Crystal, and got away with a lot of money. I say don't stop now."

"All right, you've been right so far. I'll listen to what you have to say. But the best idea now is breakfast. I could eat a horse." Pushing through the door, Harley started to step down off the porch.

"Don't you think you ought to get dressed first?" Dinkins asked.

"Oh," Harley replied, turning around to go back into the crib where he had left his clothes. "Yeah, I guess so."

Fifteen minutes later the two men were having a breakfast of ham and eggs in a café that identified itself only by a big sign that said EATS. Neither Frank nor Travis Slater had awakened yet.

"What you got in mind? Another bank?"

"No, not a bank, a stage coach," Dinkins said.

"Banks are better," Harley said. "You know they've got money, and they ain't movin'."

"Yeah, but they are also in the middle of town. And we lost a man in each of the last two banks we robbed. Putnam in Gothic, and Parnell in Crystal."

"That's the chance you take when you are in this kind of business," Harley reminded him.

"Look at this," Dinkins said. "I tore it out of the newspaper yesterday." He took the article from his shirt pocket, then handed it to Harley.

"What is it?"

"Just read it. This is our next job."

Harley unfolded the article and began to read.

Money Transfer

The sum of five thousand dollars is to be transferred from Escalante to Suttle on Friday next, said funds to be used to run the city business. The loan was negotiated by the Bank of Suttle, and will be repaid, it is said, by a series of bonds to be passed by the Suttle City Council.

"You think the money will go by stage coach?" Harley asked.

"That's the only way it can go. And, since there ain't but three stages per week between Escalante and Suttle, it ain't goin' to be hard to figure out which one it's on."

Harley smiled. "It's nice of them to tell us about the money, ain't it?"

"Yeah, I don't imagine the stagecoach people are all that pleased with the article."

Escalante, Colorado

Stan McVey, the driver of the Escalante to Suttle stagecoach, had been making that particular run for the last four years, and he knew every creek, hill, turn in the road, rock and tree along the sixty-two mile route. He stood out in front of the depot for a few moments, watching as the team of six horses was attached to the coach.

"Mr. McVey, I put Ole Dan on the off side like you told me," one of the hostlers said.

"Thanks, Jake. He tends to pull to the left all the time and if he is on the off side, well, the near horse will keep him going straight. Do you know if Lonnie took a look at the reach?" As McVey asked the question, he knelt down and looked at the bar that connected the rear axle with the front part of the coach. Stretching out his hand, he grabbed hold of the reach and tried to shake it. It felt secure.

"Yes, sir, he said he tightened up the bolts."

"Good enough," McVey said.

"I'll loop the ribbons around your whip," Jake said.

Looking over toward Burt Conway, he saw his shotgun messenger receiving a canvas bag from Mr. Dempster, the owner of the Escalante Bank. McVey had read in the paper about the transfer of money, which meant that anyone who might have an idea about robbing the coach also read it. He knew that the stagecoach supervisor, Mr. Sinclair, had complained about it, but he was told by G. E. Hastings, editor of the newspaper, that he enjoyed "freedom of the press," and there was nothing Sinclair could do to prevent him from publishing such information.

Satisfied that all was well with the coach, McVey walked into the depot to address the six passengers—three men and three women. It was an unusual mix of passengers, for none of the men were married to any of the women.

The station manager brought McVey a cup of coffee and he took a couple swallows as he looked at his passengers. The two older women, Mrs. Gray and Mrs. Johnson, were talking. Mr. Evans, a salesman, had made the trip many times. He was making notes of some sort. Mr. Calhoun, a rancher from near Suttle, and Dr. Potter, a local physician, were engaged in conversation. Miss Dawson, who was about seventeen, was with her mother, who had come to see her off.

McVey finished his coffee, then glanced up at the big clock that stood by the back wall. It was ten minutes before departure, time for him to give the passengers his normal pre-run briefing. "Folks, can I have your attention? Can I have your attention, please?"

All the conversation stopped as the passengers looked toward him.

"My name is Stan McVey. I'm your driver for this trip, so if you would, I'd like for you to gather 'round for a moment or two so's I can talk to you about this here trip you'll be takin' today. It's eight and a half hours from here to Suttle, if ever'thing goes like it's s'posed to go. Gents, I'd prefer that you don't drink no liquor durin' the run, but there ain't no law agin' it, so there ain't no way I can stop you. But, if you are goin' to drink, then I ask that you share the bottle with them that might want it, on account of sometimes arguments get started over that.

"Since we got ladies present, I'm also goin' to ask that you don't smoke no cigars or pipes inside the coach without the ladies tellin' you it's all right. That's 'cause the smell sometimes irritates the ladies. You can chew if you like, but when you spit, make sure you spit with the wind, and not agin' it, 'cause iffen you spit agin' it, why it will come right back into the coach. I don't care if it gets on you, but it's the others in the coach I'd be worryin' about.

"I'm goin' to ask you not to be cussin' none either, 'cause oft time the women gets offended by that.

"Now, are any of you gents wearin' guns?"

Only Calhoun indicated that he was.

"Then I'll be askin' you not to be shootin' your gun out the window at rabbits, or deer or anythin' like that, 'cause the gunshots tend to scare the horses and they might commence to runnin'. Oh, and if for some reason the horses do take off a' runnin', then for sure don't be jumpin' out of the coach. It might be a little frightenin' to you, but trust me, you're a heap safer off stayin' inside.

"And finally, I want to say this, and you'd best listen to me, 'cause I am real serious about it. If any of you men does or says anything that upsets or offends any of the ladies, I'll put you off the coach and you'll be walkin' back to the depot. And believe me, you ain't goin' to like that. Now, if there ain't no one got 'ny questions to ask, we'll be loadin' up in"—McVey glanced at the clock—"about three minutes. That means you just barely got time to get there."

Young Mary Dawson turned to her mother and they embraced. "You tell your grandmother we'll be expectin' her and grandpa around the Fourth of July," Mary's mother said.

"I will," Mary promised.

"Are you sure you'll be all right? I mean, this is a pretty long trip to be taking all by yourself."

"Mama, I have friends who have gone back East for a whole year to go to school. I'm a big girl. I can take care of myself."

"I'm sure you can. It's just that I worry so."

"Don't worry. I have to go now. Bye."

"I'm coming outside to see you off," Mary's mother said.

The men, whether responding to the words of the driver, or out of authentic gentlemanly concern, were most solicitous of the ladies as they boarded the coach. The shotgun guard kissed his wife good-bye, then climbed up on the box, sitting on the left side.

"You drive safely now, Stan," Mrs. Conway said as McVey grabbed hold to climb up into his seat. "And you two look out for each other."

"We'll do that, Martha." He turned to Conway. "I saw you pick up the bag from the bank. Is everything all set?"

"Yeah, we're ready. It's stowed under the seat,"

Conway said. "Woulda been better though, if there hadn't been anything about it in the paper."

"You got that right," McVey replied.

Removing his whip from its holder, McVey whirled it around once over his head, then snapped it over the head of his team, causing it to pop loudly.

Inside the coach, Mary jumped at the sound of the popping whip. "Oh! What was that?"

Calhoun chuckled. "Don't worry 'bout that, miss. That was just the driver snapping his whip over the team.

"Heah, team!" McVey shouted, his exhortation clearly heard by all who were inside the coach.

It pulled away from the station, exiting Escalante at a rapid clip. There would be no way MeVey could hold this speed for any length of time, but he liked to depart and arrive in great fashion, and having the horses gallop as he drove out of town was a way of doing that.

Bridgeport, Colorado

Jericho Taggart was a regulator, a man who made a living by hunting wanted men. He specialized in hunting those who were wanted Dead or Alive, because the rewards were generally higher for such a person. Also the Dead or Alive provision gave him all the cover he needed to bring in his quarry dead. With live prisoners there was always the chance they could get away, and with it, the reward money. Also a live prisoner would, if he had the chance, kill the man who was attempting to bring him in.

There was no such problem with dead prisoners.

The men Taggart brought in weren't just dead, they were very dead—because his weapon of choice was a Sharps .50 caliber buffalo rifle. He could stand half a mile off from his quarry, and with the energy generated by the large, heavy .50 caliber bullet, a hit almost anywhere would generate enough shock to kill, often before his victim even realized he was in trouble.

A week ago, Taggart learned there was a fifteen hundred dollar reward for a man named Elliot Simpson. He also learned that Simpson had an old mother who lived all alone about a mile outside the town of Bridgeport. When it was safe for Simpson to come see his mother, she would hang a pair of red long johns on the clothesline as a signal.

For the last three days Taggart had stationed himself just outside the Simpson house. This morning he watched as the old woman came out, looked around, then pinned a pair of red long johns onto the clothesline.

Taggart lay down on a flat rock, five hundred yards from the house and waited until late afternoon, before someone came riding up. The old woman come out onto the porch, holding her arms out wide in welcome.

Taggart squeezed the trigger.

The bullet hit Simpson in the side of the head, and even from so far away Taggart could see the spray of blood and brain matter exploding from Simpson's head.

Simpson's mother began screaming hysterically, and was still screaming when Taggart rode down to pick up Simpson's body and drape it over his own horse.

"You killed my boy! You killed my boy!" she shouted at him.

Taggart didn't bother to answer her.

Five minutes later he rode away, leading Simpson's horse, over which the body lay. Half an hour later he saw another wanted poster.

$5,000

SMOKE JENSEN

WANTED

FOR MURDER

$5,000 REWARD

to be paid by
Sheriff of La Plata County

CHAPTER TWENTY-ONE

On the road to Suttle

Shortly after the coach got underway, Calhoun pulled his pistol and spun the cylinder to make certain it was fully loaded.

"Sir, I wish you would be a bit more judicious in the handling of that firearm," Mrs. Gray said.

"Madam, if we are attacked by road agents, you will be thanking me for this gun," Calhoun said.

"Road agents?" Mary asked. "Are we likely to be attacked by road agents?"

"I think not, miss," Dr. Potter said. "I've made this trip several times and there has never been any problem."

"You should be ashamed of yourself, frightening the child," Mrs. Gray said.

"Didn't mean to frighten you none, miss," Calhoun said. "I apologize."

Mary grinned back at him. "It's all right. I shouldn't be such a fraidy cat."

Stage, as in stagecoach, was actually a term that expressed distance. Way stops and swing stops were "staged" along the route approximately every fifteen miles. Swing stops consisted of nothing but a stable and small shack for the hostler who would have a fresh team ready upon the arrival of the coach. The team could be changed in about ten minutes, then the coach would be on its way. Way stops not only provided for a change of horses, but the passengers could take their meals, and even spend the night if they were on a trip that required such a thing. Although there would be no overnight stays on this trip of eight hours, there would be a noon meal at the way station that was halfway between the two towns.

Some four hours later, they heard the driver blowing upon his horn, a signal to the way station that they were arriving. Most of the time the signal was sent so a new team could be assembled, and the coach would require less than ten minutes to proceed on with fresh steeds. But this would be a stop for lunch, so it signaled the way station proprietors of the eminent arrival so they could make all accommodations ready for the travelers.

When the coach came to rest just in front of the way station, McVey called down to his passengers. "Folks! We will be here for one half hour and one half hour only. I suggest you eat quickly then take care of anything that needs took care of."

The door was opened from the outside by Don

Pratt who, with his wife, Marian ran the way station. "Oh, my, did you folks choose a good day to travel," he said. "My wife made three apple pies this mornin'. But I suggest you eat quick, before McVey sees them. I've known that man a long time, and Lord does he like to eat."

The passengers enjoyed their meal, and laughed at the good-natured jibes tossed back and forth between the Pratts and the driver and shotgun guard. Less than thirty minutes after they arrived, McVey stood and hitched up his trousers. "Miz Pratt, I tell you, if you don't stop feedin' me so well here, I'm not goin' to be able to get into my britches much longer. There ain't no restaurant anywhere that sets a better table than you do."

Marian Pratt blushed at the compliment.

"All right, folks, let's go," McVey called to his passengers. "We got a long way to go and I aim to be there before sundown."

The passengers, thanking Mrs. Pratt for her hospitality, filed out of the way station and climbed back into the coach, connected now to a fresh team.

As the trip progressed, the passengers conversed, sharing not only their names and background, but the purpose of their journey. Mary Dawson was going to Suttle to spend some time with her grandmother and grandfather. Mrs. Gray and Mrs. Johnson were both from Suttle. They were members of the Colorado Ladies' League, and were returning home after a most productive and successful meeting in Escalante. Dr. Potter was from Escalante, but he was going to Suttle to visit with a friend, another doctor, who wanted to discuss a patient with him. Calhoun had come to Escalante to make arrangements with the railroad for a cattle shipment. Evans planned to show a sample of his wares—cooking utensils—to housewives in Suttle.

The coach had been underway for some six hours. The passengers, having recently partaken of a rather large meal at the way station, and having exhausted nearly all subjects of conversation, were quiet. All but Mary and Dr. Potter were asleep, and the lulling sway of the coach, the sound of the hooves, and the whirling wheels were lulling her to sleep as well. To keep herself awake, Mary thought of her grandmother, always so appreciative of gifts. Mary anticipated the joy she would experience in giving her a shawl that she had knit with her own hands.

The coach slowed considerably, and the passengers could feel it going uphill. The change in motion and sound awakened the others.

"Oh, great," Calhoun said irritably. "I suppose we'll have to get out and walk again."

His observation was born of the fact that twice previously, the driver had asked the passengers to get out and walk in order to reduce the weight the animals had to pull up the hill.

"No, we'll be all right for this hill," Evans said. "I've made this trip dozens of times. We've never had to leave the coach for this hill."

On the train from Big Rock to Parlin

Smoke, convinced that Sally's recovery was well underway, left again on his quest to find Dinkins and his group of outlaws. His horse was in the stock car, and he sat looking out the window of the train as the terrain rolled by.

Rugged hills and sage covered meadowland, but he wasn't seeing it, so occupied was his mind with thoughts of Sally. He had nearly lost her. He had never fully recovered from losing Nicole. He didn't know what he would do if something like that ever happened again.

The train stopped, and a young cowboy who was wearing an ivory-handled pistol, a fancy vest, and a hat with a silver hatband came aboard. He swaggered back and forth through the car a few times, as if trying to make himself the center of attention, but Smoke paid little attention to him.

At the next stop a very pretty young woman came aboard the train. She smiled prettily, shyly, at Smoke as she took her seat near the front of the car. Politely, Smoke nodded to her, then turned his attention back to the scenery outside. The swaggering cowboy moved quickly to sit next to the young girl and Smoke smiled, wondering if he had ever been that young and that eager around pretty girls. He put the cowboy and the girl out of his mind, then leaned his head back and tipped his hat down over his eyes for a little nap.

Smoke was asleep when the conductor tapped him on the shoulder. "Mr. Jensen, I thought you might want to know we'll be coming in to Parlin in about fifteen minutes or so."

"Thanks. Oh, if you don't mind, I'd like to go forward to be with my horse," Smoke said.

"I thought you might. Just be careful stepping across the platform going from car to car."

"I will, thanks."

When Smoke got up from his seat, he saw that the young girl and the cowboy were gone. He thought nothing more of it until he stepped outside where he saw the two of them standing on the platform between the cars.

"Please," the young girl was saying. "I want to go back into the car."

"No ma'am, you done played fast and easy with me, and I intend to see the elephant."

Smoke was just about to go into the next car when he heard the exchange, and he stopped and looked back at them. He didn't like butting in where it was none of his business, but the expression on the girl's face indicated she was not a willing participant in what was going on. Still, what could happen to her on a train? He reached for the door to go into the next car.

"What are you hanging out here for, mister?" the cowboy asked irritably. "What's goin' on here ain't none of your business, so you just get on now."

Smoke sighed. He had already decided that what was going on was none of his business, but he didn't appreciate this young polecat pointing that out to him.

"Now, get on out of here before I throw you off this train," the cowboy said.

That's it. Now the little son of a bitch has made it my business. "I think I will go on," Smoke said. "But if I do, the young woman is going to go with me."

"What? What the hell did you just say?" the cowboy asked.

"It seems pretty obvious to me that the young lady doesn't want to be out here. I'm merely offering her my protection."

"Haw! Your protection?"

"Yes, such as it is," Smoke said. "I haven't made a mistake, have I miss? I did hear you say you wanted to go back into the car, didn't I?"

"Yes, but please go. I don't want you to have any trouble because of me." The tone of the girl's voice betrayed the fear she was feeling.

"There will be no trouble, miss," Smoke said.

"You better listen to her, mister, and leave while you are still in one piece," the cowboy replied.

"Come with me, miss," Smoke said. "Don't be afraid of him."

"I warned you!" The cowboy stepped across the vestibule and took a wild swing at Smoke. Smoke leaned back, easily avoiding the swing, then, capitalizing on the momentum of the young man's swing, gave the young cowboy a swift kick in his behind.

The cowboy might have yelled, but so quickly did it happen that by the time he hit the down slope of the berm, the train had moved forward enough so that he couldn't be heard.

Smoke leaned out and looked to the rear to

see the young cowboy regain his feet and look on in utter shock as the train continued down the track without him.

"Oh!" The young girl put her hand to her mouth. "I hope you didn't kill him!"

"Take a look," Smoke invited. "He's all right."

The girl started toward the edge of the platform, then stepped back. "I'm too frightened to look."

"Give me your hand, I'll hold you," Smoke said. "Then, take a look so you can ease your conscience."

The young woman offered Smoke her hand, and he held it firmly as she leaned out to look toward the rear. She giggled. "He looks really mad."

"I didn't butt in where I wasn't wanted, did I?" Smoke asked.

"No, no, not at all. He was being very boorish. I'm glad you stepped out here when you did."

The girl's smile and the expression in her eyes suggested that she would be more than willing to express her gratitude in other ways, but Smoke just returned her smile, then touched the brim of his hat before he went on forward to see to his horse.

Bridgeport

"You say you killed him in front of his mama?" Sheriff Adams said as he identified the body of Elliot Simpson. Identification wasn't all that easy. The bullet had entered the back of Simpson's head, and exited through his face. The resultant wound left his face very disfigured.

"Yeah, that's how I knew for sure who he was," Taggart answered.

"I don't suppose you bothered to try and bring him in alive?" the sheriff asked.

"I don't write the posters, Sheriff," Taggart said. "The poster says dead or alive, it doesn't say alive or dead. And you know what I figure?"

"What's that?"

"I figure anytime a poster says dead or alive, what it really means is they want him dead. Think of all the money and time you save by not having a trial."

"His mama must have taken it some hard," the sheriff said.

"She knew her son was an outlaw. She had to expect somethin' like this sometime."

"Yes, but not right in front of her," Sheriff Adams said. "Noni Simpson is a good woman."

"A good woman who raised a bad son. Are you going to authorize the payment or not?"

"Yeah, I'm going to authorize the payment." Sheriff Adams took a sheet of paper from his desk drawer and wrote on it.

> *Received of Jericho Taggart, the body of Elliot Simpson, wanted criminal. The reward of $1,500 dollars, said amount to be charged to the account of the state, is hereby authorized. Ty Adams, Sheriff, Delta County*

Taggart took the receipt down to the bank where it was paid without question. From the bank, he went to the saloon where he had a few drinks, and played some cards. "Any of you have any idea where Smoke Jensen might be?"

"Like as not he's at his ranch, Sugarloaf," one of the other players said.

"I bet he ain't," another said.

"What makes you think he ain't?"

"Ain't you been readin' the papers none? Someone shot his wife."

"Damn, I ain't heard that. Was she kilt?"

"I don't know, but it don't really make no never mind. If someone shot his wife, whether it kilt her or not, he'll be goin' after 'em."

CHAPTER TWENTY-TWO

Purple Peak Pass

Bill Dinkins, Wes Harley, Travis and Frank Slater were waiting at a turnout at the top of the hill the coach from Escalante to Suttle had just started to navigate. Harley climbed to the top of a rock that enabled him to see the various switchback turns in the road leading up to the pass.

"Can you still see the coach?" Dinkins called up to Harley.

"Yeah, they've made the last switchback. They'll be here in a couple more minutes."

Travis laughed out loud.

"What are you laughing at?" Dinkins asked.

"I just pissed a grasshopper off a weed. That makes him a pissed-on grasshopper."

"So?"

"Don't you get it? A pissed-on grasshopper is a pissed-off grasshopper." Travis laughed again.

"Get ready," Dinkins said without joining in the laughter. "The coach will be here in just a couple more minutes."

"It means he's mad," Travis said, still trying to explain his joke.

"Get ready," Dinkins said again.

Harley came back down from the rock. "They're real close now."

"Yeah, I can hear 'em," Dinkins said.

The coach was close enough they could hear the driver's shouts, whistles, and popping of the whip, as well as the clatter of hooves, and the squeaking and jarring of the coach itself.

"Heah! Heah! Giddap there, hosses! Just a little way and you can take a breather! Heah!"

"Get ready!" Dinkins hissed.

When the coach reached the top of the grade the driver called the team to a halt. The horses could be heard, breathing hard. The driver was putting the whip back in its holder when the four men stepped out from behind the rocks. Each of them was wearing a kerchief around the bottom half of his face, and holding a pistol, leveled at the coach.

"You folks inside, climb out here!" Dinkins shouted.

Three men climbed down, and as they did so, Calhoun produced a pistol and fired at the robbers, but missed. Dinkins and the others returned fire, riddling the coach with bullets. The rancher and the salesman went down. When the messenger made a move for his shotgun, he was killed. McVey jumped down from the driver's seat, and ran off the road and into the rocks along with the doctor. Dinkins and the others pointed their guns at them and pulled the triggers, but all the firing pins fell on empty chambers. Not one of them had a charged cartridge remaining.

"Damnit!" Dinkins shouted angrily. Quickly, he and the others reloaded, but it was too late, the driver and passenger had already gotten away.

"Travis, look in the coach!" Dinkins ordered.

Cautiously, Travis approached the coach, then peered in through the window. He saw three women, drenched with blood.

"What's in there?"

"Just women," Travis called back. "And all three are dead."

As Travis was checking inside the coach, Harley climbed up onto the driver's seat. Looking underneath the seat he found a canvas bag, marked ESCALANTE BANK. With a whoop, he held it up.

"Look here boys, what I found!"

"What is it?"

Harley cut through the canvas, stuck his hand inside, and pulled out a handful of greenbacks. "Money, boys! Lots of money!" Harley shouted.

"Now what did I tell you? When Bill Dinkins plans a job, he does it right. Come on down, Wes. Let's get out of here."

Inside the coach, Mary Dawson lay uninjured, but pinned to the floor of the coach by the bodies of the other two women. She lay quietly until she was sure the outlaws had left. Only then did she start trying to work her way free. When she raised up and looked down at the two women whose bodies had held her down, she nearly gagged over what she saw. Both women had multiple gunshot wounds, and there was so much blood it was almost an inch thick on the floor of the coach.

Mary felt sick to her stomach at the grizzly sight, and knew she had to get out of the coach. By the time she climbed out, McVey and Dr. Potter were returning.

"Good Lord, Miss Dawson, how badly are you hurt?" Dr. Potter asked, seeing all the blood on her.

"I'm not hurt," Mary replied. "But I think the other two ladies, Mrs. Gray and Mrs. Johnson, are dead."

Dr. Potter checked on the two women, then nodded. "They're dead." He checked Evans and Calhoun. "They are, too."

As Dr. Potter was checking on the passengers, McVey had climbed up to the box to check on Conway. "Doc, you want to come up here and take a look at Burt?"

Using the spokes of the front wheel, Dr. Potter climbed up to the box to stand beside McVey. Although there were no visible wounds on the shotgun guard's body, he was very still, and his eyes were open and opaque. Dr. Potter put his hand on Conway's neck, but could find no pulse. Then he saw the wound, a bullet hole over his heart, not immediately visible because of the way he was positioned. "There's the wound."

"How is he?" Mary called up to him.

"He's dead," Dr. Potter called back down.

"Doc, if you will help me, we'll get the bodies laid out up here," McVey said quietly. "I think it would be better for Miss Dawson, and for you, if you didn't have to ride in the coach with them."

"I'll be glad to help you," Dr. Potter said, climbing back down.

McVey looked down at Calhoun's body. He was still clutching the pistol in his hand, the pistol from which only one shot had been fired.

"Here is the dumb son of a bitch who caused all this," McVey said.

"That's not fair, Mr. McVey," Dr. Porter replied. "He didn't cause it. The road agents caused it. He was just doing what he thought was right."

"It was Bill Dinkins," Mary said.

"What?" McVey asked. "Bill Dinkins? Are you sure?"

"Yes. I heard his name."

"Then I take it back," McVey said. "Dinkins is a cold-blooded murderer. Like as not he would have shot us all whether Mr. Calhoun took a shot at him or not."

It took a good ten minutes to get the four bodies lifted up to the top of the coach to join with Conway's body, which was already lying there.

"Are we going back to Escalante?" Dr. Potter asked.

"No," McVey said. "We are going on. We are only two hours from Suttle, six hours back to Escalante. We'll send a telegraph message back when we reach Suttle."

One of the reasons this was the coach turnout was because of proximity of water, from Tomichi Creek. A pipe from the creek kept a watering trough filled for livestock that passed through. Dr. Potter wet his handkerchief in the trough, then used it to wash away the blood from Mary's face, hands, and arms. "There's nothing I can do about your dress, I'm afraid."

"Thank you," Mary replied. "Grandma will wash it. Poor Mrs. Gray and Mrs. Johnson. They were so excited about the meeting they attended in Escalante. They were going to tell their friends all about it." Tears began to slide down Mary's cheeks. "I'm sorry. I'm crying like a baby."

"No you aren't, child," Dr. Potter said reassuringly. "You are crying like a compassionate woman."

"If you folks are ready, we'll get underway," McVey said, the tone of his voice much more gentle than it had been at the start of their journey.

Suttle, Colorado

The first thing the people noticed about the arrival of the coach was that McVey did not come galloping in as he normally did. Then someone saw the bodies lying on top of the coach, as well as bullet holes in the sides. "Hey, look at the coach!"

"What happened?"

"I bet they was held up!"

The forward progress of the coach down Center Street was so slow the citizens of the town who were curious and aggressive enough to do so, were able to keep pace with it.

"What happened?" someone called.

"Was you held up?" another asked.

McVey made no reply. He continued to stare straight ahead, concentrating on driving the team as resolutely as he could. Finally he pulled to a stop in front of the Dunn Hotel, which also served as the stagecoach office for Suttle. The crowd that had followed him drew up there as well, so by the time McVey set his brake there were close to a hundred people gathered around the coach.

Caleb Stallings, the station manager, stepped onto the front porch. When he saw the blood, the bodies, and the holes in the side of the coach, he got a horrified expression on his face. "Stan, my God!" he called up to the driver. "What happened?"

"We was waylaid," McVey said. He stood, then pointed his hand toward the top of the coach. "These folks was all kilt, I'm afraid."

"Good Lord, Stan, are you the only one left alive?"

The door to the coach opened then, and Dr. Potter stepped down. He reached back into the coach to help Mary down.

"Mary!" an older woman called and broke from the crowd rushing toward Mary, who met her halfway. The two women embraced, weeping as they did so.

"Juanita?" a gray haired old man said, his voice cracking. "Where is Juanita Gray, my wife?"

"I'm sorry, Mr. Gray," Dr. Potter said. "Mrs. Gray and her friend, Mrs. Johnson, were both killed. So were Mr. Calhoun and Mr. Evans."

"Pop!" a young boy of about sixteen called. "No! I came to town to get him! What will I tell Ma?"

As news spread through the town, bringing realization that five people had been killed, three of whom were from Suttle, anger and sorrow became pervasive.

There were resolute shouts to form a posse to go after the perpetrators, but nothing progressed beyond the shouts. The real finality of the event occurred when Gene Welch, the undertaker, arrived at the scene, not with a hearse, but with an open wagon large enough to accommodate all five bodies.

"Would someone give me a hand, please?" he asked, and a dozen or more willing souls stepped up to help pass the bodies down from the top of the coach.

* * *

Harold Denman, editor of the *Suttle Sentinal* didn't even bother to write out the story first. He composed the story as he set the type, which was not that difficult a job for him. He had grown up in a print shop, and had been setting type for as long as he could remember. Because of that he was able to read the type in reverse as easily as he could read it forward.

Inking the platen, Denman brought down the press to make the first impression. Then he pulled the first page of the press and looked at the story he had written, putting it out as a special edition.

Coach Holdup
Between Escalante and Suttle
FIVE ARE MURDERED IN COLD BLOOD

In a most dastardly fashion, Bill Dinkins and his gang of murderers and thieves lay in wait at Purple Peak Pass on Friday of the week previous. When the driver, Stan McVey, reached the top of the grade, he stopped, as all good drivers do, to give his team an opportunity to catch their breath.

It was there, according to Mr. McVey, that four masked men showed themselves. Without so much as one word, they began shooting, the balls taking fatal effect not only on Mr. Evans and Mr. Calhoun, but also on Mrs. Gray and Mrs. Johnson, they being passengers. Burt Conway, the messenger, was also killed. The robbers relieved the coach of its money pouch, containing five thousand dollars.

Miss Dawson, who survived the attack, told Sheriff Jones she overheard one of the men say the name *Bill Dinkins*. It is this comment, uttered by one of the perpetrators of the evil deed, which has enabled the sheriff to declare it to be the work of the Dinkins gang.

CHAPTER TWENTY-THREE

Delta, Colorado

There was nothing specific about the little town that caused Smoke to go there. It was just one of the many fly-blown towns he hadn't checked out before. It was one week after he left Sugarloaf, this time convinced that Sally was fully on the mend. He had spent the last six nights out on the trail, so the thought of a bed and bath was all the incentive he needed, whether Dinkins was there or not.

After making certain that Seven was stabled and fed at Fadley's Corral, he checked in to the Central House Hotel.

"Yes, sir, Mister"—the clerk turned the register to examine it—"Jensen? Mr. Jensen, welcome to Delta and the Central House Hotel. I hope you find the accommodations satisfactory."

"I'm sure I will, thank you," Smoke said. "I see

that you have a restaurant here in the hotel. Is it one that you would recommend? I mean, beside the fact that you are working here?"

"I do indeed recommend it, and it is not just because I work here," the clerk replied.

"No need to apologize for being loyal to your employer. I admire loyalty. Suppose, after dinner, I would like to have a drink or two. Which saloon would you recommend?"

"We have three saloons in town, but I would recommend the Palace Sampling Room. You can't miss it. It is right across the street from the Farmers and Merchants Bank."

"Thank you." Smoke saw a stack of newspapers on the corner of the desk. "Local paper?"

"Yes, sir, this is the *Delta Free Press*, printed right here in town, once a week."

Smoke picked up one of the papers. "How much is it?"

"Oh, the paper is free for the hotel guests, sir," the clerk said.

Smoke nodded, then went into the dining room. Selecting a table where he could place his back in the corner, he read it as he waited for his dinner to be served.

One article had the headline Outlaw Cole Parnell Hurled into Eternity in Legal Hanging.

He felt no particular need to read that article, as he had been present when the hanging took place. But the next article did catch his attention.

Coach Holdup
Between Escalante and Suttle
FIVE ARE MURDERED IN COLD BLOOD

Smoke smiled. Escalante was the next town over from Delta. He was on the trail, all right.

As Smoke started into the dining room, the clerk reached under his desk and pulled out a circular someone had brought him a few days earlier.

WANTED

FOR MURDER

SMOKE JENSEN

$5,000 REWARD

DEAD OR ALIVE
to be paid by
Sheriff of La Plata County

The desk clerk scrawled a quick note, then signaled to one of the bellhops. As the young bellhop approached the desk, the clerk held the note out toward him. "Kenny, here is a quarter for you. I want you to run down the street to the Palace Sampling Room and give this to Loomis Coltrane."

Kenny nodded, then left the hotel on his mission.

Ten minutes later Loomis Coltrane came into the lobby. Coltrane was a medium-sized man, unprepossessing in appearance with a sweeping mustache and evil looking eyes. He strode over to the desk. "The note said you wanted to see me."

"Do you remember the wanted poster you brought me the other day?"

"Yeah, what of it?"

"Suppose I told you that I know where you can find Kirby Jensen?"

"Kirby Jensen? I ain't interested in him. It's Smoke Jensen that the reward is for."

"They are one and the same."

"The hell you say."

"Yes, I say."

"So, what if I am looking for him?" Coltrane asked.

"It might be that I know where to find him," the clerk said.

"Where?"

"Information like that should be worth something, don't you think?"

"Where is he?"

"Like say, a thousand dollars?"

"A thousand dollars? Are you crazy? I ain't got that kind of money."

"I'm willing to wait until after you collect the reward."

"That's too much money. There are already three of us involved," Coltrane said.

"That will give you thirteen hundred and thirty dollars apiece. Surely you can be satisfied with that."

Coltrane stroked his jaw for a moment, then nodded. "All right, I'll go along with it. That is, if your information tells us how to find him."

The clerk leaned around to look into the dining room. At first he didn't see Smoke, then he spotted him in the far corner.

"Do you see that man back in the corner, reading the newspaper?"

"Yeah, what about him?"

"That's Smoke Jensen."

Coltrane studied him for a moment longer. "Hmm. He don't look all that tough to me."

"I'm sure there has been many a man who has made that same judgment, or should I say, misjudgment?"

Coltrane took a step toward the dining room.

"No," the clerk said sharply. "Whatever you have planned, don't do it here."

"Don't worry, I ain't goin' to do anything here," Coltrane said. "Not without Grange and Stallings."

"For your information, he will be going down to the saloon after his dinner."

"How do you know?"

"We discussed it as he was signing in," the clerk said.

Coltrane hurried back to the saloon. It was early evening, and the saloon was at its busiest, with drinkers, card players, and even a few who were eating their dinner. He saw Stallings talking with one of the bar girls, and motioned him over. Grange was standing at the far end of the bar, nursing a drink, and Coltrane walked down to join him. He waited to speak until Stallings joined them.

"Jensen is here," Coltrane said.

"Where?"

"Right now he is having his supper. Then he's coming down here, so I suggest we get ready for him."

Coltrane moved to stand just inside the door of the saloon watching for Jensen. When he saw him coming, he gave a signal to the others, who hurried to get into position.

The saloon had a wide boardwalk flanking the dusty street, a couple hitching posts out front, and bat wing doors through which Smoke pushed his way inside.

When he entered the saloon, he stepped to the side and made a quick perusal before he walked up to the bar to order a beer. At one time saloons such as this one had become so much a part of his day-to-day existence they had become part of his heritage. From Denver to Cheyenne to Phoenix to Dodge City, one saloon was like another.

Since he'd married Sally that was no longer the case. He still spent a lot of time in Longmont's, but that was because Louis was his friend. And Longmont's was so superior to the ordinary saloon, it was more like a private club than a public watering hole.

"What will it be, mister?" the bartender asked.

Smoke saw that, for some reason, the bartender seemed more than a little nervous. "What's wrong?"

"Nothing, I . . . ," the bartender started, then his eyes darted to the rear of the saloon, so quickly Smoke couldn't tell whether it was a reflexive action or a signal.

Curious and cautious, he glanced toward the rear of the saloon.

"He's seen us!" someone yelled at the top of his voice from the upper level floor. He was wielding a double-barrel shotgun, which he had turned toward Smoke.

"Shoot the son of a bitch!" someone else shouted and the shotgun boomed loudly.

Alerted by the shout, Smoke fell to the floor and rolled to his right, just as the man at the top of the stairs fired. The heavy charge of buckshot tore a large hole in the top and side of the bar, right where Smoke had been standing but a second before. Smoke shot at the man before he could pull the trigger on the second barrel. The would-be assailant tumbled over the railing and crashed onto the piano below.

As Smoke and the man on the overlook were firing at each other, Coltrane took the opportunity to go for his own gun. Suddenly the saloon was filled with the roar of another gunshot as Coltrane fired.

The presence of a second gunman did not surprise Smoke, for he had heard the first shooter yell out, "He's seen *us!*" Smoke was able to react so quickly, his gunshot and the shot fired by Coltrane sounded like one.

Smoke hit exactly what he was aiming for. Coltrane was knocked backward onto a table where he lay sprawled out on his back, his head hanging down on the opposite side of the table. The table was covered by green felt, the easier for card playing. At the moment, however, it was soaked in blood.

A third man ran out of the saloon without even attempting a shot. Smoke didn't know if he was running to get out of the line of fire, or if he had been a part of the team of ambushers who lost his courage when he saw the other two cut down.

Hearing the shots, the town marshal and his deputy came running into the saloon with guns drawn. Smoke had already holstered his pistol and was standing calmly with his back to the bar, his arms up, resting his elbows on the bar. The other customers in the saloon, those who had dived under the tables, or behind the piano, were milling around the two dead bodies, looking down at them with a cross between morbid curiosity and guilty appreciation of still being alive.

Noticing that Smoke was the only one not milling around with the others, the marshal and his deputy holstered their own pistols, then stepped over to talk to him.

"I have a feeling you are a part of this," the marshal said.

"I was," Smoke agreed. "But not by choice."

"You want to tell me what happened?"

"These two men shot at me," Smoke said. Moving to one side, he pointed to the damaged bar. "I believe there may have been a third, but he ran when the shooting started."

"You're Smoke Jensen, aren't you?"

"Yes."

"I guess you are used to this by now. Getting shot at, I mean."

"I don't know if you ever get used to it," Smoke replied.

"Hey, Marshal, look at this!" one of the saloon patrons said.

He brought over a piece of paper and showed it to the marshal. The marshal read it, looked up at Smoke, then back down at the paper. To Smoke's surprise, the marshal drew his pistol and pointed it at Smoke.

"What's that for?" Smoke asked. "You can ask anyone in here and they will tell you these two men started the shooting."

"That may be so," the marshal said. "But it doesn't make any difference whether they started it or not, as long as they had justification for it."

"What can justify one man dry gulching another?" Smoke asked.

"This, perhaps?" The marshal showed Smoke the wanted poster, stating that a five thousand dollar reward would be paid for him, dead or alive.

"Where did that come from?" Smoke asked, surprised to see the poster.

"Coltrane had it on him," the saloon patron said.

"It's not real," Smoke said.

"What do you mean, it's not real?" the marshal asked. "I'm holding it in my hand, looking at it. It's real."

"Look, it's no secret that I'm after Bill Dinkins and his gang. I've been told he put out a one thousand dollar reward, payable to anyone who killed me. I haven't heard about this, but he has to be behind this as well."

The marshal shook his head. "According to this, it's the sheriff of La Plata County who has put out the reward."

"Do you get reward posters in the mail to post in your office?" Smoke asked.

"Yes."

"Have you gotten this flyer on me?"

"No, not yet. But that don't mean nothin'. It could be days, even weeks before I might get a poster that's bein' sent out. It looks like I'm goin' to have to lock you up in jail until we get to the bottom of this."

"I don't think I would like that," Smoke said.

"Well, Mr. Jensen, I don't care what you would like," the marshal replied. "I've got a duty to this badge. And right now, I've got the drop on you. So I reckon we'll just do it my way."

In a move that was totally unexpected, and incredibly fast, Smoke reached out and jerked the marshal's pistol out of his hand. Even as he was doing that, he drew his own gun.

"Uh-uh." Smoke cautioned the deputy with a warning glance, and the deputy who looked as if he might go for his own gun, stopped in mid-move. "We'll do it my way."

"And what way is that?" the marshal asked, his voice edged with fear.

"We are going to go down to the telegraph office and send a wire to the sheriff of La Plata County. I want you to ask him if he has authorized this poster."

"His name is on it," the marshal said. "He must have approved it."

"You think so?"

"If he didn't approve it, where did it come from?"

"I told you that Dinkins had a thousand dollar reward on me. It looks like he just upped the ante."

"You think he has that much money?" the marshal asked.

"It doesn't matter. He doesn't intend to pay it," Smoke said. "That's why he put it out over the sheriff of La Plata's name."

Smoke handed the marshal's pistol back to him. "Shall we go find out what this is all about?"

Surprised to have his gun returned to him, the marshal put it back in his holster, then nodded. "Yes. Let's go find out."

Half an hour later, the telegrapher handed the marshal a telegram.

THIS OFFICE HAS ISSUED NO FLYERS
OFFERING A REWARD FOR SMOKE JENSEN
ANY SUCH REWARD POSTERS AS MAY EXIST
ARE FORGERIES

"It looks like you are right," the marshal said.
"I'm sorry I didn't believe you."

"That's all right," Smoke said. "You were just
doing your job. Or at least, you thought you were
doing your job."

"Yes, but I could have killed you."

Smoke chuckled. "No, you couldn't have."

For a moment the marshal was confused by the
answer, then realized that Smoke was right. Smoke
had actually taken his pistol away from him.

"Come to think of it, I don't guess I could have
killed you after all."

Smoke had no idea what woke him up. Since it
was his first night in a real bed in over a week, and
since he was sleeping soundly, there was no dis-
cernible reason why he suddenly awoke. But he
was lying in bed, staring into the darkness overhead, wide awake.

He did not hear anything, nor did he see anything, but the same sixth sense that had awakened him told him to get out of bed. Rolling over
quietly, Smoke pulled his pistol from the holster,
then stepped over to the wall, backing up against
it, right next to the door.

No sooner had he done that, than he heard the sound of a key being inserted in the lock of his door. The key was turned slowly, but he heard the click of the tumblers. The door opened, and in the ambient light cast through the window, dim as it was, Smoke saw the man walk over to the bed. He raised his hand over his head, and Smoke saw the soft gleam of moonlight on the blade of a knife.

"What the hell?" the man said, when he realized nobody was in the bed.

Smoke had stepped up behind him, no more than foot away. "Are you looking for me?"

"Ahh!!" the man cried, startled by the unexpected sound behind him. He turned quickly trying to bring his knife around in a slashing arc, but he was too late. Smoke took him down with a crushing hard right to the jaw.

Half an hour later they were in the marshal's office. The deputy had awakened the marshal who was clearly agitated by being awakened in the middle of the night. "Stallings, you want to tell me why you were in Mr. Jensen's room in the middle of the night with a knife?"

"I was trying to kill him."

"Why?"

"Maybe you don't know it, but there is a price on his head. The sheriff over in La Plata County has offered five thousand dollars, dead or alive, for Smoke Jensen."

"And of course you were planning on taking him in dead, is that it?"

"Yeah. It don't say he has to be alive."

"You might be interested in this." The marshal showed Stallings the telegram he had received from the sheriff of La Plata County.

Stallings read the telegram, then looked up at the marshal. "Does this mean there ain't no reward?"

"That is exactly what it means."

"So what you are saying is, Coltrane and Grange, they both got themselves kilt for nothing."

"That's right."

"Stallings, where did you get that flyer?" Smoke asked.

"I don't know. They're all over. I think we got this one offen' an old abandoned shack about ten miles east of here."

"You said they are all over," Smoke said. "What do you mean by all over?"

"I mean this ain't the only one we seen. After we took this one, we seen at least five, maybe ten more, on trees, old buildings, an abandoned mine."

"All of them east of here?"

"Yeah, pretty much."

Smoke nodded. "Then that's where they are."

"That's where who are?"

"Bill Dinkins and his men."

CHAPTER TWENTY-FOUR

Sapinero, Colorado

At ten-thirty p.m. the eastbound train number 20 arrived at the Sapinero station. Harley and the two Slater brothers, Frank and Travis, were waiting in the darkness on the opposite side of the railroad tracks from the station. They had hidden their horses a mile out of town, and the plan was to get on the train and force it to stop where their horses were.

When the train stopped at the station, the three men climbed onto the platform just behind the tender. They remained there, unseen in the dark, as the train pulled out of the station. Travis climbed up over the tender and dropped down behind the engineer and fireman, both of whom were illuminated by the yellow cab lantern. They were staring straight ahead.

"Hello, boys!" Travis called.

Startled, the engine crew turned toward him.

"What the hell are you doing here?" the engineer asked.

"You might say I've taken over as the conductor," Travis said. "I want you to get ready to stop where I tell you to stop."

"The hell I will," the engineer said angrily.

Travis shot the fireman in the leg, and he let out a yelp of pain, grabbing his leg where the bullet struck.

"My next shot will be to his head," Travis said.

The engineer stuck both hands out in front of him. "All right, all right. Don't shoot him again."

"Brake this train, right now," Travis said.

The engineer set the brakes, and the train squealed to a halt. Travis leaned out through the engineer's window and looked ahead. He saw a bonfire with a man standing in silhouette in front of it. The man was carrying a rifle, and he held it up, then pointed it to the right.

Travis smiled. That was the agreed-upon signal, which meant the switch had been thrown.

"All right, start her up again, but go slow."

After proceeding forward for several feet, the train took the switch track and veered to the right.

"Where are we going?" the engineer asked. "I ain't never left the main line."

"Slow down, way down," Travis said. "But don't stop."

"What's going on?" the engineer asked.

"Haven't you figured that out yet, Mr. Engineer? We're robbing your train," Travis said. "Slower, slower, slower."

The engineer complied with Travis's order until the train was barely moving. "Now stop," Travis said.

The train stopped, as it bumped up against the track guard at the end of the spur. It had been switched onto a siding that would allow cars to be backed up to a loading pen.

"Get out," Travis ordered. "Both of you."

"I'm not sure I can get down, what with my leg," the fireman said.

Travis pointed his gun to the other leg. "I can even it up for you if you want me to."

"No, no!" the fireman said. "I'll get down!"

"I thought you might see it my way."

Travis stayed in the cab until both the engineer and the fireman were on the ground. The engineer, thinking it was his opportunity to run, started to do so. Travis shot at him and the engineer went down.

Harley and Frank had come out from their place on the platform behind the tender. The conductor and several passengers were also coming alongside the train to see why it had stopped as abruptly as it did.

Harley turned toward them. "Get back on the train."

"See here, I'm the conductor. I want to know what's going on here?"

Harley shot the passenger who was coming with the conductor.

"Get back on the train and keep your passengers there," Harley said. "I'll kill the next person who sticks his head out."

Frightened, the conductor and the other passengers who had come out with him hurried to get back onto the train.

"You," Dinkins said to the fireman, who was staring down at the body of the engineer. "Come here."

The fireman limped over to him. "Ernie is dead."

"You're going to be dead too, if you don't do what I tell you to do," Dinkins said. "Tell the messenger to open the express car."

The fireman tapped on the door of the express car. "Miller," he called. "Miller, this is Jasper. Open the door."

"I ain't goin' to do it," a muffled voice replied from inside.

"Open the car or we'll blow it up!" Dinkins said.

"You go to hell!" the voice from inside replied.

Dinkins pulled a stick of dynamite from the bag he was going to put the money in, and wedged it into the door frame. The dynamite had a short fuse, and Dinkins gave a match to the fireman. "Light it."

"That fuse is too short, and I've got a shot leg," the fireman protested. "If I light that thing, I won't get away in time."

Dinkins pointed his rifle at the fireman. "At least you will have a chance to get away. If you don't light it, I'll blow your head off, right here."

Dinkins and the other robbers stepped back from the train several feet, but Dinkins kept his rifle aimed at the fireman. With shaking hands, the fireman struck the match, lit the fuse, then, as best he could, ran several paces away from the train before he threw himself on the ground.

The dynamite exploded, tearing off the door and opening a big hole in the side of the express car.

Inside the train, everyone heard the loud, stomach shaking explosion.

"Oh! What is it?" one woman called loudly. "What is happening?"

"Listen to me!" the conductor said, holding out his hands. "The train is being robbed!"

"Oh, my God! We'll all be killed!" another woman said. Some of the children began to cry.

"They don't want to kill us, they just want the money," the conductor said. "Hide most of your money, but keep a little on your person and if they come aboard, give 'em that."

"Why not hide it all?" one of the men passengers asked.

"If you hide all of it, they will know what you have done and like as not they'll start shooting. You have to keep a little so they won't suspect anything."

"Where can we hide it?" someone asked.

"Give it to me," a porter said. "They ain't goin' to be searchin' no colored man for money."

"Julius is right," the conductor said. "Give him all your money."

Quickly the men and women began taking out their money and handing it to the porter, who stuffed it into his voluminous pockets.

"How are you going to know who the money belongs to?" another man asked.

"Mister, I reckon we just all got to be honest," Julius said.

While all that was going on inside the passenger cars, outside the train the four robbers started shooting through the open door of the express car, even before all the smoke cleared. Then they rushed up to the car and while Dinkins and Harley stayed outside, Frank and Travis Slater climbed in to the car.

Two of the four kerosene lanterns had been extinguished by the blast, but two remained, though the thick billow of smoke made it impossible to see inside the car when they first entered. As the smoke drifted away, they saw Miller, the messenger, getting up on his hands and knees and shaking his head groggily.

"Open the safe," Travis ordered.

"There's not much in there," Miller said.

"You let us be the judge of that. Open the safe."

Miller got to his feet, then went over to the safe. "It looks damaged. I don't know if I will be able to get it open."

Travis pulled the hammer back on his pistol and the click as the sear engaged the cylinder was loud. "I think you will be able to open it."

Miller turned the combination lock, then swung the door open.

"Ha!" Travis said. "I knew you could open it if

you tried. Clean it out, Frank, while I keep him covered."

Frank reached into the safe, and started pulling out the contents. He found a money bag and, with a big grin, opened it. The grin disappeared. "Travis, there ain't nothin' here."

"What?"

"I mean there's some here. Don't look like it's much over a hunnert dollars though."

"Where's the rest of the money?"

"I'm just the messenger," Miller replied. "We don't ever know what's in these bags. This is what I was given when I came aboard this evening."

Travis stepped over to the open door of the car. "Hey, Dinkins. Ain't more'n a hunnert dollars here!"

"Are you sure?"

"You can come in and look for yourself," Travis said. "But there ain't no more than a hunnert dollars in the money pouch."

"Damn," Dinkins said. "All right, you and Frank stay with the messenger and the engineer. Wes and me will go through the train and see what we can take offen the passengers."

Dinkins and Harley boarded the first car, which was a sleeper car. They were met by a black porter.

"You gentlemen got no right to be wakin' up my passengers," the porter said.

"What's your name, darkie?"

"It ain't darkie," the porter bristled. "It's Julius."

"All right, Julius, I tell you what," Dinkins replied. "You come along with us, and we'll make this as easy as we can. You tell us which berths have women, and we won't be disturbin' them none."

They stopped at the first set of berths.

"There is only ladies in these berths," the porter said.

"All four of 'em? The two on each side?" Dinkins asked. "'Cause if I open one of these curtains you say has women, and I see a man, I won't ask no questions. I'll kill the man that's in the berth."

"These two has men," Julius said quickly.

"Well now, that's more like it."

Dinkins jerked open the curtain. "Let me have all your money," he said to the frightened man who was sleeping in the berth.

The man gave him eleven dollars.

"Eleven dollars? What did you do, hide the rest of it?"

"That's all I have," the man said.

"Hop down out of that berth," Dinkins said. "I'm goin' to look around and if I find so much as a nickel hid, I'm goin' to shoot you. Now, you want to give me the rest of the money?"

"Eleven dollars is all I have," the man repeated.

After the man hopped down, Dinkins searched under the mattress, but found nothing. "All right, you can get back in bed."

He took money from nine other men in the sleeping car; in every case the amount was disappointingly low. He searched one more berth without success.

When they reached the end of the car, the porter stopped.

"What are you stoppin' for?" Dinkins asked.

"This here is my car. I ain't supposed to leave it."

"You're comin' with us through the rest of the train." Stepping across the vestibule, Dinkins pushed the porter in first, and called, "Folks! We're goin' to be movin' through the car collectin' the fare." He laughed. "You may think you've already paid your fare, but this is what you might call an extry fare. Oh, and if anyone tries anythin' funny, I'm goin' to shoot this here darkie. You got that?"

The passengers, their faces varying in expressions from fear, to anger, even to a sense of excitement, all nodded in the affirmative.

"Julius, you hold the bag for us," Dinkins said, and as they proceeded through the cars, the porter held the bag open, passing it from passenger to passenger to get their donation.

"I don't believe this is all the money you have," Dinkins said when one man dropped a dollar bill into the bag.

"It's all I have on me," the man answered.

"I'm going to search you. And if I find any more money on you, I'll shoot you for lying to me."

The man stared at Dinkins without blinking and without a change of expression on his face.

Dinkins stuck his hand in every pocket, but came away empty.

After going through two cars and getting the slimmest of pickings, Dinkins spoke out again. "What the hell?" he said loudly. "How can you people travel with so little money?"

"This is all the money my mama gave me," one young girl, who was about fifteen, said.

"You travelin' alone, girl?" Dinkins asked.

"Yes, sir."

Dinkins smiled. "Well now, when you are an old woman with grandkids, you are goin' to be able to tell 'em that you was robbed by Bill Dinkins. Think about that."

Dinkins and Harley reached the rear of the train, then stepped onto the back platform with the porter still with them. Dinkins took the bag from the porter, then he and Harley stepped down on to the ground.

"Are you finished with us, Mr. Dinkins? Can I tell the conductor we can go on, now?" Julius asked.

"Get on back in there now, darkie, before I blow your head off," Dinkins said with a growl.

CHAPTER TWENTY-FIVE

Risco

Dinkins and the others came upon a large cottonwood tree standing just outside the town. Hanging from a limb was a corpse. His hands were tied behind his back and his head and neck were misshapen from the effect of the hanging. The corpse was twisting slowly at the end of the rope.

"Son of bitch!" Travis said. "What the hell is this? I didn't think there was any law in Risco."

Whoever hanged the man did not bother to put a hood over his face, leaving the grotesque visage of a violent death for all to see. The man's skin was black, though it did not appear that he had been a black man in life. His cheeks were puffed, his mouth was open, and flies were crawling in and out of it. The worst part about him was his eyes. They were bulging nearly out of their sockets.

"He sure is an ugly son of a bitch, ain't he?" Frank asked.

"Does anyone know who he is?" Dinkins asked.

"I don't know him," Travis replied. "But him bein' all black and puffed like he is, I don't think I would recognize him even if I did know him."

"He's got a sign pinned to his pant leg there," Dinkins said, pointing to a piece of paper.

Frank rode up to the hanging corpse, then, standing in the stirrups, reached up to pull off the sign.

"What does it say?" Travis asked.

Frank read it aloud. "This is the corpse of Frank Marlow. Do not assume that because we have no law in this town means we have no law. Mr. Marlow carved up and killed one our soiled doves, and for that, has paid the extreme penalty."

"Better pin the sign back on him," Dinkins said.

Frank did, then the four men rode on into Risco, stopping in front of the saloon.

Inside they got two bottles of blended whiskey, then found a table. When the whores they had stayed with before saw them, they came over to the table to join them. The dissipation of years on the line told in all four of them. There was not one who was in the least attractive, and none of them could have been able to make a living in their profession anywhere else but Risco.

The irony was that they were making more money than they had ever made before in their lives. But the money did them little good, since it cost so much to live in Risco.

"I see you boys are back." Wanda was the largest of the four, the one Dinkins had awakened with the last time he was in Risco. Because of that, she established a proprietary attitude toward him.

"You know why they're back, don't you, Wanda?" Emma said. Emma was running her hand through Travis's hair. "They fell in love with us, and they can't live without us."

The four women laughed at Emma's joke, but none of the men found it particularly funny.

"Go away," Harley said to the women.

"Oh, honey, you don't really want us to—" Wanda started to say, but that was as far as she got before Harley, without getting up from his chair, backhanded her. The sound of the slap was heard all over the saloon, and though Wanda gasped in shock and pain, she neither cried out, nor cried.

"I said go away," Harley repeated.

The four women left.

"You didn't have to do that, Wes," Travis said. "I kinda like havin' the women around."

Harley glared at Travis, but he said nothing.

"Of course, I reckon if we want the women, we can always ask 'em to come back," Travis said.

"We need to decide where we're goin' to go from here," Dinkins said.

"I hope you ain't got no more ideas about holdin' up another train," Frank said. "'Cause we sure didn't get much from the last one."

"Yeah," Travis said. "This was about as bad as the bank in Gothic was."

"You can't win 'em all," Dinkins said. "And we ain't done all that bad. We got six thousand dollars from the bank in Crystal, and another five thousand from the coach hold-up."

"So what do you have in mind next?" Travis asked.

"I figure we won't do anything for a while," Dinkins said. "We got some money, we'll just stay here until somethin' else comes up."

Sapinero

It was nearly ten o'clock, and the night creatures were calling to each other as Smoke stood looking toward Sapinero. The cloud passed over the moon and moved away, bathing in silver the little town that rose up like a ghost before him. The main street was fronted on both sides by buildings, more than half of which were dark. The biggest and most brightly lit building was the saloon at the far end of town.

Inside the saloon someone was playing a guitar, and Smoke could hear the music all the way out to the edge of town. The player was good, and the music spilled out in a steady beat with two or three poignant minor chords at the end of each phrase. An overall, single string melody worked its way in and out of the chords like a thread of gold woven through the finest cloth.

Between Delta and Sapinero, he had found ten of the DEAD OR ALIVE dodgers, which were posting a five thousand dollar reward on his head. He had destroyed every one of them, but he wondered if there were any reward posters in this town. Well, if there were, he would just have to deal with them.

Smoke passed by a coach sitting in front of the stage depot. The coach was dark and there was no team attached, but it had obviously moved into position to be able to leave town at first light. He heard a cat screech and a dog bark. A baby cried, and a woman's loud and angry voice cut through the night.

He rode on through the town, the only one out on the street at that hour, and the hollow-sounding clops of his horse's hooves echoed back loudly from the buildings that stood on either side of the street. He stopped in front of the saloon, then wrapped the reins around the hitching rail before stepping up onto the porch.

Two men came through the front door, laughing and talking as they continued the conversation they had started inside. In the lantern light that spilled out from the interior, Smoke studied them. He had no idea what Bill Dinkins looked like, and he only knew Wes Harley by description. "He's one of the ugliest men you'll ever see. His head looks just like a skull, with skin stretched over it," he had been told.

He knew what Travis and Frank Slater looked like, because he had studied their pictures. He studied the two men as they exited the saloon, their private conversation so intense they took no notice of Smoke.

"I'm Al Frakes," the gray-haired man said by way of introduction. "I publish the newspaper here. The banker is Ollie Lynch. Ollie is a messenger for Wells Fargo. And the gentleman who challenged you is Jim Saddler. He owns the leather goods and saddle shop, which I think is most appropriate for someone with the name Saddler."

"Who might you be?" Saddler asked.

"The name is Jensen. Kirby Jensen. But most folks just call me Smoke."

The three players looked at him in shock.

"You are Smoke Jensen?" Ollie asked.

"Yes."

Jim Saddler stuck his hand across the table. "It is an honor to meet you, Mr. Jensen. I hope you don't hold it against me that I asked if you had the means to play in this game."

"Not at all," Smoke said. "If I didn't have enough money to play, it would have been a friendly gesture."

Saddler was the dealer and on the first hand, Smoke drew two pair, which was enough to keep him in the game. He wasn't able to convert it into a full house though, and he lost to Frakes, who had drawn three tens.

Over the next half hour Smoke won some and lost some so that he stood at about ten dollars ahead in the game.

The conversation flowed easily, mostly about the game, but often coming back to an article that had been published in Al Frakes' newspaper about the train robbery.

"What article is that?" Smoke said.

"Well now, I just happen to have a copy of that newspaper with me," Frakes said. "It is, in my humble opinion, the best newspaper published between Denver and San Francisco."

"Your opinion isn't all that humble, when you figure that you are the publisher," Saddler said, and the others laughed.

Frakes gave Smoke the newspaper, then pointed out the article that appeared on the front page.

Bold Train Robbery Near Sapinero

BILL DINKINS GANG THE CULPRITS

It was lacking five minutes of eleven in the evening when one of the outlaws, believed to be Travis Slater, climbed over the tender and ordered engineer Ernest Gibson to slow the train. Complying with the request the train was slowed, then diverted to a side track where it was ultimately brought to a halt.

Engineer Gibson jumped down from the engine cab and attempted to escape, but was shot down and killed by Travis Slater. When conductor Martin Kraft and passenger Thad Wallace exited the train to see what was the reason for the unscheduled stop, passenger Wallace was shot and killed.

The robbers then dynamited the express car and ordered the messenger, Sy Miller, to open the safe, from which the robbers took one hundred and thirty-six dollars. They then proceeded to pass through the train, ordering the passengers to "give it up," but were able to gather less than two hundred dollars in that operation, making their entire haul for the robbery, just over three hundred dollars.

What the robbers did not know was that, when the train was stopped, Mr. Miller, anticipating a robbery, had opened the safe and removed a money shipment of twenty thousand dollars, hid same in the express car, then closed the safe again, fooling the robbers into believing the money they found was all the money that was being transferred.

They fared little better in robbing the passengers, for the quick thinking conductor convinced the passengers to entrust their funds with the Negro porter, Julius Jackson. Jackson, while pretending to help the robbers by carrying their loot bag from car to car was, unbeknownst to them, carrying over three thousand dollars of the passengers' money on his person.

The robbers were so bold as to make no effort to conceal their identity, and Bill Dinkins even suggested to Lydia Lane, a young, fifteen-year-old girl making the trip alone, that she could someday brag to her grandchildren that she was robbed by Bill Dinkins.

A mounted posse went in pursuit of the gang by the next morning, but they lost the trail and returned empty handed.

"I'll bet they were some mad when they found out the messenger had hidden the money shipment," Frakes said.

"Ha! And that the porter had hidden all the passengers' money," Saddler added.

"They ain't likely to find out," Ollie said. "Not where they are now. There's no newspapers."

"Where they are now?" Smoke said. "Why do you say that? Do you know where they are?"

"More'n likely they are in Risco," Ollie said.

"Risco?" Frakes asked.

"It's a little town on Cebella Creek, about halfway between here and Powderhorn," Ollie said.

"I've never heard of it," Frakes said.

"It's not on any map," Smoke said. "And that's by design. They don't want anybody to know they're there."

"Why, that beats all I've ever heard," Saddler said. "Why would a town not want anybody to know of its existence?"

"It's what some might call a Robbers' Roost," Smoke said. "Men who are running from the law go there, knowing there is little chance anyone from the law will trace them there."

"You know the town, Mr. Jensen?" Ollie asked, surprised by Smoke's response.

Smoke had visited the town once when he was on the dodge, going by the name of Buck West. "Yes, I know the town." He gave no further explanation.

"How is it that you know the town, Ollie?" Frakes asked.

"I wasn't always an agent for Wells Fargo. At one time in my life I was a different kind of agent."

"My God," Saddler said. "You mean you were a road agent?"

"I was nineteen," Ollie said. "And I fell in with the wrong crowd. I served two years, and I've been straight ever since."

"Does Wells Fargo know about this?" Frakes asked.

"They know." Ollie smiled. "That's why they let me handle their money, just as you men are doing in this card game."

The others laughed.

"I would like to ask you something, Ollie," Smoke said. "When you say you fell in with the wrong crowd, would that be Bill Dinkins?"

"I don't have anything to do with Dinkins anymore," Ollie said.

"What?" Saddler said. "Ollie, are you telling me that you were not only a road agent, but that you actually rode with Bill Dinkins?"

Ollie folded his cards and drummed his fingers on the table for a moment. "If you gentlemen would rather I not play cards with you anymore, I will understand. I don't want to cause any trouble."

"We aren't saying that, Ollie. We aren't saying that at all, are we, Jim?" Frakes asked the question pointedly, challenging Saddler.

"No, I, uh, didn't mean to imply anything like that."

"Mr. Lynch, I don't mean to be pushy or anything, but I have a personal interest in locating Bill Dinkins and the men who are riding with him," Smoke said.

"I know you do, Mr. Jensen. I doubt there is anyone in Colorado who doesn't know that Dinkins shot your wife. It's been in all the papers. How is she, by the way?"

"She has had a hard time of it. But she's doing quite well now."

"I figured she must be, or you wouldn't be huntin' for him. You would be back home with your wife."

"You think he might be in Risco, do you?"

"I can't be for sure, because I haven't seen him in over five years. But when I was ridin' with him, we used to spend quite a bit of time there."

"May I ask what was the attraction of such a place?" Frakes asked.

"Well, think about it, Al. What is the good of holding up a stagecoach, or robbing a bank, if you can't spend your money? And if you are a wanted man, you can't spend it in a town like a normal person would—you can't even go into a regular town without fear of bein' recognized.

"So, ever'one winds up in Risco at one time or another. Risco has restaurants, hotels, drugstores, general stores, saloons, gambling halls, and whore houses. In short, ever'thing a man might need.

Only thing is, ever'thing costs 'bout three or four times more there than it does anywhere else."

"Mr. Lynch, I thank you kindly for the information," Smoke said. "I just don't know why I hadn't thought of Risco myself."

"You'll be goin' there, will you, Mr. Jensen?" Lynch asked.

"Yes."

"Maybe you're goin' after Bill Dinkins, and I know why you are. But he ain't the one you got to worry about. The one you got to worry about is Wes Harley. I reckon you've heard of him."

"Yes, I have heard of him. Cole Parnell told me about him, before he was hanged. Parnell said he was Dinkins' brother."

"Yes sir, he is. They got the same ma, but their pa is different."

"I'm not looking for Harley. He isn't the one who shot Sally."

"That don't matter none. Like as not, he knows you are after them, so he'll be lookin' for you now. And here's the thing. He's like Dinkins, in that he would just as soon kill you, as look at you. What makes him different from Dinkins is that he is good at it."

"Thanks for the warning," Smoke said.

"It's not goin' to stop you from lookin' for him though, is it?" Ollie asked.

"Not for a minute." Smoke said.

"I didn't think so."

CHAPTER TWENTY-SIX

Risco

In the three days since the train robbery, Dinkins and his men had been living lavishly on the money they had taken from the bank in Crystal and from the stagecoach.

With the increased prices of everything in town, they were paying a dollar for a glass of beer and twenty-five dollars for a bottle of whiskey. The women were charging them fifty dollars, but as long as the men had the money, they spent it, unaware the high prices had been fixed for them alone.

They had gotten very little money from the train robbery, and the money they had taken from the bank and the stagecoach was diminishing rapidly as they spent it foolishly and gambled unwisely. As they saw the money going, their attitude toward the citizens of Risco became more and more belligerent.

Thus it was that James Webb had a talk with Bill Dinkins.

Risco had neither mayor nor sheriff, but even a city without law had to have some sort of leader, and James Webb had assumed that role. A graduate of Washington University in St. Louis, Webb had studied for the law and had been a circuit judge in Missouri when he was caught taking bribe money to affect the outcome of a major case.

The date for the trial was set and Webb, because he was an important and influential figure, was given bail. There was no doubt in his mind that he would be sent to prison, where he'd face many of the hardened criminals he'd sent there. He was convinced that he would not live a year in prison, so he jumped bail. Abandoning his wife and two children, he headed west, winding up in the lawless town of Risco.

"What do you want to talk about?" Dinkins asked.

"You, and the men with you," Webb replied. "You, Harley, and the Slater brothers are, well, to put it as delicately as I can, upsetting the equilibrium of our little town."

"I tell you the truth, Webb, I don't have an idea in hell what you just said," Dinkins said.

"All right, let me reword it. Our little community is unique. We have neither law nor governing structure, and we ask no questions about anyone's past. But, just because we have no law, does not mean you can behave any way you want while you are staying with us. No doubt, you noticed the corpse of the recently deceased Frank Marlow when you rode into town?"

"Yeah, it was kind of hard to miss."

"That's good. Mr. Marlow, you see, is an object lesson. We left him there as a reminder to others that there is a limit to our tolerance. He carved up and killed one of our whores. The rest of the town took umbrage with that."

"Yeah, well, what are you talking to me for? We ain't done nothin' like that."

"You have been, however, rather brutal with the ladies. And you have been belligerent to the ones who serve us here, the bartenders, the cooks, the clerks in our stores."

"They have been charging us too much," Dinkins said.

"I am sure you can understand there must be added costs to living here, and enjoying the freedom that we enjoy."

"So, what you're saying is you want us to be nicer to the hired help."

"I'm just giving you a few words of advice," Webb said. "You know, there are some people who don't want you here at all. You have a string of murders behind you that might attract enough lawmen here that we won't be able to discourage them."

"Wait a minute. Are you telling me that among the horse thieves, cattle rustlers, bank, coach, and train robbers here, there ain't none of them ever kilt anyone?"

"I am sure that quite a few of our citizens have killed," Webb replied. "But generally they have killed because they were forced to. With you and your men, it is almost as if you have killed for no other reason than the pleasure it gives you."

"Is that what you think?"

"It is, indeed. Oh, and one final thing, Mr. Dinkins. As a result of the string of killings you and your men have left behind, the reward money being offered now is fifteen hundred dollars for you, dead or alive. It is one thousand dollars for Mr. Harley, dead or alive, and five hundred dollars each for Frank and Travis Slater. That makes the four of you worth a total of thirty-five hundred dollars, and I must warn you, that sum is enough to tempt some of our citizens."

"What you are saying is we should leave town. That is what you are saying, ain't it?"

"Let us just say I am making a strong suggestion to that effect," Webb replied.

Smoke removed his U.S. deputy marshal's badge and put it in his saddlebag before he rode into town. It had been a long time since he was last in Risco, but as he rode down Outlaw Way, the main street of the little town, the years seemed to fall away. The town, inbred and festering, serviced by neither railroad nor stagecoach, had not changed. The purpose for which it existed meant it was better off remaining unheralded, unnoticed, and for the most part, unknown.

Looping Seven's reins around the hitching post in front of the saloon, Smoke loosened the pistol in his holster, then pushed through the swinging doors to step inside. To his amazement, the man tending bar was the same one who had been tending bar when he was there last.

He stepped up to the bar, and when the bartender moved toward him, Smoke greeted him with a smile. "Hello, Dixon. Are you still watering the whiskey?"

Dixon, who appeared to be in his mid-sixties, was confused for a moment, then his face reflected recognition. "Buck West." He smiled and stuck his hand across the bar. "I haven't seen you in so long, I thought you had gone straight. Actually, I hoped you had gone straight."

"So far I've managed to stay out of trouble," Smoke said. When he was on the vengeance trail, and on the dodge because of it, Buck West was the name he was known by during his stay in Risco.

Like many of the other tradesmen in town, Dixon was not a wanted man, and had never committed a criminal act other than the technical crime of harboring wanted fugitives. Since all he was doing was tending bar, Smoke doubted if he could have been charged with that.

Dixon drew a beer without being asked, then put it in front of him. "Well, if you ain't wanted, what are you doing here? Risco ain't the kind of place someone visits for pleasure."

"Maybe it's for old time's sake," Smoke replied. "You know, to see you, and a few other old friends?"

"I doubt there is anyone here now that was

here when you were, except for me. Most of the merchants make a killin' here, sell out, and move on. And most of our residents—well, to tell you the truth, Buck, they don't generally live that long. They wind up hung or shot. I'm surprised to see that you are still alive."

"Sometimes I'm surprised myself."

"I'll ask you again, what are you doing here?"

"I'm looking for some people. And I was sort of hoping I might find them here."

"Have you turned bounty hunter, West? Are you looking to cash in on the reward for someone? Because I can't help you, you know that. If I turned someone over to a bounty hunter, my life wouldn't be worth a wooden nickel."

"I'm not a bounty hunter, Dixon," Smoke said. "This is personal."

"Do you see that man sitting over there, reading?"

Smoke had seen him when he first came into the saloon. In fact, he had checked everyone out when he first came in, not only to see if he might recognize the Slater brothers, or Harley, but to make certain there was nobody who might recognize him.

"Yeah, I saw him when I came in."

"His name is Webb. He's a judge."

"A judge? Here?" Smoke asked, surprised by the pronouncement.

"Yeah, well, I didn't say he was an honest judge," Dixon said with a little chuckle. "But, he sort of runs things here, or at least, keeps things even.

Maybe you seen the corpse hangin' from the tree when you come into town."

"I did see it. Smelled it too."

"Yeah, some of the people are already complainin' about the smell. Anyway, Judge Webb is the one that held the trial and sentenced him to hang. So, if you got somethin' personal against someone here, I'd suggest you talk to the judge."

"All right, I will. Thanks," Smoke said. "Oh, what does the judge drink?"

"Whiskey. Blended," Dixon said.

"Pour me a shot."

Carrying his beer and a shot of whiskey, Smoke walked over to Webb's table. "May I join you for a few minutes, Your Honor?"

Webb looked up from his book. "Please do not call me Your Honor. There is no longer anything about me that is honorable."

"All right." Smoke put the glass of whiskey in front of Webb and, with a nod of thanks, Webb picked it up and tossed it down.

"Now, sir, what can I do for you? But I must tell you before we begin to talk, that as I am not a conventional outlaw—I do not steal or rob—my only source of income is the money I get by providing legal advice."

"I'm not asking for legal advice per se," Smoke said. "But I am perfectly willing to pay you for engaging in this conversation."

"Per se? My, one does not often hear language like that here. It is refreshing. Are you an educated man, sir?"

"My wife is a schoolteacher. She has done what she could to educate me."

"You are also married. I must say, you are an unusual specimen for this settlement. What can I do for you, Mister . . ." He left the word blank for Smoke to fill in.

"When I was in this town before, folks knew me as Buck West." Smoke nodded toward Dixon. "That is how Mr. Dixon addressed me a few moments ago. I'm going to tell you my real name, Judge, and in doing so, I am, in a manner of speaking, putting my life in your hands."

"Are you a lawman?" the judge asked.

Smoke shook his head. "Not by profession, though from time to time I have been deputized. My name is Smoke Jensen."

The judge was silent for a moment. "So you are the famous Smoke Jensen."

"Yes. And I'm here to—"

"You don't have to tell me why you are here, Mr. Jensen. I know why you are here."

"You do?"

"We may be isolated, but from time to time newspapers find their way here. I am aware that your wife was shot, either by Dinkins, or one of the men with him. I expect you are after them."

"Yes," Smoke said. "But not for any reward. My quest is a personal vendetta."

"And what do you want from me, Mr. Jensen? Do you want some legal action, similar to that which was dispensed to Frank Marlow?"

"Frank Marlow?"

"The gentleman hanging from the cottonwood tree."

"Not exactly."

"I see. You want to dispense your own justice, do you?"

"Yes. And what I want from you, Judge, is your permission. This is your town, and as long as I am in your town, I am willing to play by your rules."

"Interesting," Webb said. "All right, you have my permission. You do know, do you not, that Wes Harley is one of the men who is associated with Bill Dinkins?"

"I have heard that. But he had no hand in shooting my wife."

"That doesn't matter. I expect that you are not going to be able to get to Dinkins, without first going through Wes Harley. And I think you would find him to be quite a formidable adversary."

"I have never seen him, but I have heard him described," Smoke said. "Is he in this room now?"

"He is not. I believe he is visiting in one of the cribs out back."

"Thank you. I guess that means I'm going to have to take care of him first."

Smoke stood up then, and looked out over the men, and the few women, who were in the crowded saloon. Pulling his pistol, he shot it into the floor. The sound of the gunshot got everyone's attention, as he expected it to.

"Folks. I have a bone to pick with Wes Harley. I have reason to believe he is out back with"—he looked at one of the women, whose face reflected her fear, and smiled at her—"with a lady friend. If one of you would be so kind as to summon him, please tell him I will be waiting for him in the street out front."

Wanda watched as the tall, handsome cowboy pushed his way through the bat wing doors. She recognized him, having seen him once, several years ago. She knew if there was anyone in the country who could face up to Wes Harley, Buck West would be that man. And that, she would like to see.

She went out behind the saloon to Emma's crib, which was the second from the end, and knocked on the door.

"Who is it?" Emma called.

"Emma, honey, it's me. Wanda. Is Mr. Harley in there with you?"

A second later the door opened, and Harley stood there, wearing only his pants and boots. Wanda had never been with Harley and for a second, she was struck dumb seeing just how hairless his body was. Even though Emma had said, "*He doesn't even have hair around his pecker. You should see him. He is as hairless as a baby,*" she really wasn't prepared for what she was seeing.

"What is it?" Harley asked gruffly. "What do you want?"

"There is someone who wants to meet you in the street," Wanda said.

"What do you mean, meet me in the street?"

"I think he wants to have a gunfight with you."

To her surprise, Harley smiled. "Well now, a gunfight. Good. It was getting a little boring around here. Who is it?"

"I don't have any idea," Wanda lied.

CHAPTER TWENTY-SEVEN

Word had spread, not just through the saloon, but all through town, that someone had challenged Wes Harley to a gunfight in the street. The name of the man who had challenged him, Dixon informed the others, was Buck West, a long-ago resident of Risco.

"Why does this West fella want to go up agin' Harley for?" someone asked.

"I don't know. Maybe he just wants to make a name for himself. Whoever kills Wes Harley is goin' to be famous, that's for sure."

"No. What you mean is, whoever goes up agin' Wes Harley is goin' to be dead. And that's what's about to happen here. We're about to see this Buck West fella get hisself kilt by Wes Harley."

Outlaw Way was lined on both sides with spectators, as every resident of Risco had turned out to watch the gunfight.

Smoke was standing in front of the saloon. He

felt a little exposed. No doubt there were people in the crowd who had one reason or another to want him dead. But there was also an intense interest running through the crowd, the excitement of seeing a gunfight take place between two men who had far-reaching reputations as to their skills with a pistol.

"Here comes Harley!" someone shouted, and the excitement of the crowd grew more pronounced.

Someone had told Smoke that Wes Harley looked like a walking skeleton, and he thought that description was apt. Harley was a gangly-looking man, that was true, but it wasn't the fact that he was skinny, as much as that he was hairless, and his head really did look like a skull.

He walked into the middle of the street in front of the general store. He stood, not facing Smoke, but with his side to him, presenting much less of a target that way.

"Before I kill you, mister, you want to tell me who you are?" Harley asked.

"The name is Jensen. Smoke Jensen."

Smoke's name arced through the crowd, from man to man, like an electric spark jumping between the telegraph key and the sounder.

"Smoke Jensen!"

"Jensen!"

"If there is anyone who could face Harley even up, it would be Jensen."

"I hope he kills Harley. I haven't liked that son of a bitch since he got here."

"Hell, I wish they would just kill each other."

Laughter greeted the last comment.

"Folks! Folks, let me have your attention!" Judge Webb shouted, stepping into the street between Smoke and Harley. He held his arms up in the air. "Your attention, please!"

"You got our attention, Judge. Say whatever it is you are a'plannin' on sayin'," someone from the crowd called back.

"Mr. Jensen came to me a little while ago. He has assured me he is not here in pursuit of bounty, nor does he want to arrest anyone. Oddly enough, his fight is not with Harley, but with Dinkins, and Frank and Travis Slater, they being the men who shot his wife. But, I pointed out that I do not think he can get to them without going through Mr. Harley, thus bringing about the confrontation we are all about to witness.

"I'm going to say now that if anyone in the crowd violates the integrity of this duel, I will see to it that you join Mr. Marlow in hanging from the tree."

"So," Harley said. "You are the famous Mr. Smoke Jensen. Yes, sir, killing you is going to be quite a feather in my cap."

Smoke said nothing.

"You have nothing to say to me, Mr. Jensen?" Harley came down hard on the word *mister*.

"I'm not here to have a conversation with you, Harley. I'm here to kill you," Smoke said calmly.

Because of the way Harley was standing,

presenting his left side to Smoke, his gun hand was hidden. Smoke couldn't be sure when Harley started his draw. When he saw Harley twist around toward him, he realized Harley had already pulled his gun, getting it out stealthily as they were talking.

Harley fired even as Smoke was drawing, but the bullet missed, flying past his ear with a loud pop. Smoke returned fire and didn't miss.

Harley went down on his back, his arms extended on either side, his gun sliding out several inches from his hand.

Smoke held the smoking pistol in his hand for a moment longer. When he was convinced Wes Harley was dead, he holstered his pistol.

Several of the crowd gathered around Harley, looking down at him with morbid curiosity, thus leaving Smoke standing alone, several feet away.

"Mr. Jensen?" The woman who called out to him was short, fat, and aging.

"Yes?"

"You don't remember me, Mr. Jensen, but my name is Wanda. I met you once many years ago when you were playing cards in a saloon where I was working."

Smoke smiled, and touched the brim of his hat. "Well, it's nice to see you again, Wanda."

"Thank you, but I'm not trying to call back old memories or anything. I understand you are looking for Dinkins and his men?"

"Yes, I am. Do you know where they are?"

"They rode out of town about fifteen minutes ago, soon as they heard your name."

It wasn't hard to pick up the trail of three horses moving quickly. Smoke was too far back, and they were moving too fast for him to catch a glimpse of them, but he didn't need to see them to know where they were going. The trail was leading into a canyon. Black Canyon.

One of the steepest, darkest, and most rugged of all canyons, Black Canyon was formed by the Gunnison River as it flowed through hard ancient rocks at the western edge of the Rocky Mountains on its way to joining the Colorado River at Grand Junction. Smoke had been there before. He knew the canyon walls, composed of volcanic schist, were predominantly black in color, and because the gorge reached a depth of over 2,000 feet and because it was no more than 1,500 feet across, the walls seldom received any direct sunlight. For that reason it was called Black Canyon.

Smoke was a little leery as he approached the canyon. He knew it would be an ideal place for the outlaws to set up an ambush. He stopped for a moment and listened hard, trying to hear anything from ahead . . . the whicker of a horse, a voice, even the scratch of iron-shod hooves on stone. If there had been any sound, it should have carried to him quite easily, as the canyon walls had the effect of a megaphone.

But, listen though he did, he could hear nothing.

He reached down and patted his horse on the neck. "What do you think, Seven? You up to going in there?"

Seven whickered, as if he understood what Smoke was saying. The horse was exceptionally intelligent with an innate awareness of things. Smoke knew that Seven sensed danger, but he also knew the horse wouldn't falter.

Smoke took a deep breath and pulled his rifle from the saddle sheath, then started into the canyon. He hadn't ridden more than one hundred yards into the canyon before Seven stopped.

"I know, boy, I feel it too." Smoke neither heard nor saw anything. But, in that sixth sense developed by men who constantly live on the edge of danger, he felt something. Suddenly a bullet whizzed by not six inches in front of his face. It hit a big rock on the other side of the trail, then whined off into space, while the canyon reverberated with the flat crack and high-pitched scream of the missed rifle shot.

With his rifle in his hand, Smoke slid down quickly. "Get back, Seven."

As the horse whirled around and galloped out of the canyon, Smoke ran toward a nearby line of large rocks, diving for cover just as another shot rang out. Like the first one, it was so close he could hear the bullet passing.

"Jensen, is that you?" a voice called from a

position partway up the canyon wall. "Did you kill my brother?"

Like the rifle shots before, the last word echoed back and forth through the canyon.

Brother . . . brother . . . brother . . .

"If Wes Harley was your brother, I killed him."

Killed him . . . killed him . . . killed him . . .

As soon as he shouted, Smoke rolled to his right to deny them a target. As it turned out, it was the right thing to do. A bullet kicked up sand and pebble at the exact spot where he had been but a second earlier.

Moving to the end of the row of rocks, he studied the canyon wall on the opposite side. He was on one side of the trail and they were on the other. There was no way he could cross the open space unseen.

"We didn't know the woman we shot was your wife!" the voice yelled.

Wife . . . wife . . . wife . . .

"Besides, she ain't kilt!"

Kilt . . . kilt . . . kilt . . .

"No thanks to you," Smoke shouted.

You . . . you . . . you . . .

He rolled to his left and coming out of the roll, had the rifle to his shoulder, looking out across the barrel at the canyon wall toward the sound of the outlaw's voice. He saw the puff of smoke from the outlaw's rifle, then saw the outlaw raise up slightly to have a look. He only stayed up for a second, but that was all Smoke needed. He squeezed the trigger. The Winchester roared and kicked back against his shoulder. A second later the outlaw tumbled down the wall on the other side of the canyon.

"Frank! Frank!" a frightened voice called. "Dinkins, he got my brother! He got Frank!"

Frank . . . Frank . . . Frank . . .

"Yeah? Well, he shoulda kept his head down," Dinkins replied.

"We shouldn't have come into this canyon," Travis said. "We ain't got no way out!"

Out . . . out . . . out . . .

"Travis is right, Dinkins," Smoke called up to him. "You boys are in trouble. You have no way out of here, without coming through me."

Me . . . me . . . me . . .

"Seems to me you're the one in trouble. We got you trapped down there," Dinkins replied.

"Uh-uh," Smoke said. "I've got my water and food with me. I'll just bet you fellas left yours with your horses."

"He's right, Dinkins! We ain't got no water or nothin' up here."

"Shut up, Travis. Don't be such a yellow belly! See if you can get a look at where he's at."

"Uh-uh, I ain't movin' from here and I ain't stickin' my head up, neither," Travis replied. "I seen what happened to Frank. Jensen kilt my brother."

"Well he kilt my brother, too."

"The difference is, you run out on your brother,"

Travis said. "Me 'n Frank didn't run out on each other."

Dinkins began firing wild and unaimed shots, which gave Smoke a chance to improve his own position without fear of being hit. Crouching over, he ran behind the line of rocks, then darted across the little open gap so he was on the same side of the trail as the outlaws.

"Did you get him?" Travis called.

From the sound of Travis's voice, Smoke knew he was no more than fifty or sixty yards away. He began looking around for a way up to him.

"I don't think so," Dinkins called back. Clearly, Dinkins was farther back in the canyon.

"You musta got him. I don't see him or hear him movin' around down there. I think you got him," Travis said.

Smoke smiled at their confusion.

"Shoot again," Travis called.

"You shoot," Dinkins replied. "I'll keep an eye open and if he returns your fire, I'll have him."

"I ain't got nothin' to shoot at. He's like a ghost or somethin'."

"Take a look, Travis, see if you can see him!" Dinkins called out again.

"I ain't movin'," Travis said again.

"Shoot at him, you sonofabitch, or I'll shoot at you," Dinkins said angrily.

Smoke saw Travis lift his head up. Unlike the others who had rifles, Travis was armed only with a pistol. He began shooting, wild, unaimed shots at the rocks on the other side of the canyon where Smoke had been earlier. The bullets hit the rocks then careened off, screaming long, descending wails that echoed and reechoed and reechoed through the canyon.

"Do you see him?" Dinkins shouted.

Him . . . him . . . him . . .

"No!"

No . . . no . . . no . . .

Smoke managed to climb up a fissure until he was just a few feet away. He waited until the hammer on Travis's gun fell on an empty chamber.

"All right, I shot at him," Travis called. "Now it's your time to shoot at him. I'm out of bullets! I have to reload!"

"You dumb bastard, you didn't do nothin' but waste your bullets," Dinkins replied.

Smoke stepped out in front of Travis at that moment.

"No!" Travis screamed. He raised his pistol and pointed it at Smoke, snapping the trigger even though his gun was empty.

Smoke took him down with a vertical butt stroke of his rifle.

"Travis! Travis, what's goin' on over there? What were you yellin' about?"

Smoke remained quiet.

"Travis, what is it? Answer me!"

"He can't answer you, Dinkins," Smoke said.

"What? What are you talking about? Where are you? Where is Travis?"

Smoke looked down at Travis and could tell by the twist in his neck, and his open, but sightless eyes, still fixed in his last instant of terror, that Travis was dead.

"Where is Travis?" Dinkins called again.

"He's dead," Smoke answered. "He's dead, Frank is dead, and Wes Harley is dead. Now there is only you."

"I give up!" Dinkins said. "Don't shoot, I'm comin' down. I give up! Do you hear me?"

"I hear you," Smoke said. "Come on out here with your hands high."

Dinkins came walking down a path that led up to a higher ridge. His hands were up as Smoke had ordered, but he was holding a rifle in his right hand.

Smoke noticed that, though Dinkins was holding the rifle over his head, his hand was wrapped around the narrow part of the stock and the receiver, his finger was inside the trigger guard, and actually on the trigger itself. Smoke also noticed that the hammer was cocked.

"Throw down the rifle," he ordered.

Dinkins looked up at his rifle, then back toward Smoke, and smiled. "Ahh, no foolin' the great Smoke Jensen is there? You seen the rifle cocked. Well, you can't blame me for tryin', can you?"

"Throw it down," Smoke ordered.

Dinkins pulled the trigger, firing the rifle.

Though as it was over his head and aimed to one side, it represented no danger to Smoke.

"That was just to keep it from goin' off when it hits the ground. Wouldn't want that to happen now, would we? It might have gone off on me. Or you." Dinkins chuckled, then tossed the rifle aside.

"Tell me, Jensen, do you know any good lawyers?" he asked. "Whoever it is, I hope it ain't the same one that defended Parnell. Poor old Parnell got hisself hung. But I'm sure you know that."

All the time Dinkins was talking to Smoke, he was going down the path—an easy walk sometimes. Other times, where the path made a steep drop, or in some other way made its transit difficult, Dinkins put one or two hands on a rock to help him negotiate the obstacle.

When Dinkins was no more than thirty feet from Smoke the path stepped down about three feet. It was too far to step directly down, but a rock outcropping provided Dinkins with some leverage when he put his hand on it. He stepped down with some difficulty.

Smoke had been watching him descend, almost lulled into the slow, laborious operation, when all of a sudden a pistol appeared in Dinkins' hand.

Dinkins wasn't wearing a holster. That was one of the first things Smoke had checked. So, where did the pistol come from?

That wasn't a thought Smoke dwelled on for more than a split second, for a split second is all the time he had to respond. He fired, his bullet hitting Dinkins in the middle of his chest.

Dinkins fell headfirst down the drop, his head hitting the stone ground below. He flipped over on his back, then stared up through open, but sightless eyes.

CHAPTER TWENTY-EIGHT

Sugarloaf Ranch

"There's no need for you to go into town, Miss Sally," Cal said. "Whatever you need, I'll get for you."

"What if I told you I want to go to Amy's Ladies' Shop to buy a new camisole?" Sally said. "Would you buy that for me?"

"Well, I, uh, I mean if you told me what kind, uh, I could, uh . . ." Cal blushed profusely as he tried to respond to Sally's question.

She laughed. "See, you can't get whatever it is I might need. I have to do it myself."

"But I don't think you should be ridin' yet. It ain't been, I mean, it hasn't been that long since you got shot."

"Nonsense, the wound is completely healed and I feel fine. Smoke has been through this a dozen times. So have you and Pearlie. Besides, I'm getting cabin fever. I have to get out of the house."

"Yes ma'am, well, I reckon I can understand that all right. I can ride along with you."

"For heaven's sake, Cal, are you saying there isn't enough to keep you busy here at the ranch?"

"Well, yes, ma'am, I reckon there is, it's just . . ."

"It's just nothing," Sally said. "Don't worry about me. I will be all right. Nothing is going to happen."

"Yes, ma'am. Well, I'll hitch up the buckboard. Or would you rather take the surrey?"

"Neither," Sally said. "I'm going to ride. You can saddle my horse if you would like."

"But don't you think it would be better if—"

Whatever question Cal was going to ask was cut off by a direct stare from Sally.

"Yes, ma'am. I'll get your horse saddled."

"Cal, saddle the filly."

"Yes, ma'am. I know you have a particular like for that horse."

As Sally rode into town, she felt an exhilarating sense of freedom. For the first time since she had been shot, she felt like her old self and, in her enthusiasm, she urged her horse into a gallop. Leaning down over the horse's neck, she galloped at full speed for at least a quarter mile, enjoying the wind in her face and hair.

Finally she stopped the gallop and allowed the horse to continue at a gait needed to cool her down. She patted the horse's neck, and spoke soothingly. "Good girl. Smoke won't race us, because I think he is afraid you could beat Seven. I don't just think, I know you could beat him. But, between us girls, there's no need to be showing up the men now, is there? Sometimes we just have to grin and bear it."

Big Rock

Jericho Taggart was sitting in the Brown Dirt Cowboy nursing a beer. He knew this was where Smoke lived. All he had to do was hang around town until he showed up.

"Well, look there," one of the saloon patrons said, pointing through the front window. "That's Mrs. Jensen riding down the street just as sassy as you please. She sure don't look none the worse for bein' shot now, does she?"

A couple others moved to the front to watch as Sally rode by.

"That's Smoke Jensen's wife, is it?" Taggart asked.

"Yes. Oh, you was askin' about him, wasn't you? Well sir, if you was to go ask Mrs. Jensen, I'll bet she could tell you where he is, and when he is gettin' home."

"Where is Jensen, anyhow?" one of the others asked. "I ain't seen him around in more'n a month. 'Course, this here ain't the saloon he comes to. I reckon he's too high tone for it."

"Not a bit of it," the bartender said. "Smoke Jensen is as fine a man as there is anywhere in this world. He don't come in here 'cause he and Longmont are just real close friends."

"Yeah, but he ain't even been down there in a month of Sundays."

"He's been on the trail of them that shot his wife," the bartender said. "He'll be back when he has them all took care of."

"*If* he takes care of all of 'em."

"When," the bartender insisted.

Taggart finished his beer, then walked to the livery stable where he rented two saddle horses, complete with saddles and gear. After that, he left town going in the direction of Sugarloaf Ranch, riding one horse and leading the other.

Somewhere between Big Rock and Sugarloaf

Sally was on her way back to the ranch, her purchases for the day in a bag hanging from the saddle horn. She was about halfway home when she heard a loud bang. To her shock and horror, her horse's head seemed to explode in front of her, as blood, bone, and brain matter burst out.

The horse fell. It happened so fast Sally was barely able to get her leg out from under her. In doing so, she was out of position, and her head hit the ground hard.

Everything went black.

Sally was aware that she was sitting in the saddle of a horse being led by another rider who was in front of her. Almost at the same moment, she realized that her hands were tied together, and her ankles were tied to the stirrups. She was confused as to why and how she had gotten there.

Then she remembered hearing a shot, and seeing her horse's head explode in front of her. How long ago was that?

She was able to lift her hands and found her watch, still pinned to the bodice of her dress. Pulling it out, she examined it. It was five minutes after eleven. It was ten o'clock when she left town to start back home, and it couldn't have been more than fifteen minutes later when she was ambushed on the road.

How long had she been on this horse? She could not remember a thing beyond her horse being shot, but she must have been conscious. Unless the man in front of her put her on the horse while she was unconscious. She had no memory of any of that.

"Who are you?" she called to the rider. "Where are we going?"

The rider stopped, then looked back at her. "Oh, so you are not too high and mighty to talk to me now, are you? I've been trying to get you to say something for the last hour."

"I-I don't remember anything about the last hour," Sally said. "Why am I tied up? What do you want with me?"

"Oh, I don't want you for anything," the rider said. "It's your husband I want."

"What is your name?"

"My name is Taggart. Jericho Taggart."

"Why do you want my husband, Mr. Taggart?"

"Because he is worth five thousand dollars, dead or alive."

"That's ridiculous! My husband isn't a wanted man. He is an outstanding, law-abiding citizen."

"Someone wants him," Taggart said. "And they are willing to pay five thousand dollars for him."

"Well, if you want him, why have you taken me?"

"He will be coming for you, won't he?"

"You better believe he will."

"That's what I'm counting on," Taggart said.

Big Rock

Smoke was at the depot, waiting for Seven to be off-loaded from the stock car, when Sheriff Carson saw him.

"Smoke, welcome home!" Carson smiled broadly, extending his hand.

"Hello, Monte." Smoke took the deputy U.S. marshal's badge from his pocket, and handed it to the sheriff. "I won't be needing this anymore."

"I take it your quest came out to your satisfaction?"

"Let's just say that Dinkins and his gang will rob no more banks, and shoot no more women."

"Oh, that reminds me. Sally is in town."

"To see the doctor? Is something wrong?"

"No, no, didn't mean to cause you any worry. She is looking fine. She rode in herself. Told me she was doing a little shopping, and had never felt better."

"Where is she now, do you know?"

"I don't have any idea, to be honest. It's been a little over an hour since I saw her," Sheriff Carson said.

"Good. I hope she is still in town. We can ride home together."

Mounting Seven, Smoke rode up and down the main street, looking for Sally's horse. When he didn't see it anywhere, he stepped into Amy's Ladies' Shop. He knew Sally never came to town without stopping there. Even if she didn't buy anything, she would stop to visit with Amy.

"Hello, Smoke."

"Hi, Amy. Have you seen Sally today?"

"She was in here about an hour ago, but she said she was going home next."

"All right, thanks. I guess I'll catch up with her there."

Somewhere between Big Rock and Sugarloaf

Four miles out of town, Smoke saw several buzzards circling. In order to attract that many buzzards, he knew there had to be something dead, and bigger than a rabbit, or even a coyote. He urged Seven into a gallop and a moment later, saw a horse down.

It was Sally's horse!

When he reached the horse, he jumped down from the saddle. Sally was nowhere to be seen, and his first thought was that she had walked on home. But the bag of her purchases was still attached to the saddle horn, and he knew she wouldn't have left . . . oh my God! What happened to the horse?

The horse's head was laid open like a smashed watermelon. That was no accident!

As Smoke examined the dirt road around the horse, he saw footprints coming from the side of the road to the horse, then going back to the side of the road from the horse. The footprints were made by a man's boot. He saw no sign of Sally.

Following the direction of the footprints, Smoke saw the print of two horses. And he saw something else—the empty cartridge of a .50 caliber bullet.

What happened to Sally's horse was no longer a mystery. Someone had waited until Sally came along, then killed Sally's horse. The fact that he didn't kill Sally meant she wasn't his principal target. Whoever it was, was after Smoke, and he was using Sally as bait.

"All right, Mr. Bushwhacker," Smoke said aloud. "I'm going to take the bait, so you better be ready for me, 'cause I'm damn sure ready for you."

Ahead of Smoke the brown land lay in empty folds of rocks, dirt, and sage. Smoke picked up the tracks of two riders, but the ground was hard and the tracks so indistinct he couldn't tell very much about them. He couldn't be sure Sally was one of the riders, but it was the best he had to go on. He saw a piece of green calico hanging on some sage, and knew he was on the right track. It also told him that she was all right.

"Good girl, Sally." He pulled the cloth off the branch and stuck it in his pocket.

Fifteen minutes after he found the first bit of cloth he found another. It not only told him he was still on the right trail, it saved his life. The second piece of cloth was lying on the ground and he got off his horse to pick it up. Just as he was dismounting, a rifle boomed and the heavy ball whistled by, taking his hat off and fluffing his hair. The bullet hit a rock and knocked a huge chunk out of it.

That had to be a .50 caliber bullet, meaning he had found the man he was looking for. Or, the man had found him. If that bullet had hit him, it would have taken off the top of his head and he would be as dead as Sally's horse.

Moving quickly, Smoke slapped Seven's flank to get him out of the line of fire, then dived for a nearby rock just as a second shot whizzed by. Again, the bullet was so heavy that even though it missed him, he could feel the concussion from the shock wave.

Smoke wriggled his body under cover, then raised himself slowly to take a look around. He saw the crown of a hat poking over the top of a rock so he aimed and shot. The hat went sailing away.

"You're pretty good with that little pea shooter, Jensen," the shooter called out to him. "But face it, you don't have a chance against my Sharps fifty."

"Who the hell are you?" Smoke asked.

"The name is Taggart. Jericho Taggart. I reckon you've heard of me."

"I reckon not," Smoke replied. "Is Sally with you?"

"Yeah, she's with me."

"Sally! Sally, are you there?"

"She can't answer you, Jensen. I've got a gag stuffed in her mouth."

"Taggart, if you are after the five thousand dollar reward, maybe you should know there is no such thing. I'm not wanted. That's a poster Bill Dinkins put out."

"Whether Dinkins pays the reward or the sheriff does, makes no difference to me," Taggart replied.

"Dinkins can't pay the reward. He's dead."

"You killed him, I suppose?"

"I killed him, his half brother Wes Harley, and the two Slater brothers," Smoke said.

"My, you have been a busy man, haven't you, Jensen?"

"Since that dodger was put out by Dinkins, and not by the sheriff of La Plata County, and Dinkins is dead, there's no money for you in killing me."

Taggart fired again and the bullet was as close as the first one. It hit the rock right in front of Smoke and kicked pea-sized chunks of rock into his face, opening up wounds. The impact was so great that, for a moment Smoke thought he had been hit. But he knew that couldn't be right. If he had actually been hit, he would be dead. Smoke turned around and slid to the ground.

Taggart laughed. "This fifty will chew up some rock, won't it?"

"What are you still shooting for? I told you, there's no money in it."

"Well, let's just say once it gets out that I'm the one who killed the famous Smoke Jensen, I'll find a way to turn it into money," Taggart said.

Again, the .50 boomed, the shot sounding like thunder.

"I want to hear Sally's voice," Smoke said.

"Do you, now?"

"Let me hear her say something."

"Don't worry about her. After I kill you, I'll let her go."

"Do you think killing me with a fifty caliber rifle from fifty yards away is going to make you famous?" Smoke taunted.

"I don't know," Taggart replied. "Maybe you have a point. Folks do say that you are as fast as greased lightning with that gun of yours. Is that right?"

"You want to try me?"

"Do I want to try you?" Taggart laughed. "No, that would be foolish now, wouldn't it? I like to do my killin' with a Sharps fifty. This isn't exactly the kind of gun you use in fighting a duel."

"I see. Tell me, Taggart, have most of your kills been from half a mile away? Have you ever had the courage to face a man down, and look him in the eyes? At least Harley was man enough to do that."

"That's the way it is."

"That's the coward's way," Smoke said.

"You can call me whatever you want, Mr. Jensen. But the truth is, I've got your woman, and the only way you are going to get her back, is to come through me."

Smoke raised up just a bit and Taggart fired again. But the sound was sharper, higher, less explosive than the other. The bullet hit the rock in front of him, then careened off with a high pitched skirling sound.

"Oh, yeah, maybe I should have told you," Taggart called across the gap separating them. "My fifty is a single shot. So, just to keep me safe between shots, I also have a Winchester."

"You have it all figured out, don't you, Taggart?"

"I have to. Killin' folks is my profession."

"You sound as if you are proud of that."

"How about you? I'll bet if truth were known, you've killed more people than I have," Taggart replied.

"It's not something I take pride in." Smoke moved around, trying to get into position to see his assailant.

"I tell you what, Jensen. What do you say me 'n you meet each other out in the open? You with your pistol, me with my Winchester. You got the guts to try that?"

"What?" Smoke asked, surprised by the challenge.

"Let me get this straight. You're offering to go up against me?"

"Yeah. I'm a sportin' man. Step out now, with your pistol in your holster. I'll step out with my Winchester, and we'll go agin' each other. To make it more even, I'll toss my Sharps out on the ground."

Smoke looked around the rock and saw Taggart hold the big buffalo rifle up, then toss it.

"There, see, I wasn't lyin' to you. There's my fifty, lyin' on the ground. Come on out, now."

Smoke hesitated.

"Ah," Taggart said. "I understand. You are afraid that if you come out, I'll shoot you, right? Just to make you feel better, I'll come out first."

Smoke raised up again to take a look, and saw Taggart, coming out from behind the rock. Then he saw Taggart reach back and pull Sally out from behind the rock. She was gagged, and her wrists were bound together. Her ankles were tied together with a short piece of rope that would let her shuffle, but not walk, and certainly would not let her run.

"All right, Mr. Jensen, as you can see, I'm already out here."

Smoke holstered his own pistol, then stepped out from behind the rock. "Well, I'll be damned. I didn't really think you'd do it."

"Well, I'm a surprising man." Taggart grinned evilly. "But I am not a dumb man." He reached for Sally and pulled her over to stand in front of him.

"Now, let's see if you are good enough to hit

me, without hitting your wife." Taggart laughed. "Interesting challenge, isn't it?"

Smoke looked into Sally's eyes and saw, not fear, but determination. She was trying to tell him something, but what? She blinked a couple of times and stared pointedly, and all of a sudden he realized what she was saying. Smoke smiled at her, and she smiled back.

"Anytime, Mr. Jensen," Taggart said.

"Now!" Smoke shouted.

Sally threw herself to the ground. Her sudden, and unexpected move not only exposed Taggart, it surprised him into a split second of indecision.

That split second was all Smoke needed. He drew and cocked his gun at the same time, then fired. The bullet slammed into Taggart's chest, severing arteries and plowing through one of his lungs. Taggart dropped his rifle and fell to the ground.

Smoke stood quietly as the echo of his shot came rolling back from a nearby rock wall. When the last echo was a subdued rumble off a distant hill, the silence returned. The leaves of a nearby aspen rustled. A distant eagle shrieked. A rabbit scurried under a clump of sagebrush.

Smoke saw Sally trying to get back up and hurried over to her. He lifted her up, then removed the gag. Not only had Taggart bound a cloth around her mouth, he had also stuck a sock in it. She reached up with her bound wrists and pulled the sock out, then coughed and gasped for air.

"Ohhh, that was awful! I don't think that sock has ever been washed." She began spitting.

"If you'll stop spitting, I'll kiss you." Smoke smiled at her.

"You'll taste sock," Sally warned.

"No, I'll taste only you."

They kissed, then Sally held up her hands. "Untie my wrists. I can't kiss properly with my hands tied."

Smoke laughed, but he untied her hands. "What makes you think you need your hands to kiss?"

"So I can do this." She leaned into him, put her arms around him and her hands on the back of his head to pull him closer.

They kissed deeply, then all of a sudden Sally stiffened and pulled away from him. Smoke looked at her in surprise, but before he could say anything, she pulled his pistol from his holster. He whirled around then and saw that Taggart had sat up and cocked his Winchester.

Sally fired four times, the shots coming so close together it sounded almost like one sustained roar.

Taggart fell back with one bullet hole in his forehead, one in each cheek, and one in his chin.

The gunshots echoed and reechoed back from the mountain walls, as Sally stood there, holding the pistol in her hand, staring down at Taggart's body.

She continued to stare as Smoke got down on his knees long enough to untie the rope that had her ankles bound together. Then he stood up and took his pistol from her hand. Because it was empty, he opened the cylinder gate, poked out all the spent cartridges, then reloaded.

Sally had not spoken one word since she killed Taggart.

"What do you say we go home?" Smoke suggested.

"What about him?" Sally pointed to Taggart's body.

"Leave him for the critters."

TURN THE PAGE
FOR AN EXCITING PREVIEW OF

A LONE STAR CHRISTMAS
by William W. Johnstone
with J. A. Johnstone

**SMOKE JENSEN. MATT JENSEN. FALCON
AND DUFF MACCALLISTER—TOGETHER
FOR THE FIRST TIME**

**They just wanted to get home for Christmas . . .
but fate had other plans.**

The year is 1890. A Texas rancher named Big Jim
Conyers has a deal with a Scottish-born, Wyoming
cattleman named Duff MacCallister. Along with
Smoke and Matt Jensen, the party bears down on
Dodge City, Kansas, to make a cattle drive back to
Fort Worth. Soon the drive turns into a deadly
pursuit, then a staggering series of clashes with
bloodthirsty Indians and trigger-happy rustlers.
And the worst is yet to come—the party rides into
a devastating blizzard, a storm so fierce their very
survival is at stake.

From America's greatest Western author, here is an
epic tale of the unforgiving American frontier
and how, amidst fierce storms of man and nature,
miracles can still happen.

CHAPTER ONE

Marshall, Texas, March 12, 1890

It was cold outside, but in the depot waiting room, a wood-burning, potbellied stove roared and popped, glowing red as it pumped out enough heat to make the room comfortable, if one chose the right place to sit. Too close and it was too hot, too far away and it was too cold.

Two weeks earlier, Benjamin Conyers, better known as Big Ben, had taken his twenty-one-year-old daughter Rebecca into Fort Worth to catch the train to visit with his sister in Marshall. It was time for Rebecca to return home, and her aunt Mildred had come to the depot with her to see her off on the evening train.

Everyone agreed that Rebecca Conyers was a beautiful young woman. She had delicate facial bones and a full mouth. She was slender, with long, rich, glowing auburn hair, green eyes, and a slim waist. She was sitting on a bench in the Marshall depot, the wood polished smooth by the many passengers who had sat in the same place over the last several years. Just outside the depot window, she could see the green glowing lamp of the electric railroad signal.

"Rebecca, I have so enjoyed your visit," Mildred said. "You simply must come again, sometime soon."

"I would love to. I enjoyed the visit as well."

"I wish Ben would come with you some time. But I know he is busy."

"Yes. Pa always seems to be busy."

"Well, he is an important man. And important men always seem to be busy." Mildred laughed. "I don't know if he is busy because he is important, or he is important because he is busy. I imagine it is a little of both."

"Yes, I would think so as well." Rebecca turned to her aunt. "Aunt Mildred, did you know my mother?"

"Julia? Of course I know her, dear. Why would you ask such a thing?"

"I don't mean Julia," Rebecca said. "I mean my real mother. I think her name is Janie."

Mildred was quiet for a long moment. "Heavens, child, why would you ask such a thing now? The only mother you have ever known is Julia."

"I know, and she is my mother in every way," Rebecca said. "But I know, too, that she isn't my birth mother, and I would like to know something more about her."

Mildred sighed. "Well, I guess that is understandable."

"Did you know her? Do you remember her?"

"I do remember her, yes. I know that when Ben learned that she was pregnant, he brought her out to the house. You were born right there, on the ranch."

"Pa is my real father though, isn't he? I mean he is the one who got my real mother pregnant."

"Oh yes, there was never any question about that," Mildred replied.

"And yet he never married my mother," Rebecca said.

"Honey, don't blame Ben for that. He planned to marry her, but shortly after you were born Janie ran off."

"Janie was my birth mother?"

"Yes."

"What was her last name?"

"Garner, I believe it was. Yes, her name was Janie Garner. But, like I said, she ran off and left you behind. That's when Ben wrote and asked me to come take care of you until he could find someone else to do it."

"That's when Mama, that is Julia, the woman I call Mama, came to live with us?"

"She did. She and Ben had known each other before the war, and everyone was sure they were going to get married. But after the war, Ben seemed—I don't know—restless, I guess you would say. Anyway, it took him awhile to settle down, and by that time he had already met your real mother. I'll tell you true, she broke his heart when she left. Julia came after that, when you were two months old."

"Why did my real mother leave? Did she run away with another man?"

"Nobody knows for sure. All we know is that she left a note saying she wasn't good enough for you. For heaven's sake, child, why are you asking so many questions about her now? Hasn't Julia been a good mother to you?"

"She has been a wonderful mother to me," Rebecca said. "I couldn't ask for anyone better, and I love her dearly. I've just been a little curious, that's all."

"You know what they say, honey. Curiosity killed the cat," Mildred said.

Hearing the whistle of the approaching train, they stood up and walked onto the depot platform. It was six o'clock, and the sun was just going down in the west, spreading the clouds with long, glowing streaks of gold and red. To the east they could see the headlamp of the arriving train. It roared into the station, spewing steam and dropping glowing embers from the firebox. The train was so massive and heavy it made Rebecca's stomach shake as it passed by, first the engine with its huge driver wheels, then the cars with the long lines of lighted windows on each car disclosing the passengers inside. Some looked out in curiosity, others read in jaded indifference to the Marshall depot, which represented but one more stop on their trip.

"What time will you get to Fort Worth?" Mildred asked.

"The schedule says eleven o'clock tonight."

"Oh, heavens, will Ben have someone there to meet you?"

"No, I'll be staying at a hotel. Pa already has a room booked for me. He'll send someone for me tomorrow."

"Board!" the conductor called, and Rebecca and her aunt shared a long good-bye hug before she hurried to get on the train.

Inside the first car behind the express car, Tom Whitman studied the passengers who were boarding. He didn't know what town he was in. In fact, he wasn't even sure what state he was in. It wasn't too long ago he left Shreveport. He knew Shreveport was in Louisiana, and he knew it wasn't too far from Texas, so he wouldn't be surprised if he was in Texas.

"We are on the threshold of the twentieth century, Tom," a friend had told him a couple months ago. "Do you have any idea what a marvelous time this is? Think of all those people who went by wagon train to California. Their trip was arduous, dangerous, and months long. Today we can go by train, enjoying the luxury of a railroad car that protects us from rain, snow, beating sun, or bitter cold. We can dine sumptuously on meals served in a dining salon that rivals the world's finest restaurants. We can view the passing scenery while relaxing in an easy chair, and can pass the nights in a comfortable bed with clean sheets."

* * *

At the time of that conversation, Tom had no idea he would actually be taking that cross-country trip. He was in one more town of the almost countless number of towns—and ten states—he had been in the last six days.

The town wasn't that large. Although there were at least ten people standing on the platform, only four were boarding, as far as he could determine. One was a very pretty young, auburn-haired woman. He watched her share a good-bye hug with an older woman, whom Tom took to be her mother.

One of the passengers who had boarded was putting his coat in the overhead rack in front of Tom.

"Excuse me," Tom said to him. "What is the name of this town?"

"Marshall," the passenger answered.

"Louisiana, or Texas?"

"Texas, mister. The great state of Texas," the man replied with inordinate pride.

"Thank you."

"Been traveling long?"

"Yes, this is my sixth day."

"Where are you headed?"

"I don't have any particular destination in mind."

"Ha, that's funny. I don't know as I've ever met anyone who was travelin' and didn't even know where they was goin'."

"When I find a place that fits my fancy, I'll stop," Tom said.

"Well, mister, I'll tell you true. You ain't goin' to find any place better than Texas. And any place in Texas you decide to stop is better than any place else."

"Thank you. I'll keep that in mind." In the week since he had left Boston, Tom had shared the train with hundreds of others, none of whom had continued their journey with him. He had managed to strike up a conversation with some of them, but in every case, they were only brief acquaintances, then they moved on. He thought of the passage from Longfellow.

> *Ships that pass in the night, and speak each*
> * other in passing,*
> *Only a signal shown and a distant voice in the*
> * darkness;*
> *So on the ocean of life we pass and speak one*
> * another,*
> *Only a look and a voice; then darkness again*
> * and a silence.*

With a series of jerks as the train took up the slack between the cars, it pulled away from the station, eventually smoothing out and picking up speed. Once the train settled in to its gentle rocking and rhythmic clacking forward progress, Tom leaned his head against the seat back and went to sleep.

* * *

Once Rebecca boarded, found her seat, and the train got underway, she reached into her purse to take out the letter. She had picked the letter up at the post office shortly before she left Fort Worth to come visit her aunt Mildred. The letter, which was addressed to her and not to her father, had come as a complete surprise. Her father knew nothing about it, nor did she show it to her aunt Mildred. The letter was from her real mother, and it was the first time in Rebecca's life she had ever heard from her.

Rebecca's first instinct had been to tear it up and throw it away, unread. After all, if her mother cared so little about her that she could abandon her when Rebecca was still a baby, why should Rebecca care what she had to say now?

But curiosity got the best of her, so she read the letter. Sitting in the train going back home, Rebecca read the letter again.

Dear Becca,

This letter is going to come as a shock to you, but I am your real mother. I am very sorry I left you when you were a baby, and I am even more sorry I have never attempted to contact you. I want you to know, however, that my not contacting you is not because you mean nothing to me. I have kept up with your life as best I can, and I know you have grown to be a very beautiful and very wonderful young woman.

*That is exactly what I expected to happen
when I left you with your father. I did that, and I
have stayed out of your life because I thought it
best. Certainly there was no way I could have
given you the kind of life your father has been
able to provide for you. But it would fulfill a
lifetime desire if I could see you just once. If you
can find it in your heart to forgive me, and to
grant this wish, you will find me in Dodge City,
Kansas. I am married to the owner of the Lucky
Chance Saloon.*

> *Your mother,*
> *Janie Davenport*

Rebecca knew about her mother. She had been
told a long time ago that Julia was her step-
mother. But she didn't know *anything* about her
real mother, and the few times she had asked, she
had always been given the same answer.

"Your mother was a troubled soul, and things
didn't work out for her. I'm sure she believed,
when she left you, that she was doing the right
thing," Big Ben always said.

"Have you ever heard from her again?" Rebecca wanted to know.

"No, I haven't, and I don't expect I will. To tell
you the truth, darlin', I'm not even sure she is still
alive."

That had satisfied Rebecca, and she had asked
no more questions until, unexpectedly, she had
received the letter.

From that moment, she had been debating with

herself as to whether or not she should go to Dodge. And if so, should she ask her father for permission to go? Or should she just go? She was twenty-one years old, certainly old enough to make her own decision.

She just didn't know what that decision should be.

She read the letter one more time, then folded it, put it back in her reticule, and settled in for the three and one-half hour train trip.

Fort Worth, Texas

The train had arrived in the middle of the night, and when Tom Whitman got off, he wondered if he should stay, or get back on the train and keep going. Six and one-half days earlier he had boarded a train in Boston with no particular destination in mind. His only goal at the time was to be somewhere other than Boston.

As he stood alongside the train, he became aware of a disturbance at the other end of the platform. A young woman was being bothered by two men. Looking in her direction, Tom saw that it was the same young woman he had seen board the train in Marshall.

"Please," she was saying to the men. "Leave me alone."

"Here now, you pretty little thing, you know you don't mean that," one of the men said. "Why, you wouldn't be standin' out here all alone in the middle of the night, if you wasn't lookin' for a little fun, would you now? And me 'n Pete here are just the men to show you how to have some fun. Right, Pete?"

"You got that right," Pete said.

"What do you say, honey? Do you want to have a little fun with us?"

"No! Please, go away!"

"I know what it is, Dutch," Pete said. "We ain't offered her no money yet."

"Is that it?" Dutch asked. "You're waitin' for us to offer you some money? How about two dollars? A dollar from me and one from Pete. Of course, that means you are going to have to be nice to both of us."

"I asked you to go away. If you don't, I will scream."

Pete took off his bandanna and wadded it into a ball. "It's goin' to be hard for you to scream with this bandanna in your mouth."

Tom walked down to the scene of the ruckus. "Excuse me, gentlemen, but I do believe I heard the lady ask you to leave her alone."

Tom was six feet two inches tall, with broad shoulders and narrow hips. Ordinarily his size alone would be intimidating, but the way he was dressed made him appear almost foppish. He was wearing a brown tweed suit, complete with vest, tie, and collar. He was also wearing a bowler hat and was obviously unarmed. He could not have advertised himself as more of a stranger to the

West if he had a sign hanging around his neck proclaiming the same.

The two men, itinerant cowboys, were wearing denim trousers and stained shirts. Both had Stetson hats on their heads, and pistols hanging at their sides. When they saw Tom, they laughed.

"Well now, tell me, Dutch, have you ever seen a prettier boy than this *Eastern* dude?" Pete slurred the word *Eastern.*

"Don't believe I have," Dutch replied. To Tom he said, "Go away, pretty boy, unless you want to get hurt."

"Let's hurt him anyway," Pete said, smiling. "Let's hurt him real bad for stickin' his nose in where it don't belong."

"Please, sir," the young woman said to Tom. "Go and summon a policeman. I don't want you to get hurt, and I don't think they will do anything if they know a police officer is coming."

"I think it may be too late for that," Tom replied. "These gentlemen seem rather insistent. I'm afraid I'm going to have to take care of this myself."

"Ha!" Pete shouted. "Take care of this!"

He swung hard, but Tom reached up and caught Pete's fist in his open hand. That surprised Pete, but it didn't surprise him as much as what happened next. Tom began to squeeze down on Pete's fist, putting viselike pressure against it, feeling two of Pete's fingers snap under the squeeze.

"Ahhh!" Pete yelled. "Dutch! Get him off me! Get him off me!"

Dutch swung, and Tom caught Dutch's fist in his left hand, repeating the procedure of squeezing down on the fist. Within a moment he had both men on their knees, writhing in pain.

"Let go, let go!" Pete screamed in agony.

Tom let go of both men, and stepped back as they regained their feet. "Please go away now," he said with no more tension in his voice than if he were asking for a cup of coffee.

"You son of a . . ." Pete swore as he started to draw his pistol. But two of his fingers were broken, and he was unable to get a grip on his pistol. It fell from his hand.

The young woman grabbed it quickly, then pointed it at the cowboys. "This gentleman may be an Eastern dude, but I am not. I'm a Western girl and I can shoot. I would like nothing better than to put a bullet into both of you. If you don't start running, right now, I will do just that."

"No, no. Don't shoot! Don't shoot!" Pete cried out. "We're goin'! We're goin'!"

The two men ran off, and the young woman laughed. To Tom, her laughter sounded like wind chimes.

She turned to him with a broad smile spread across her face. "I want to thank you, sir." She thrust her hand toward him, but when he shied away she looked down and saw that she was still holding the pistol. With another laugh, she tossed the gun away, then again stuck out her hand. "I'm Rebecca Conyers."

"I'm Tom—" He hesitated before he said, "Whitman."

"You aren't from here, are you, Mr. Whitman?"

He chuckled. "How can you tell?"

Rebecca laughed as well. "What are you doing in Fort Worth?"

"This is where the train stopped," Tom replied.

Rebecca laughed again. "That's reason enough, I suppose. Are you looking for work?"

"Well, yes, I guess I am."

"Meet me in the lobby of the Clark Hotel tomorrow morning. Someone will be coming to fetch me from my father's ranch. Pa is always looking for good men. I'm sure he would hire you if you are interested."

"Hire me to do what?"

"Why, to cowboy, of course."

"Oh. Do you think it would matter if I told l him I have never been a cowboy?"

Rebecca smiled. "Telling him you have never been a cowboy would be like telling him you have blond hair and blue eyes."

"Oh, yes. I see what you mean."

"It's easy to learn to be a cowboy. Once he hears what you did for me tonight, you won't have any trouble getting on. That is, if you want to."

"Yes," Tom said. "I believe I want to."

As Rebecca lay in bed in her room at the Clark Hotel half an hour later, she wondered what had possessed her to offer a job to Tom Whitman. She had no authority to offer him a job; her father did the hiring and the firing, and he was very particular about it.

On the other hand, before she left to go to Marshall, she heard him tell Clay Ramsey that he might hire someone to replace Tony Peters, a young cowboy who had left for Nevada to try his hand at finding gold or silver. Rebecca had a sudden thought. What if he has already hired someone to replace Peters?

No, she was sure he had not. Her father tended to be much more methodical than to hire someone that quickly. But that same tendency of his to be methodical might also work against her, for he would not be that anxious to hire someone he knew nothing about.

Well, she would just have to talk him into it, that's all. And surely when her father heard what Tom Whitman had done for her, he would be more than willing.

Rebecca wondered why she was so intent on getting Mr. Whitman hired? Was it because he had been her knight in shining armor, just when she needed such a hero? Or was it because he might be one of the most handsome men she had ever seen? In addition to that, there was something else about him, something she sensed more than she saw. He had a sense of poise and self-assuredness she found most intriguing.

* * *

Because Tom liked to sleep with fresh air, he had raised the window when he went to bed. He had taken a room in the same hotel as Rebecca because she had suggested the hotel to him. He was awakened by a combination of things, the sun streaming in through his open window and the sounds of commerce coming from the street below.

He could hear the sound of the clash of eras—the whir of an electric streetcar, along with the rattle and clatter of a freight wagon. From somewhere he could hear the buzz and squeal of a power saw, and the ring of steel on steel as a blacksmith worked his trade. Newspaper boys were out on the street, hawking their product.

"Paper, get the paper here! Wyoming to be admitted as state! Get your paper here!"

Tom got out of bed, shaved, then got dressed. Catching a glimpse of himself in the mirror, he frowned. He was wearing a three-piece suit, adequate dress if he wanted to apply for a job with a bank. But he was going to apply for a job as a cowboy, and his outfit would never do.

Stepping over to the window, he looked up and down Houston Street. On the opposite side, he saw the Fort Worth Mercantile Store. Leaving his suitcase in his room, he hurried downstairs, and then across the street and into the store.

A tall, thin man with a neatly trimmed mustache and garters around his sleeves stepped up to him. "Yes, sir, may help you?"

"I intend to apply for employment at a neighboring ranch," Tom said. "And I will need clothes that are suitable for the position."

"When you say that you are going to apply for employment, do you mean as an accountant or business manager?" the clerk asked.

"No. As a cowboy."

The expression on the clerk's face registered his surprise. "I beg your pardon, sir. Did you say as a cowboy?"

"Yes," Tom said. "Why, is there a problem?"

"No, sir," the clerk said quickly. "No problem. It is just that, well, sir, you will forgive me, but you don't look like a cowboy."

"Yeah," Tom said. "That's why I'm here. I want you to make me look like a cowboy."

"I can sell you the appropriate attire, sir," the clerk said. "But, in truth, you still won't look like a cowboy."

"Try," Tom said.

"Yes, sir."

It took Tom no more than fifteen minutes to buy three outfits, including boots and a hat. Paying for his purchases, he returned to the hotel, packed his suit and the two extra jeans and shirts into his suitcase, then went downstairs, checked out, and took a seat in the lobby to wait for the young woman he had met last night.

As he waited for her, he recalled the conversation he had had with his father, just before he left Boston.

* * *

"*You are making a big mistake by running away,*" his father had told him. "*You will not be able to escape your own devils.*"

"*I can try,*" Tom said.

"*Nobody is holding it against you, Tom. You did what you thought was right.*"

"*I did what I thought was right? I can't even justify what I did to myself by saying that I did what I thought was right. My wife and my child are dead, and I killed them.*"

"*It isn't as if you murdered them.*"

"*It isn't? How is it different? Martha and the child are still dead.*"

"*So you are you going to run away. Is that your answer?*"

"*Yes, that is my answer. I need some time to sort things out. Please try to understand that.*"

His father changed tactics, from challenging to persuading. "*Tom, all I am asking is that you think this through. You have more potential than any student I ever taught, and I'm not saying that just because you are my son. I am saying it because it is true. Do you have any idea of the good that someone like you—a person with your skills, your talent, your education, can do?*"

"*I've seen the evil I can do when I confuse skill, talent, and education with Godlike attributes.*"

His father sighed in resignation. "*What time does your train leave?*"

"*At nine o'clock tonight.*"

His father walked over to the bar and poured a glass of Scotch. He held it out toward Tom and, catching a *beam of light from the electric chandelier, the amber fluid emitted a burst of gold as if the glass had captured the sun itself. "Then at least have this last, parting drink with me."*

Tom waited until his father had poured his own glass, then the two men drank to each other.

"Will you write to let me know where you are and how you are doing?"

"Not for a while," Tom said. "I need to be away from everything that can remind me of what happened. And that means even my family."

Surprisingly, Tom's father smiled. "In a way, I not only don't blame you, I envy you. I almost ran off myself, once. I was going to sail the seven seas. But my father got wind of it, and talked me out of it. I guess I wasn't as strong as you are."

"Nonsense, you are as strong," Tom said. "You just never had the same devils chasing you that I do."

Tom glanced at the big clock. It showed fifteen minutes of nine. Shouldn't she be here by now? Had she changed her mind and already checked out? He walked over to the desk.

"Yes, sir, Mr. Whitman, may I help you?" the hotel desk clerk asked.

"Rebecca Conyers," Tom said. "Has she checked out yet?"

The clerk checked his book. "No, sir. She is still in the hotel. Would you like me to summon her?"

"No, that won't be necessary. I'll just wait here in the lobby for her."

"Very good, sir."

Huh, Tom thought. *And here it was my belief that Westerners rose with the sun.* As soon as he thought that, he realized she had gone to bed quite late, having arrived on the train in the middle of the night. At least his initial fear that she had left without meeting him was alleviated.

When Rebecca awakened that morning she was already having second thoughts about what she had done. Had she actually told a perfect stranger that she could talk her father into hiring him? And, even if she could, should she? She had arisen much later than she normally did, and as she dressed, found herself hoping he had grown tired of waiting for her and left, without accepting her offer.

However, when she went downstairs she saw him sitting in a chair in the lobby. His suitcase was on the floor beside him, but he wasn't wearing the suit he had been wearing the night before. He was wearing denims, a blue cotton shirt, and boots. If anything, she found him more attractive, for the denims and cotton shirt took some of the polish off, giving him a more rugged appearance.

Although Tom had gotten an idea the young woman was pretty, it had been too dark to get a really good look at her. In the full light of morning he saw her for what she was—tall and willowy, with long, auburn hair and green eyes shaded by long, dark eyelashes. She was wearing a dress that showed off her gentle curves to perfection.

"Mr. Whitman," she said. "How wonderful it is to see you this morning. I see you have decided to take me up on my offer."

"Yes, I have. You *were* serious about it, weren't you? I mean, you weren't just making small talk?"

Rebecca paused before responding. If she wanted to back out of her offer, now was the time to do it. "I was very serious," she heard herself saying, as if purposely speaking before she could change her mind.

"Do we have time for breakfast? If so, I would like to take you to breakfast."

Rebecca glanced over at the clock. "Yes, I think so. And I would be glad to have breakfast with you. But you must let me pay for my own."

"Only if it makes you feel more comfortable," Tom said.

"Let's sit by the window," Rebecca suggested when they stepped into the hotel restaurant. "That way we will be able to see when Mo comes for me."

"Mo?"

"He is one of my father's cowboys. He is quite young."

They settled at a table and ordered breakfast, drinking coffee and making small talk until their meals arrived. Rebecca had a poached egg and toast. Tom had two waffles, four fried eggs, a rather substantial slab of ham, and more biscuits than Rebecca could count.

"My, you must have been hungry," Rebecca said after Tom pushed away a clean plate. "When is the last time you ate?"

"Not since supper last night," Tom said, as if that explained his prodigious appetite. "Oh, I hope I haven't embarrassed you."

"Not at all. Tell me about yourself, Mr. Whitman. Where are you from? What were you doing before you decided to come West?"

"Not much to tell. I'm from Boston. I'm more interested in you telling me about the ranch."

"Oh, there's Mo," Rebecca said. "I won't have to tell you about the ranch, we'll be there in less than an hour."

Tom picked up his suitcase and Rebecca's, then followed her out to the buckboard.

"Hello, Mo," Rebecca greeted.

Mo was a slender five feet nine, with brown eyes and dark hair, which he wore long and straight.

"Hello, Miss Rebecca," Mo said with a broad smile. "It's good to see you back home again. Ever'one at the ranch missed you. Did you have a good visit?"

"Oh, I did indeed," Rebecca answered.

Seeing Tom standing there with the two suitcases, Mo indicated the back of the buckboard. "You can just put them there." Turning to Rebecca, he whispered, "Uh, Miss Rebecca, you got a coin? I come into town with no money at all."

"A coin?"

Mo nodded toward Tom. "Yes ma'am, a nickel or a dime or somethin' on account of him carrying your luggage and all."

"Oh, we don't need to tip him, Mo. His name is Tom, and he's with me. He'll be comin' out to the ranch with us."

"He's with you? Good Lord, Miss Rebecca, you didn't go to Marshall and get yourself married up or somethin', did you?" Mo asked.

Rebecca laughed out loud. "No, it's nothing like that."

"Sorry I didn't bring the trap," Mo said to Tom. "This here buckboard only has one seat. That means you'll have to ride in the back."

"That's not a problem," Tom said. "I'll be fine."

"I hope so. It's not all that comfortable back there and we're half an hour from the ranch."

Tom set the luggage in the back of the buckboard, then put his hand on the side and vaulted over.

"Damn," Mo said. "I haven't ever seen anybody do that. You must be a pretty strong fella."

"You don't know the half of it," Rebecca said.

CHAPTER TWO

Live Oaks Ranch

Just north of Fort Worth, 120,000 acres of gently rolling grassland and scores of year-round streams and creeks made Live Oaks Ranch ideal for cattle ranching. Two dozen cowboys were part-time employees, and another two dozen were full-time. Those who weren't married lived in long, low bunkhouses, painted white with red roofs. At least ten of the permanent employees who were married lived in small houses painted green with red roofs, adjacent to the bunkhouses. There was also a cookhouse large enough to feed the single men, a barn, a machine shed, a granary, and a large stable. The dominating feature of the ranch was what the cowboys called "The Big House." It was a stucco-sided example of Spanish Colonial Revival, with an arcaded portico on the southeast corner, stained-glass windows, and an elaborate arched entryway.

Inside the parlor of the Big House, the owner of Live Oaks, Rebecca's father, was standing by the fireplace. Big Ben Conyers was aptly named, for he was six feet seven inches tall and weighed 330 pounds. Rebecca had just introduced Tom to him, explaining how he had come to her aid when she had been accosted by two cowboys.

"I thank you very much for that, Mr. Whitman." Big Ben shook Tom's hand. "There are many who would have just turned away."

"I'm glad I happened to be there at that time," Tom replied.

"Mr. Whitman is looking for a job, Pa," Rebecca said. "I know that Tony Peters left a couple weeks ago, and when Mo picked me up this morning, he told me you hadn't replaced him."

"I don't know, honey. Tony was an experienced cowboy," Big Ben said.

"Nobody is experienced when they first start," Rebecca said, making Big Ben laugh.

"I can't deny that," he said. "Where are you from, Mr. Whitman?"

"I'm from Boston, sir."

"Boston, is it? Can you ride a horse?"

For several years Tom had belonged to a fox hunting club. Uunlike the quarter horses, bred for speed in short stretches that were commonly seen out West, fox-hunting thoroughbreds were often crossed with heavier breeds for endurance and solidity. They were taller and more muscular, and were trained to run long distances, since most hunts lasted for an entire day. They were also bred to jump a variety of fences and ditches. Tom was, in fact, a champion when it came to riding to the hounds.

The sport got mixed reactions, from those who felt sorry for the fox, to those who thought it was a foolish indulgence, to those who did not understand the skill and stamina such an endeavor required.

"Yes, sir, I can ride a horse," he said.

"You don't mind if I give you a little test just to see how well you can ride, do you?" Big Ben asked.

"Pa, that's not fair," Rebecca said. "You know our horses aren't like the ones he is used to riding. At least give him a few days to get used to them."

"I don't have a few days, Rebecca. I have two hundred square miles of ranch to run, and a herd of cattle to manage. I need someone who can go to work immediately. Now, maybe you're right, everyone has to get experience somewhere, so I'm willing to give him time to learn his way around the ranch. But if he can't even ride a horse, I mean a Western horse, then it's going to take more time than I can spare."

"I'm sorry, Mr. Whitman," Rebecca said. "If you don't want to take Pa's test, you don't have to. We'll all understand."

"I'd like to take the test," Tom said.

"Good for you," Big Ben said. "Come on outside, let me see what you can do."

A tall, gangly young man with ash-blond hair

and a spray of freckles came up to them. "Hello, Sis. I heard you were back."

"Did you stay stay out of trouble while I was gone?" Rebecca asked. Then she introduced the boy. "Mr. Whitman, this is my brother, Dalton."

"Are you going to work for Pa?" Dalton asked.

"I hope to."

"Then I won't be calling you Mr. Whitman. What's your first name?"

"Dalton!" Rebecca said.

"I don't mean nothin' by it," Dalton said. "I'm just friends with all the cowboys, that's all."

"My name is Tom. And I would be happy to be your friend."

"Yes, well, don't the two of you get to be best friends too fast," Big Ben said. "First I have to know if Tom can ride well enough to be a cowboy. Clay!" Big Ben called.

A man stepped out of the machine shed. "Yes, sir, Mr. Conyers?"

"Get over here, Clay, I've someone I want you to meet." To Tom, Big Ben added, "Clay is the ranch foreman. I'll leave the final word as to whether or not I hire you up to him."

"Good enough," Tom said.

Clay Ramsey was thirty-three-years-old with brown hair, a well-trimmed mustache, and blue eyes. About five feet ten, he was wiry and, according to one of the cowboys who worked for him, as tough as a piece of rawhide.

"Saddle Thunder for him," Big Ben said, after he explained what he wanted to do.

"Pa, no!" Rebecca protested vehemently.

"Honey, I'm not just being a horse's rear end. If he can ride Thunder, he can ride any horse on the ranch, and there wouldn't be any question about my hiring him."

"I can ride a horse, Mr. Conyers," Tom said. "But I confess I have never tried to ride a bucking horse. If that is what is required, then I thank you for your time, and I'll be moving on."

"He's not a bucking horse," Clay said. "But he is a very strong horse who loves to run and jump. If you ride him, you can't be timid about it. You have to let him know, right away, that you are in control."

"Thank you, Mr. Ramsey. In that case, I will ride him."

"Ha!" Dusty McNally, one of the other cowboys, said. "I like it that you said you *will* ride him, rather than you will *try* to ride him. That's the right attitude to have."

Thunder was a big, muscular, black horse who stood eighteen hands at the withers. Although he allowed himself to be saddled, he kept moving his head and lifting first one hoof, then another. He looked like a ball of potential energy.

"Here you are, Mr. Whitman." Clay handed the reins to Tom.

"Thank you." Tom pointed toward an open area on the other side of a fence. "Would it be all right to ride in that field there?"

"Sure, there's nothing there but rangeland." Clay pointed. "The gate is down there."

"Thank you, I won't need a gate." Tom slapped his legs against the side of the horse and it started forward at a gallop. As he approached the fence, he lifted himself slightly from the saddle and leaned forward.

"Come on, Thunder," he said encouragingly. "Let's go see if we can find us a fox."

Thunder galloped toward the fence, then sailed over it as gracefully as a leaping deer. Coming down on the other side Tom saw a ditch about twenty yards beyond the fence, and Thunder took that as well. Horse and rider went through their paces, jumping, making sudden turns, running at a full gallop, then stopping on a dime. After a few minutes he brought Thunder back, returning the same way he left, over the ditch, then over the fence. He slowed him down to a trot once he was back inside the compound, and the horse was at a walk by the time he rode up to dismount in front of a shocked Big Ben, Clay, and Dusty. Rebecca was smiling broadly.

Tom patted Thunder on his neck, then dismounted and handed the reins back to Clay. "He is a very fine horse," Tom said. "Whoever rides him is quite lucky."

"He's yours to ride any time you want him," Big Ben said. "That is, provided you are willing to come work for me."

"I would be very proud to work for you, Mr. Conyers."

"Come with me. Tom, is it?" Clay invited. "I'll get you set up in the bunkhouse and introduce you to the others."

"Tom?" Rebecca called out to him.

He looked back toward her.

"I'm glad you are here."

"Thank you, Miss Conyers. I'm glad to be here."

Tom ate his first supper in the cookhouse that evening. Mo introduced him to all the others.

"Where is Mr. Ramsey?" Tom asked. "Does he eat somewhere else?"

"Mr. Ramsey?" Mo asked. Then he smiled. "Oh, you mean Clay. Clay is the foreman of the ranch, but there don't any of us call him Mr. Ramsey. We just call him Clay 'cause that's what he wants us to call him."

"Clay is married," one of the other cowboys said. "He lives in that first cabin you see over there, the only one with a front porch."

"He married a Mexican girl," another said.

"Don't talk about her like that," Mo said. "Maria is as American as you are. Emanuel Bustamante fought with Sam Houston at San Jacinto."

"I didn't mean nothin' by it," the cowboy said. "I think Señor Bustamante is as fine a man as I've ever met, and Mrs. Ramsey is a very good woman. I was just sayin' that she is Mexican is all."

"I assume that none of you are married," Tom said. "Otherwise you wouldn't be eating here in the dining hall."

"Ha! The dining hall. That's sure a fancy name for the cookhouse."

"I don't mean any disrespect for Clay," Mo said. "But it don't make a whole lot of sense for a cowboy to be married. First of all, there don't none of us make enough money to support a family. And second, when we make the long cattle drives, we're gone for near three months at a time."

"And Dodge City is too fun a town to be in if you are married, if you get my meanin'," one of the other cowboys said, and the others shared a ribald laugh.

A couple cowboys decided to razz the tenderfoot that first night. Tom had been given a chest for his belongings, and while Tom and the rest of the cowboys were having supper, Dalton and one of the cowboys slipped into the bunkhouse and nailed the lid shut.

When Tom and the others returned, Tom tried to open the lid to his footlocker, but he was unable to get it open.

"What's the matter there, Tom? Can't get your chest open?" Dalton asked.

He had told the others what he did, and all gathered around to see how Tom was going to react. Would he get angry, and start cursing everyone? Or would he be meek about it?

Tom looked more closely at the lid, and saw

that it had been nailed shut by six nails, two in front and two on either side. "That's odd. It seems to have been nailed shut."

The others laughed out loud.

"Nailed shut, is it? Well, I wonder who did that?" Dalton asked.

"Oh, I expect it was a mistake of some sort," Tom said. "I don't really think anyone would nail the lid shut on my chest as a matter of intent."

"Do you think that?" Dalton asked, and again, everyone laughed at the joke they were playing on the tenderfoot.

"All right, fellas, you've had your fun," Mo said. "Wait a minute, Tom, I'll get a claw hammer and pull the nails for you so you can get the lid open."

"Thank you, Mo," Tom said. "I don't need the claw hammer to get the lid open."

"What are you talking about? Of course you do. How else are you going to open the lid if you don't pull the nails out first?"

"Oh, it won't be difficult. I'll just open it like this." Reaching down with both hands, Tom used one hand to steady the bottom of the chest and the other to grab the front of the lid. He pulled up. With a terrible screeching noise as the nails lost their purchase, the lid came up. Reaching into the footlocker, Tom removed a pair of socks. "Ahh. That's what I was looking for."

"Good God in heaven," someone said reverently. "Did you see that?"

"Dalton, I don't think you ought to be messin' any more with this one. He's as strong as an ox."

Sugarloaf Ranch, Big Rock, Colorado
May 1, 1890

"Did you get a count?" Smoke asked Pearlie.

Pearlie held up the string and counted the knots. There were fourteen knots. "I make it fourteen hundred in the south pasture."

"I've got another eleven hundred," Cal added.

"And I've got just over fifteen hundred," Smoke said.

"Wow, that's better than four thousand head," Pearlie said. "We've got almost as many back as we had before the big freeze and die-up."

The big die-up Pearlie was talking about happened in January three years earlier when there had been a huge seventy-two hour blizzard. After the blizzard, the sun melted the top few inches of snow into slush, which was frozen into solid ice by minus thirty-degree temperatures the following day. Throughout the West, tens of thousands of cattle were found huddled against fences, some partially through and hanging on the wire, many frozen to death. The legs of many cows that survived were so badly frozen that, when they moved, the skin cracked open and their hooves dropped off. Hundreds of young steers wandered aimlessly around on bloody stumps, while their tails froze as if they were icicles to be easily broken off.

Humans died that year too—men who froze to death while searching for cattle; women and children in houses where there was no wood to burn and blankets could not hold back the sub-zero temperatures. The only creatures to survive and thrive that winter were the wolves who feasted upon the carcasses of tens of thousands of dead cattle.

Sugarloaf Ranch had survived, but nearly all the cattle on the ranch had died. Then Smoke heard from his friend, Falcon MacCallister. Falcon's cousin, Duff MacCallister, recently arrived from Scotland, was running a new breed of cattle—Black Angus.

He had been spared the great die-up disaster because his ranch was located in the Chugwater Valley of Wyoming, shielded against the worst of winter's blast by mesas and mountain ranges. His ranch, Sky Meadow, had no fences to prevent the cattle from moving to the shelter of those natural barriers. The Black Angus breed of cattle Duff MacCallister was raising was better equipped to withstand the cold weather than were the Longhorns.

Smoke had gone to Sky Meadow to meet with Duff, and after his visit, agreed to buy one thousand head of Black Angus cattle. That one thousand head had grown into a herd of nearly four thousand in the last three and a half years, and it had been a very good move for Smoke. Whereas the market price for Longhorn had fallen so low Smoke's neighbors, who were still raising that breed, were doing well to break even on their investment, the market price for Black Angus, which produced a superior grade of beef, was very high.

"You men take care of things here," Smoke said. "Sally is coming back today, and I'm going to meet her at the train station."

"I'll go get her," Cal volunteered.

Pearlie chuckled. "I'm sure you would, Cal. We've got calves to brand and you'll do anything to get out of a little work."

"It's not that," Cal said. "I was just volunteering, is all."

"Thanks anyway," Smoke said. "But she's been back East for almost a month and I'm sort of anxious to see her again."

When Smoke reached the train depot in Big Rock, he checked the arrival and departure blackboard to see if the train was on time. There was no arrival time listed, so he went inside to talk to the ticket agent. He was huddled in a nervous conversation with Sheriff Monte Carson.

"Hello, Monte, good evening, Hodge," Smoke said, greeting the two men. "How are you doing?"

"Smoke, I'm glad you are here," Sheriff Carson said. "We've got a problem with the train."

"What kind of problem? Sally is on that train."

"Yes, I know she is. We think the train is being robbed."

"Being robbed, or has been robbed?" Smoke replied, confused by the remark.

"Being robbed," Sheriff Carson said. "At least, we think that it what it is. The train is stopped about five miles east of here. There is an obstruction on the track so it can't go forward, and another on the track to keep it from going back."

"How do you know this?"

"Ollie Cook is the switch operator just this side of where the train is. When the train didn't come through his switch on time, he walked down the track to find out why, and that's when he saw the train barricaded like that. He hurried back to his switch shack and called the depot."

"And I called Sheriff Carson," Hodge said.

"I'm about to get a posse together to ride out there and see what it's all about," the sheriff said.

"No need for a posse. Deputize me," Smoke suggested. "Like I said, Sally is on that train."

"You are already a deputy, Smoke, you know that."

"Yes, I know. But I don't want people thinking I've gone off on my own just because Sally is on the train. I need you to authorize this in front of a witness."

"All right," Sheriff Carson said. "Hodge, you are witness to this. Smoke, you are deputized to find out what is happening with that train, and to deal with it as you see best."

"Thanks."

Hurrying back outside, Smoke jumped into the buckboard. Slapping the reins against the back of the team, he took the road that ran parallel with the railroad. He left town doing a brisk trot, but once he was out of town, he urged the team into a gallop. Less than fifteen minutes later, he saw the train stopped on the railroad tracks. Not wanting to get any closer with the team and buckboard, he tied them to a juniper tree, then, bending to keep a low profile, ran alongside the berm until he reached the front of the train. Hiding in some bushes, he looked into the engine cab and saw three men. The fireman and engineer he could identify by the pin-striped coveralls they were wearing. The third man had a gun in his hand, waving it around every now and then, as if demonstrating his authority over the train crew.

Smoke moved up onto the track, but since he was in the very front of the locomotive, he knew he couldn't be seen. He climbed up the cow catcher, then up onto the boiler itself, still unseen. He walked along the top of the boiler, then onto the roof of the cab. Lying down on his stomach, he peeked in the side window on the left side of the locomotive.

The man holding the gun had his back to that window so he couldn't see Smoke, but the engineer and the fireman could, and their eyes widened in surprise. Smoke hoped the gunman didn't notice.

"You two fellas are doin' just fine," the gunman said. "As soon as we collect our money from all your passengers, why we'll move the stuff off the track and let you go on."

Smoke leaned down far enough to make certain the cab crew could see him, then put his finger across his lips as a signal to be quiet.

"You got no right to be collecting money from our passengers," the engineer said.

"Well, the Denver and Rio Grande collects its fees, and we collect ours," the gunman said with a cackling laugh.

In mid-cackle, Smoke reached into the engine cab, grabbed the man by his shirt, and pulled him through the window, then let him fall headfirst to the ground.

"Hey, what—" was as far as the man got, before contact with the ground interrupted his protest. Looking down at him, Smoke could tell by the way the man's head was twisted that his neck was broken, and he was dead.

Smoke swung himself into the engine cab.

"Who are you?" the engineer asked.

"Smoke Jensen. I'm a deputy sheriff. How many more are there?"

"Four more," the fireman answered.

"Five," the engineer corrected. "I saw five."

"Where are they now?"

"Well, sir, after they found out we wasn't carryin' any money in the express car, they decided to see what they could get from the passengers, and that's what they are doing now."

"How about the two of you going down to move that body? I don't want any of the others to look up this way and see him lying there."

"Yeah, good idea. Come on, Cephus, let's get him moved."

As the two train crewmen climbed down to take care of their job, Smoke crawled across the coal pile on the tender, then up onto the top of the express car. He ran the length of that car, then leaped across to the baggage car and ran its length as well. Climbing down from the back of the baggage car, he let himself into the first passenger car.

"One of your men has already been here," an irate passenger said. "We gave him everything we have."

"Shhh," Smoke said. "I'm on your side. I'm a deputy sheriff. Where are they?"

"There was only one in here, and he went into the next car."

"Thanks." Holding his pistol down by his side, Smoke hurried through the first car and into the second. He saw a gunman at the other end of the car, holding a pistol in his right hand and an open sack in the other. The passengers were dropping their valuables into the open sack.

"What are you doing in here? You get back in the other car and stay there like you were told!" The gunman said belligerently.

"I don't think so." Smoke raised his pistol. "Drop your gun."

"The hell I will!" The train robber swung his pistol around and fired at Smoke. His shot went wide and the bullet smashed through the window of the door behind him.

Smoke returned fire, and the gunman dropped his pistol, staggering backward, his hands to his throat. Blood spilled through his fingers as he hit the back wall of the car, then slid down to the floor in a seated position. His head fell to one side as he died.

Women screamed and men shouted. As the car filled with the gunsmoke of two discharges, Smoke ran through the car, across the vestibule, and into the next car.

The gunman in the next car, having heard the shot, called for his partners. "Red! McDill! Slim, get in here quick!"

Smoke and the gunman exchanged fire, with the same result. The gunman went down and Smoke was still standing. Running into the next car, he saw the robber dashing out the back door. He chased after him but didn't have to shoot him. The gunman was taken down by a club wielded by the porter in the next car.

"Good job," Smoke said.

"The other two has done jumped off the train," the porter said.

Smoke jumped down from the train, then moved away from it to get a bead on the two who were running along the tracks. He snapped off a long shot, but missed. He didn't get a second shot. The outlaws were on horseback and galloping away.

Smoke stood there, holding his smoking pistol as he watched the two robbers flee.

"You need to develop a better sense of timing,.."

Turning, Smoke saw Sally standing on the ground behind him. He embraced and kissed her, then he pulled his head back. "What do you mean, a better sense of timing?"

"If you had been five minutes earlier, the robbers wouldn't have gotten my reticule."

"Sorry. How much did they get?" Smoke asked.

"Just my purse," Sally said with little laugh. "I had already taken everything out of it."

Several others came down from the train and all thanked Smoke for coming to their rescue.

"Look here!" someone shouted. "The two that got away dropped their sacks!"

"The ones inside never even made it off the train with their sacks," another said. "Ha! Ever'- thing they took is still here!"

"Cephus, how long will it take you to get the steam back up?" the conductor asked.

"Fifteen minutes," Cephus said. "Maybe half an hour."

Smoke looked at Sally. "Do you want to wait until they get the steam back up? Or do you want to come with me now? I left a buckboard just up the track a short distance."

"My luggage is on the train," Sally said.

"Ma'am, after what your man just did, if you want your luggage, I'll personally open the bag-gage car and get it," the conductor said.

Mitchell "Red" Coleman and Deekus McDill were the two robbers who got away. They got away from Smoke's avenging guns, but they did not get away with any money.

"Nothin'!" McDill said. "We didn't get a damn thing!"

"Maybe the day ain't goin' to be a total loss," Red said.

"What do you mean, it ain't a total loss?"

"Look over there."

"What, a store? What good is a store goin' to do us? We ain't got no money to buy nothin'."

"Who said we were goin' to buy anything?" Red said.

Finally understanding what Red was talking about, McDill smiled and nodded.

Fifteen minutes later they rode away from Doogan's store. Behind them, Jake Doogan and his wife lay dead on the floor. The total take for the robbery was seventy-eight dollars and thirty-five cents.

THE FIRST MOUNTAIN MAN SERIES BY
WILLIAM W. JOHNSTONE